THE FLOWING TIDE

Recent Titles by Alan Savage from Severn House

THE NAVAL SERIES

STORM WARNING
THE FLOWING TIDE

THE RAF SERIES

BLUE YONDER
DEATH IN THE SKY
SPIRALLING DOWN
THE WHIRLWIND

THE FRENCH RESISTANCE SERIES

RESISTANCE
THE GAME OF TREACHERY
LEGACY OF HATE
THE BRIGHTEST DAY

THE PARTISAN SERIES

PARTISAN
MURDER'S ART
BATTLEGROUND
THE KILLING GROUND

THE COMMANDO SERIES

COMMANDO
THE CAUSE
THE TIGER

'I must go down to the sea again, for the call of the
    running tide
Is a wild call, and a clear call, that may not be denied.'
                                        John Masefield

PART ONE
The Channel

'Strange sounds along the channel pass'd.'
Sir Walter Scott

Speed and Power

'What do you think of her?' inquired Captain Fitzsimmons, surveying with considerable satisfaction the long, sleek motor boat. 'Or have you changed your mind about staying with MTBs?'

His tone left no doubt as to the answer he required. The captain might be short and slightly built, with grey wings to his dark hair, but his sharp features and intense personality had earned him the total respect of those who worked under him. Now he stood on the pontoon in Portsmouth Harbour with his hands on his hips, awaiting a reply. Even on a sunless, chilly November morning, he wore no greatcoat.

But Lieutenant Duncan Eversham, who was wearing a greatcoat, had in any event no intention of abandoning what he liked best, and did best as well. 'I do want to stay with MTBs, sir.'

'Is that because you're a famous yachtsman? Or do you just like rushing about the place in a small boat?'

'I wouldn't describe myself as a famous yachtsman, sir,' Duncan said modestly. 'I only ever won one race.'

Over six feet tall, with heavy shoulders and powerful legs, he had in fact been a well-known rugby player before the outbreak of war in September 1939, just over a year previously, and his large, friendly features, topped by the thick black hair, only partially concealed by his cap, and lively dark eyes gave no indication that this very summer, on the premature death of his father, he had become a peer of the realm at the early age of twenty-six. Or of the extreme purpose and considerable skill he could bring to helming a fast boat under fire or in a rough sea. But he already wore the ribbon of the Distinguished Service Cross, earned for sinking a U-boat in the English Channel the previous December, within three months of the declaration of war.

'But what about *Seventy-Two*?' he asked. He had become

extremely fond of his current command, which had seen him through some difficult situations.

'*Seventy-Two*,' Fitzsimmons pointed out, 'is going to be out of action for some time. You were damned lucky that you took that shell right in the bow instead of further aft. It could have blown you out of the water.'

'I accept that, sir,' Duncan agreed. 'But—'

'And then you tried to take her to sea again too soon. Didn't you return from your last patrol with your deck awash?'

'She suddenly opened a seam.'

'Quite. Because you were driving her too fast.'

'Is there any point in having a fast motor boat and not driving her at full speed?'

'There is, when she has recently been badly damaged and has not been adequately repaired. Now she needs a new hull, if it is decided to repair her at all. I would have thought you'd be very happy. *Forty-One* –' he indicated the boat in front of them – 'is the latest and best we have. You'll see that in addition to two torpedo tubes she has a twenty-millimetre cannon up in the bow, which matches anything Jerry has in his motor boats.'

'Not quite, if the latest reports are accurate,' Duncan objected. 'Although I'll be glad to have it. But she seems to have only two depth charges. Or are the others stowed below?'

'There are only two. That is because this class is not designed for anti-submarine warfare. If you spot a U-boat you're welcome to have a go, but your main task will be combating enemy MTBs. Since Dunkirk they have been able to use all the French Atlantic ports, and flood the Channel with their small craft. There have been several reports of attacks on our coastal convoys. These S-boats, as they call them, are very fast, as you know, and our destroyers can't catch them. Quite apart from the fact that we don't have enough destroyers to guard the Channel and protect our Atlantic convoys. Now, since that mini-battle off Guernsey in September, which makes you the only one of our MTB skippers actually to have sunk one of the bastards, you are regarded as an expert in this field. You will command a flotilla of six boats, and your business will be to patrol the Channel.'

'Aye-aye, sir.' Duncan was enthusiastic. Even if he knew

that his victory over the larger and more heavily armed German boat in the rock-strewn waters off Guernsey had been a combination of luck and local knowledge, he liked to have his opponents where he could see them rather than lurking beneath the surface. But there was at the moment only one boat alongside the pontoon. 'You mentioned a flotilla of six boats . . .?'

'They'll be ready in a day or so. Then you'll have three on and three off at all times,' Fitzsimmons went on. 'Now, as you can see, this boat is slightly larger than *Seventy-Two*, thus she will have a larger crew, twelve instead of nine, and as you're a flotilla leader, you will have an executive officer to back you up. Don't worry, there are two cabins aft.'

'Hm,' Duncan commented. He was well aware that as an RNVR officer, as depicted by the two wavy stripes on his sleeve, he and all those like him who had been called up at the start of hostilities, and whatever their known talents or quickly proved abilities, were generally regarded as part-time amateur sailors by the regulars. Over the more than a year he had skippered an MTB there had been no member of his crew either able or willing to criticize his decisions and dispositions, and he had no desire for that to change.

'He'll be along as soon as he gets here,' Fitzsimmons said. 'Well, I imagine you'll want to get aboard and look her over. She's all yours.'

'What about the rest of my crew?' Duncan asked. 'The lads from *Seventy-Two*? If she's going to be out of action for the foreseeable future . . .'

'They'll have to be reassigned. Well, as you know three are in hospital as a result of your being hit. That includes Petty Officer Harris. So he is being replaced. The rest are being offered the usual choice, between continuing in MTBs or transferring to something bigger. That's all being sorted out. You'll have a crew by tomorrow. Then you'll want to get out there and shake her down. The rest of the flotilla won't be manned for another week. Then you'll want to shake them down as well. It all has to be ASAP. I'll leave you to it. Carry on, Lieutenant.'

'Aye-aye, sir.' Duncan saluted, waited while the captain went along the pontoon to the ramp leading up to the dock, aware as always that he was being overlooked by almost every window in the Command Building. Then he turned back to survey his new ship.

What memories came flooding back. His first MTB, *Seventeen*, had been a sixty-footer, a good dozen feet shorter than this. He had been given her simply because he was a yachtsman, familiar at once with small boats and the Channel waters. He could remember the first time he had taken her out, again under, it had seemed, the eyes of the entire shore establishment. He had in fact only just returned from the 1939 Cowes–Dinard Race in which he had won his class in his fifty-foot schooner *Kristin*, named after his mother, and had also just received his call-up papers.

In August 1939 Portsmouth had been one of the busiest and most crowded naval bases in the world. Today it was still busy, but the emphasis had changed. The great ships anchored in the Solent had all gone, some on constant patrol, some to the Mediterranean, most to the supposed safety of Scapa Flow in the Orkneys. This move had not been an unqualified success; one of the battleships, *Royal Oak*, had been torpedoed at anchor inside the Flow by Gunther Prien's *U 47*. But defences had been tightened up, as Duncan knew from experience; he had served out of Scapa back in the spring.

Today, Portsmouth and the Solent was mainly the home of small craft, destroyers, corvettes, minesweepers, and of course, torpedo boats. Although it was still subject to attack; the Luftwaffe, having accepted defeat in their efforts to destroy London, and with it, British morale, during the past summer, had turned their attention, more effectively, to tactical assaults on seaports and military establishments. There had in fact been a raid during the night, and although Portsmouth itself had escaped, there had apparently been considerable damage to Southampton, only a few miles away.

Fortunately, Duncan reflected, Jerry had never had either the time or the bombs to attack or strafe Lymington, the tiny yachting port at the far end of the Solent, where *Kristin* was stored for the duration, and outside of which the real Kristin lived in the family home. And before the outbreak of war in September of last year, life had been one long game, with even being a naval reservist no more than a bit of fun.

As for being given command of one of the new MTBs, that

had simply been another challenge. Used as he had been to helming a deep-keel sailing boat it had taken him a little while to cope with having less than three feet in the water and at the same time such enormous power under his hand. But he had had Leeming at his elbow. Leeming had been a regular, who had regarded the amateur with suspicion. But Duncan felt that he had earned his superiors' respect by that tragic night in April, off the Norwegian coast, when the flotilla had inadvertently attempted to take on the German invasion fleet bound for Norway. That had brought Leeming the Victoria Cross, but it had been a posthumous award, as he, and the second boat in the flotilla, had been blown out of the water.

Yet again, Duncan had been lucky. Not intentionally. He had taken part in the futile assault, had fired his torpedoes, and had even, he thought and as was generally accepted, scored a hit. And then had somehow managed to wriggle through the hail of gunfire and bring his ship home.

That had led to his appointment to the larger and more heavily armed *Seventy-Two*, and to promotion, both to full lieutenant and flotilla leader. Now, after his exploits at Dunkirk and during the Leopards' – now known as Commandos – raid on Guernsey, he was apparently considered the most effect-ive MTB skipper in the Navy. He wondered when his luck was going to run out.

He opened the gangway and stepped on board, the boat – she was only made of plywood – moving slightly beneath his weight. He walked forward to stand in the bow, immediately behind the quick-firer. Now here was a weapon. Only twenty-millimetre – about three-quarters of an inch – it wouldn't do much damage to the armoured hull of a battleship, but against light craft, or even a U-boat on the surface, it could be a handy thing to have.

There were also the two twenty-one-inch torpedo tubes, and the four machine guns, two of them heavy. These he knew were meant principally for use against aircraft, but again would be handy in a close scrap with their opposite numbers. And aft were the two depth charges. All the sort of things to tingle the blood.

He went up the short ladder to the open bridge – there was a windscreen but no roof – and surveyed the instruments, all so mysterious a year ago, but so very familiar now, then down

the ladder again and into the centre cabin, inhaling the unique
smell, a combination of fresh varnish and fresh paint, common
to all new boats. On a yacht this would have been a saloon
with a lower steering position. Here it was a mess which
would be shared by all hands. Forward, down another short
companion ladder, were the galley and crew's quarters. Aft,
as Fitzsimmons had promised, there were two small cabins,
each with a single berth, but one, the captain's, containing
also a desk and a bookcase. All the comforts of home. Well,
nearly; they shared a head.

'You like?' the woman asked, from behind him, at the foot
of the companion.

He turned, not having heard her come on board. But then,
Second Officer Alison, Lady Eversham, was only half the size,
and the weight, of her husband. Every time he looked at her,
taking in the pristinely smart Wren uniform, the hat worn
exactly straight almost to conceal the tight bun in which the
splendid, long black hair was confined, the slightly clipped
features, the radiant green eyes, the whole topping a surprisingly full figure, he had a sense almost of guilt that yet again
he had been so lucky as to inveigle so much fragile beauty
into his bed and then his family.

Alison of course would say that she, aided and abetted by
his mother, had organized the whole thing, extricating him
from that disastrous engagement to Lucinda Browning, even
if at the time – they had met when they had both been serving
at Scapa – she had been quite unaware that she was becoming
involved with the aristocracy, and had been taken aback when
she had realized the true situation. But she had learned to
cope very well, and not only as regards the ribbing she had
received from her fellow Wren officers. Now, again thanks to
Kristin Eversham's machinations, she was chief secretary to
the commander-in-chief, Portsmouth, a position from which
she could look out of her window at what was happening
below her, and therefore . . .

'I saw you come on board,' she explained. 'So I thought
I'd come down and—'

'You,' Duncan said, 'are a conniving witch. How long have
you known about this?'

Alison made a moue. 'Only a couple of days.'

'And I suppose Mother knew too?'

'Well . . . you know how friendly she is with Lonsdale.'

'But nobody thought to tell me.'

'It was top secret, until today.'

'Yet Mother knew.'

'Your mother isn't a woman. She's a phenomenon. That's why I love her, even if she terrifies me.'

'Snap.'

Alison had remained standing in the doorway. He took off her hat and threw it on to the desk, put his arms round her, lifted her from the deck, and laid her on her back on the bunk. Then he pushed her skirt up to her waist and pulled down her navy blue drawers. 'You know, under this heavy, wind-proof skirt, you really could wear something sexy. I mean, who's to know?'

She raised her hips to help him. 'It'd be against regulations. And you do realize that it is also against regulations for ships' officers to have sex in their cabins.'

'So put me on a charge.' He nuzzled her groin, then raised his head as the ship trembled. 'What was that?'

'Someone coming on board.' She moved his head to pull up the drawers.

'Shit!' He stood up, went to the door and to the bottom of the companion, closing the cabin door behind him.

'Permission to come aboard, sir.'

'Jamie?'

Duncan peered at the young man. Jamie Goring always looked a little older than his nineteen years, his fair hair being offset by his strong features. Almost as tall as Duncan himself, he had a slim build but powerful shoulders, and although there was an enormous gulf, both social and financial, between the Third Lord Eversham and the son of a small garage owner, the two were fast friends. Goring's Garage outside Lymington had serviced the Eversham cars ever since either could remember, and Duncan was well aware that Jamie, with his skill as a motor mechanic and even more the navigational knowledge gained from years of crewing on his father's modest thirty-footer, was the man who was chiefly responsible for his successes of the past year, from that last Cowes–Dinard to the more recent naval exploit off Guernsey. Having him as crew – the result of another of the Dowager Lady Eversham's remarkable machinations – had been the most important facet of his naval career.

'You're joining?'

'Well, of course I am, sir. If you'll have me.'

'Silly boy. What about the others?'

'The orders that you had a new ship were only read out an hour ago. I came straight over, but I think most of the others will be along. May I have a look, sir?'

'You may indeed. I haven't had a look yet, myself.' He opened the door to the engine room, which was situated under the cabin floor, and did not have quite sufficient headroom for the two tall men as they peered at the huge piece of machinery that occupied the centre of the deck.

'Wowie!' Jamie commented.

'Any good?'

'That is a Packard three-shaft, sir. It should deliver four thousand brake horsepower. Have you had an estimate of possible speed?'

'No I have not. What would you say?'

'We should get forty knots at full revs.'

'Wasn't *Seventy-Two* faster?'

'A knot or two. But here we'll be shifting forty tons, I'd say.' He went to the side panel to gaze at the huge fuel tank; there was a matching sister on the starboard side. They both had sight gauges that were presently indicating less than half full, but his practised eye could estimate. 'I'd say twelve fifty in each of these. Two and a half thousand full load, burning say twenty an hour cruising . . . we could damn near cross the Atlantic in this, sir.'

'I don't think that's what their lordships have in mind.'

Jamie was continuing to explore the tanks. 'And look at this, sir, a sheet of steel running right round the outside, inside the hull. That should stop a bullet, certainly after it's had to find its way through the wood first.'

'That's brilliant.' The vulnerability of the fuel tanks had always been the biggest problem with MTBs. 'Makes me feel a lot safer. Welcome again. But look, we won't be in commission for a couple of days. So you can run off home, if you like. Report on Thursday and we'll take her out.'

'Aye-aye, sir. Ah . . .' He looked at the doorway, in which Alison, once again smartly dressed, save for a few wisps of hair escaping her bun and her hat, had appeared. 'Milady! I'm sorry. I didn't know you were aboard.'

'Good afternoon, Jamie.' Although only a recent addition to the Eversham world Alison was already familiar with the Goring relationship. 'I think, when I'm in uniform, you should address me as ma'am, rather than milady.'

'Yes, mi . . . ma'am.'

'Well,' Alison said, 'I gather you like the ship.'

'She's a beaut.'

'I agree with you. I'll see you later, Duncan.'

'Hang about,' Duncan said. 'There's something I want to show you. Jamie's just leaving,' he added, meaningfully.

Jamie got the message. 'Aye-aye, sir. I'll report Thursday morning. Good afternoon, mi . . . ma'am.'

'Now, then,' Duncan said. 'Where were we?'

'Breaking regulations. I really should get back. People will be wondering where I am.'

'Most of them will know.' He lifted her from the deck, carried her back into the cabin, and kicked the door shut. Then he laid her on the bunk again, and again lifted her skirt.

'Ahoy, *Forty-One*. Anyone aboard?'

Duncan raised his head. 'How in the name of God does a chap get to shag his wife around here?'

'Usually by waiting until she gets off duty, and then taking her home to her own bed.'

'Every time I see you I can't wait.'

'After five months of marriage? I like that. But hadn't you better see who it is?'

'Don't move. Whoever it is, I am going to get rid of him.'

He straightened his tunic and climbed the ladder, looking through the windows of the cabin at the pontoon, and the man standing there. He was terribly young, even younger than Jamie Goring, and wore the uniform of a Naval officer, with the single band of a second lieutenant, but the band, as Duncan had feared, was straight-edged. He opened the door and went on deck.

'Lieutenant Lord Eversham?' the newcomer inquired.

'Correct.'

He saluted. 'Second-Lieutenant Arnold Cooper, sir. I am to be your executive officer.'

There was nothing for it. However much his only immediate interest lay in his cabin, Duncan recognized that if they were to be living together in close proximity, and possibly fighting shoulder to shoulder, he had to be both polite and welcoming to this youth. He returned the salute. 'I hadn't expected you so soon,' he said. 'But welcome aboard.'

'Thank you, sir.' Cooper slung his kitbag over the rail, and followed it.

Duncan shook hands. 'You don't have to move on board right this minute. We won't be ready for sea for the next few days.'

'With your permission, sir, I'd like to stay on board. Sort of get used to her.'

'Point taken. But you'll be all alone.'

'That's all right, sir. I can use the officers' mess ashore for eating and ablutions.'

'Well, then, you'd better make yourself at home. You'll find there's not a lot of room. What was your last ship?'

'I'm from Dartmouth, sir.'

'Good lord! I do apologize. But this is rather an extreme step for starters.'

'I did have a cruise on a battleship last year, sir. As a snotty.'

'This will be a little different. I'll show you your quarters.'

He could only hope that Alison had overheard the conversation, and in fact she was standing at the foot of the companion, as with Jamie fully and properly dressed. 'She seems fine,' she said, as if she had been inspecting the ship. Cooper would have to assume that she always had pink spots in her cheeks.

'Thank you, Second Officer,' he said. 'Perhaps you would complete the report.'

'Aye-aye.'

'Oh, by the way, this is Second-Lieutenant Cooper.'

They were the same rank. Alison held out her hand. 'Welcome aboard, Mr Cooper.'

'My pleasure, Miss . . . ah . . . ?'

'Eversham.'

'Ever . . . good lord. I, ah . . .'

'Second Officer Eversham is a senior secretary on the staff of Rear-Admiral Lonsdale,' Duncan explained.

'Yes, sir. But . . .' Cooper looked from one to the other.

'She also happens to be my wife.'

Now Cooper was looking flabbergasted. 'I do apologize, Lady . . .'

'Miss, when I'm in uniform,' Alison suggested. 'And you have nothing to apologize for. I'll see you later, Duncan.' She saluted and went up the steps.

Cooper stared after her, and Duncan said, 'It's a convoluted world, isn't it? There's your cabin. As I said, there's not a lot of room, but it's all yours.'

'Yes, sir.' Cooper peered into the confined space. 'Do we . . . ah . . . have . . .'

'No servants,' Duncan said. 'We have a crew of twelve, including you and me, and every man has a specialized job to do. Now tell me, did you volunteer, or were you seconded?'

'They asked for volunteers, sir.'

'Well done. But do you have any idea just what you have volunteered for? Have you any experience of small boats?'

'I've crewed on my father's boat, sir.'

'Well, that's a start. What was it? The yacht?'

'It was a motor boat, sir.'

'That could be better yet. Then you know the Channel?'

'Well, no, sir. We holidayed on the Norfolk Broads, every summer.'

'Hm. I assume you've specialized?'

'Gunnery, sir.'

'Now that is brilliant. I know nothing about guns. So when we're in action, you will command the foredeck.'

'Aye-aye, sir,' Cooper acknowledged, somewhat apprehensively. 'I have also specialized in Naval History and Design.'

'Hm. On this assignment you're more likely to make history than read about it. You don't smoke?'

'Only the odd cigarette. I'm thinking of buying a pipe.'

'Don't. Smoking is absolutely forbidden, above and below decks. This isn't prejudice. When we put to sea you will be standing on top of two thousand five hundred gallons of petrol. A single spark could send all of us into orbit.'

'Good lord! But, when we're in action . . .'

'Oh, quite. The same thing applies to a bullet in the wrong place. You are, of course, at liberty to withdraw your decision to volunteer. You haven't been officially signed on yet.'

Cooper gazed at him. 'Are you rejecting me sir?'

'No. But it is absolutely necessary for you, and every man who serves on this boat, to know exactly what he is letting himself in for. We are to be an attacking force. Our business is to seek out and if possible destroy the enemy. And we will be doing it in a five-ply wooden hull.'

'Something you have done, successfully, for over a year, sir.'

'I have been lucky. A lot of others have not. And no one's luck lasts forever.'

'I would like to serve under you, sir.'

'Then you are welcome.' Duncan shook his hand again.

Jamie caught the bus at the stop outside the dockyard gate. More often than not, when they both had time off, the skipper would give him a lift to Lymington in his Bugatti, the fantastic sports car that, like his fifty-foot schooner, had been a present from his mother. But he obviously still had things to do on the ship . . . such as christening his new bunk. Lucky bastard! But then, anyone who had the right to shag someone like Alison on demand had to be a lucky bastard.

Just as anyone who inherited a title and a lot of money had to be born a lucky bastard. Not that Duncan had inherited a lot of money, yet. His father might have been a peer of the realm, but in terms of real wealth, he had not had a lot. The money belonged to the fabulous Kristin, who had inherited it from her Spanish multimillionaire father. But that she indulged her only son in his every whim, and would undoubtedly leave him her entire estate, merely meant that he enjoyed her wealth at second-hand. As Kristin was just forty-two, looked ten years younger and lived as if she were ten years younger even than that, suggested that she might be around for a long time yet.

He chose a seat at the back of the bus – he disliked being engaged in conversation by strangers who were interested in the fact that he wore uniform – and watched the countryside slowly unfolding outside his window. It was a long ride in a stopping bus from Portsmouth, round the outskirts of Southampton – where some of the fires caused by last night's raid were still smoking – and through the New Forest, to Lymington; it would be dark before he got home. In Duncan's Bugatti it was a matter of under an hour. Or in Kristin's Bentley.

It was impossible to stop himself thinking about either the car or the woman. If he had known of her all his life, as she had patronized his father's garage for as long as he could remember, she had always been in the category of a screen goddess, there to be admired, but never to be considered in the flesh – he had never spoken to her. Until the Cowes–Dinard just over a year ago.

As he had just been coming up to eighteen – he had actually celebrated his birthday the day the race ended – it had been the first time he had crewed for Duncan Morant, as Lord Eversham had then been. It had been a tremendous experience, but it had been capped at the end by the appearance of Duncan's mother, utterly beautiful, utterly sophisticated, and utterly uninhibited, so unlike any woman he had ever dreamed could exist in the flesh. So she had a scandalous reputation. As she had happily confessed at her divorce from Lord Eversham, ten cases of adultery had been proved against her, although as his late lordship had married her after she had been expelled from her Madrid convent at the age of fifteen for becoming pregnant – by his lordship – he had to have known what he was getting into.

So had he been a fool to allow himself to be sucked into her flamboyant orbit? Actually, he supposed he had never had a chance of escaping, once she had decided that she was 'interested' in this gormless youth even younger than her adoring son. She had sailed back to England with them in a gale, and by the time they had reached Lymington he had been madly in love . . . with a woman who was twenty-three years older than himself!

The compelling aspect of Kristin Eversham was that, for all her amoral background and indeed current lifestyle, there was absolutely nothing vicious or degenerate about her. She *lived*, every moment of every day, and most nights as well. To be in her company was to be swept along on a cloud of love and laughter and above all, energy. He had not supposed he would ever have the opportunity to be as close to her again, certainly as within a month of the race England had found herself at war, and he had found himself in the Navy. But she had been there, always, in the background, pulling strings in high places, so that he had not yet completed his basic training when he had found himself posted as engineer to the MTB captained by Duncan Morant.

He had supposed it a stroke of remarkable fortune, that he should be given the chance to serve under the man he most admired as well as envied. By the time he had realized that fortune had had nothing to do with it he had been launched on a roller coaster ride of excitement and adventure, and passion. He regretted nothing of it, even if he understood that he was shamelessly taking advantage of an older woman's desires. His only fears were that one day, inevitably, Kristin would switch her interest elsewhere, and far worse, that one day, Duncan would find out about their relationship. That was too traumatic a prospect even to be considered. But, as there was no way he could now change what had happened, or wanted to change what was still happening, all he could do was let the future take care of itself . . . and hope that the present could go on forever.

At last the bus stopped, for what seemed the fiftieth time, and he was able to get down, hefting his kitbag and trudging the couple of hundred yards through the darkness to the garage. Both the office and the house were of course blacked out, but the forecourt was still operating, and Probert was just filling a tank. 'Jamie!' he cried. 'Didn't expect you back so soon.'

'I've a short furlough,' Jamie explained. 'Everything OK?'

'Here. We heard them, last night. You must have come through Southampton to get here.'

'We went round the back. But it looked pretty bad.'

'Yeah, sounded grim. If you'll come into the office, Mr Lucas.'

The customer accompanied him to the door to hand over his coupons and money, and Jamie went round to the house.

'Jamie!' In contrast to her son Mary Goring was a small woman, although she had a similar slender build. 'Now that's a funny thing.'

Jamie gave her a hug. 'What?'

'Her ladyship stopped by this afternoon. I mean the old one, not the new one. She asked after you.'

Jamie released her, and turned away so that she could not see his flush. 'What on earth did she want with me?'

'She just asked how you were. The thing is, she seemed to know you would be home. Almost as if she expected you to have this furlough.'

'She probably knew that his lordship's crew were going to be out of action for a while. She has friends in high places.'

'She was awfully nice,' Mary said. 'But then, she always is, isn't she? She actually said, if you did come home, you should give her a ring.'

'What?! Me give her ladyship a ring? Whatever for?' He hoped he sounded convincing. But then, the truth of the matter could not possibly ever have crossed Mary Goring's mind; it was outside the range of either her experience or her imagination, except perhaps in the pages of the *News of the World*. Equally, down to August of last year, it had been beyond his known horizon as well.

'She said something about her dog. You know that huge creature. A . . . ah—'

'Pyrenean Mountain Dog,' Jamie said helpfully. 'Oh, yes. She probably wants me to walk him. Well, I suppose it wouldn't do any harm to humour her. She's our best customer.'

'You haven't told me why you're home.'

'Well, you know the old *Seventy-Two* boat took a hammering off Guernsey a couple of months ago?'

'Your father and I were so worried. But . . . aren't you getting a medal for that?'

'I've been recommended for one, yes. Well, we all deserved medals. It just so happened that I got the kudos because I knew the waters and was able to navigate us in and out. But anyway . . .'

Mary was frowning. 'Wasn't her ladyship involved in that as well?'

'She happened to be in Guernsey at the time, yes. And as we had to take the Leopards in and out we were able to bring her out as well.'

'All in that small boat?'

She was getting too close to the nitty-gritty. 'She's used to small boats,' Jamie pointed out. 'She's been a yachtswoman all her life. Anyway, the point I am trying to make is that we took a hit on the bow which did a lot of damage. The boat was patched up and we were able to use her again, but they didn't do a very thorough job, and she started making water again on every patrol. So she's been taken out of service again for a complete rebuilding.'

'Does that mean you're going to be home for a spell? Your father will be so pleased.'

'No, Mother. I am home for just tomorrow. Lord Eversham

has been given a new ship, a brand new MTB, and I've signed
up to sail with him. We have trials on Thursday.'

Mary's face fell. 'You're not staying with MTBs? They're
so dangerous.'

'I'm staying with his lordship, Mother. And MTBs are only
dangerous if they're badly handled. His lordship is the best
there is. Believe me. Now I'd better give her ladyship a call.'

Alison parked the Sunbeam on the forecourt of Eversham
House – the car belonged to the Eversham collection – and
remembered to brace herself as she approached the front door.
The first time she had come here she had been knocked flat
by the mountainous creature who greeted most visitors to his
mistress's home overenthusiastically. They were now the best
of friends, but she knew he would still want to embrace her,
and as he weighed over a hundred pounds he was a lot to
stand up to.

But then, she reflected, she would have been knocked flat,
at least mentally, by everything about this place, the entire
atmosphere of careless extravagance that was this family. The
miracle was that with such a background and such a mother
Duncan should have turned out so splendidly. He might enjoy
all the good things in life, but he remained consumed with
the concept that as he was an aristocrat, he must always be a
gentleman, always say the right thing, and above all, always
do his duty. That duty had called him from being a playboy
yachtsman to the Navy at the outbreak of war, and he had
gone from strength to strength.

And picked her up on the way. That was the most miracu-
lous thing of all. In command of the cipher department at
Scapa Flow at the beginning of the year, she had found the
handsome young Lieutenant Morant – she had had no idea
he was heir to a title – attractive from their first meeting, but
they had not got together until after that traumatic week in
April when the Navy had tried to prevent the German invasion of Norway. Duncan had had to watch two of his sister
MTBs blown out of the water with all their crews, and for all
his apparent calm acceptance of the facts of war she had
known, on his return, that he was in a confused and uncertain state.

She had been happy to assist him to recover, but she had

had no idea that he would break off his high-profile engagement and want to marry her. Even that could have been considered as merely the right thing to do, because he had slept with her and discovered that she was a virgin, and therefore by her surrender had become his responsibility, whereas he had apparently never attempted to impose upon Lucinda's somewhat snooty maidenhood. But equally, as he had confessed, he had fallen totally in love with her.

Whether or not she had deserved such a remarkable change in her status and fortune was not a question she was at that moment prepared to ask herself, much less attempt to answer. The summer had been such an ongoing kaleidoscope of triumph and tragedy she still wasn't quite sure how it had all happened, but here she was, with no social background to speak of, Lady Eversham and living in a style she had not suspected actually to exist outside of magazines like *The Tatler*. As her only condition for accepting his proposal was that she should not have to give up her job and rank she had even found herself transferred to Portsmouth to be near her husband. And his mother, who had organized the whole thing.

And his dog! She opened the door and two enormous paws were placed on her shoulders, while he licked her nose. 'Please, Lucifer,' she protested as her hat fell off. 'I'm in uniform.'

He subsided down her tunic and she ruffled his head as she picked up the hat and hung it on a stand.

'I'll take him out, milady,' volunteered Harry, emerging from the pantry. Harry had been Duncan's valet before the war, but as there was no room for a valet in the Royal Navy, much less on an MTB, had become Kristin's butler, and ran the house with her Spanish maid, Lucia; the rest of the pre-war staff were all in the services.

'Off you go, sweetheart,' Alison said, and frowned. 'What's that noise?'

'Milady?'

'Listen.'

From above them there came a loud click, followed by a whirrrr, followed by a *ting*.

'Ah!' Harry said. 'That's her ladyship . . . oh, I beg your pardon, milady.' He still had not properly got the measure of having two Lady Eversham's in the house. 'I meant her dowager . . .' again he paused, realizing that he had lost his way.

'What is she doing?' Alison asked, not wishing to become involved in a semantical debate.

'It's her new game, milady. Arrived yesterday. She plays it all the time.'

'I'd better see what it is.' Alison went up the small stair-case to Kristin's private sitting room.

'Darling!' Kristin Eversham said. She had had a table placed in the centre of the room, upon which there was a long board with raised edges, covered in what appeared to be a variety of pins inserted in the varnished wood, which had numbers painted on it. Her ladyship had been studying the progress of a small steel ball bouncing from pin to pin. 'Damnation!' She raised her head. 'Duncan not with you?'

Alison kissed her mother-in-law. 'He was going to the hospital to see how Petty Officer Harris is getting on.'

'Poor Harris, I do hope he comes through it all right. You must feel like a drink.'

Kristin headed for the sideboard, while Alison took off her tunic, shook out her hair and freed her tie, watching her as she did so. Watching Kristin was always a tonic after a long day. Just watching her move was that. She was tall, with a very full figure without the least suggestion that it contained any fat; she had never spared the time to allow any to develop. That she appeared to have no dress sense, although Alison suspected that this was less ignorance than a careless contempt for clothes as anything more than neces-sary, at certain times of the year, to keep one warm – she had had a Swedish mother – merely enhanced her above-it-all personality. Thus this evening she wore brown slacks and a crimson jumper, on the bodice of which there sat a string of pearls, flopping on to the board as she bent over it. Her auburn hair was worn straight to her shoulders, and unlike the rest of her, this was carefully groomed. But the whole was dominated and made irresistible by the flawless perfec-tion of her features, the deep blue eyes, and the bubbling vitality of her every movement. Alison had of course learned something of the irregular life she had lived – Kristin had never kept it a secret – and was still living, if perhaps a little more discreetly than in the past, but she had to believe that any man on whom her mother-in-law bestowed her favours, however temporarily, would die happy.

Now she poured two scotches and handed Alison one. 'Is he pleased with his new boat?'

'I would say so, yes. But he is definitely not pleased that we should have known about it before he did, and not told him.'

Kristin sat beside her on the settee. 'Duncan is one of those men who is never quite pleased about anything. Except you, I hope. That is why he should go far. Has he got his crew together?'

'He's expecting them over the next couple of days. He's hoping most of his old lot will transfer. Except of course for Harris and the other two men who were wounded in that fight with the S-boat. Was it very frightening?'

'It was exhilarating,' Kristin said. 'Although it was a shame we got hit. I should think the old crew would be happy to rejoin him. There can be no better MTB skipper.'

'I don't think anyone is going to argue about that. But the boats are so terribly vulnerable. Not everyone finds it exhilarating to go into battle in one. I supposed not everyone has your guts.'

Kristin made a moue. 'What do they say? Only the good die young? By that criterion I should live forever. So you don't actually know if any of the crew have made the transfer.'

'Oh, yes,' Alison said. 'One has, definitely. That sweet boy Jamie Goring. You know, his father has that garage you use.'

'I remember Jamie very well,' Kristin said, quietly. 'And so should you. I, he, and you worked shoulder to shoulder getting men on board at Dunkirk. And you stopped a bullet.'

'I know,' Alison said. 'It still hurts when it rains. And I still have the scar.'

'Ah, but you must always look on the bright side,' Kristin pointed out. 'If you hadn't been wounded, you wouldn't have had the unique experience of being married while lying in a hospital bed. And you say that Jamie has stuck with Duncan. I am so pleased.'

'I think Duncan is too.'

'Of course he will be. Jamie is a top-class motor engineer.' She finished her drink 'Now come and look at this.'

'I'll make you another,' Alison volunteered, getting up. 'What is it?'

'It's called Bagatelle. It's the latest thing.' She accepted her refilled glass and gestured at the board. 'You see, it's got little legs at the top so it's on a slight slope. And you have this propulsion lever at the bottom. You place the little ball against the lever, so, and you draw it back and let it go, so, and the ball is hurled up into the board, and . . . damnation. Missed again.' The ball, having reached the top of the board, rolled back down, again bouncing from pin to pin.

'The object being?'

'Well, you see, the pins are arranged in half-cages, opening away from the bottom. The object is to get the ball, on its way back, into one of the cages. You see, they all have different values, marked on the board, according to the difficulty of getting in that each presents. The ones near the bottom, where you have more chance of scoring, are valued at twenty or thirty. Those in the middle are worth fifty or sixty. The one right at the top, with the small cage, is worth a hundred. The object is to see how much you can score with a certain number of pulls, I,' she added disconsolately, 'have only managed a total of thirty with ten shots. You have a go.'

'There's the phone,' Alison said, with some relief. 'I'll take it . . .'

But the phone was on the sideboard, and Alison was already there. 'Eversham House. Yes, she's here. May I ask whose calling? Oh. Ah . . .' she put her hand over the mouthpiece. 'It's some man. He won't give me his name, but he says you're expecting his call. His voice is vaguely familiar.'

'Yes,' Kristin agreed, taking the receiver from her hand. 'Mr Smith, is it? It is good of you to call. When can we meet?' She listened. 'I think we should make it a bit earlier than that; I hate to let the morning get away from me. Let's say eight o'clock.' She listened. 'Of course, they never run on time, do they? I'll pick you up at the Stop. Eight sharp. Adios.' She replaced the phone and gazed at Alison.

'I feel I shouldn't have been here,' Alison said, aware that she was flushing.

'My dear girl, you belong here. You must forgive an old woman her foibles. I suppose you did recognize the voice.'

Alison's flush deepened. 'Well . . .'

'And I'm sure you completely disapprove, on every possible count. But I am not going to call a halt just yet. He is the most adorable hunk of man I have ever met. And I have met a few, you know.'

'I do know,' Alison said absently. 'Isn't eight o'clock in the morning a bit early?'

'To have sex? My dear girl, it's the only time. When a man staggers home from work, overtired and probably frustrated, and encounters his wife, overtired and also probably frustrated from a day's shopping and housework, how on earth can they really enjoy a cuddle? Whereas, first thing in the morning, everyone is full of vim, vigour and vitality. Or they should be.'

'I never thought of it that way. When you meet up tomorrow morning, are you going to bring him here?'

'No. Duncan will be here. We have somewhere else we can go.'

'Does Duncan know?'

'He does not. That would be a quite impossible situation, on a small boat. Are you going to tell him?'

'Of course I won't.'

Kristin kissed her. 'I adore you. Now we share a secret.'

'But . . . isn't he bound to find out, some time? Men . . . well, they like to share their experiences.'

'Jamie is not men,' Kristin said firmly. 'He is a man, and right now he is my man.'

'Right now being?'

'Long ago I found out that it is quite impossible to cross a bridge until one comes to the river. And by the time one does, who knows? It may have flooded and be impassable anyway, or it may have dried up and no longer be there.'

Affairs of the Heart

Alison, Kristin reflected, although a lovely girl in every sense, and the ideal wife for Duncan, was a typical example of the modern young woman who had been taught to think, but who lacked the masculine facility for departmentalizing thoughts, considerations, even emotions, and calling them up as and when required, or necessary. To her, life had to be taken as a whole, the good and the bad, the beautiful and the ugly, the wanting and the possible consequences of so doing, all had to be lumped together all of the time, with an inevitable hard landing at the end of it all, because that was the inescapable nature of the beast that was humanity.

Duncan had indicated that she was very good in bed, but he had also confided that she had been a virgin when they had got together, so that undoubtedly her sexual activity was part and parcel of being his wife and not an independent entity. The young woman did not lack courage and certainly accepted that her husband might not survive the war, especially if he continued to skipper MTBs, and Kristin could tell that her acceptance of this fact was a bridge she had already half crossed in her mind. But her consideration of this likely scenario was directed to being a lonely widow, although she might hope to be a mother by then. Of course the loneliness would be cushioned by the fact that she would be the Dowager Lady Eversham, entirely lacking financial worries. But Kristin was quite sure that the idea of replacing Duncan, if it had ever crossed her mind, had immediately been rejected as unthinkable.

Well, she supposed as she pulled into the bus stop, they would have to grow old together, as gracefully as possible. Only she had no intention of doing so without masculine companionship, as long as she remained capable both of attracting the dear things and enjoying them. But the whole concept was deflating, while right this moment enjoyment should be top of the list.

Jamie was wearing a raincoat and a soft hat because it was, inevitably, drizzling. To be as anonymous as possible Kristin was driving the Sunbeam, with the roof up, and he sat beside her in a damp slither. 'No problems?'

'I told them I was going into Southampton for the day.' He grinned. 'They think I have a girl.'

'Would you like to have a girl? I mean, you must be getting pretty tired of me.'

'Tired of you, milady? That's not possible.'

She concentrated on the road. 'Then when are you going to stop calling me milady? At least when we're alone.'

'I dunno. Somehow, it's your ambience.'

'Even if it's a complete misnomer? In every possible sense. Do you like the new boat?'

'Oh, it's tremendous. Did his lordship tell you that we even have an exec?'

'At dinner last night. I haven't seen him this morning. Straight out of school, he says. Have you met him?'

'Not yet. We get together tomorrow.'

'Tomorrow,' she brooded. 'We live in a world of tomorrows.'

He frowned. 'Is there something wrong?'

She was now driving through the narrow streets of Lymington, and down the hill to the ferry port and the yacht harbour, and the boatyard where *Kristin* was stored. She glanced at him. 'Nothing is wrong when I am with you.'

'I wish I knew why. I mean . . .'

Don't tell me that he also is becoming introspective, she thought. It must be the war, having this pernicious effect upon young people. 'You are what I want,' she said. 'Everything I want. Does that upset you?'

'Well, of course it doesn't, milady. It makes me the most privileged man in the world. But . . .'

'Then no buts.' The gate to the boatyard was locked, but Kristin had a key, which she gave to Jamie, and he got out and opened it. The yard was deserted as the entire staff had joined up with the exception of the owner, and he only stopped by occasionally. Thus it was a petrified forest of yachts shrouded in tarpaulins. on their legs, their masts stacked, their canvas and fittings stowed.

'Have you ever thought what a single bomb dropped in here would do?' Jamie asked, as they stopped before the open shed in which *Kristin*, as the most expensive yacht in the yard, was kept under cover.

'It would upset an awful lot of people,' she suggested, getting out.

He followed her under the roof, gazed at the schooner; her masts lay on the ground to one side. What memories seeing her always brought back, even if he had only made one voyage in her. But, for all the action he had seen on the MTBs, that voyage remained the high spot of his life, so far. He walked round the hull to look at the gash on the lead keel, caused by striking a rock off the west coast of Guernsey. 'Still not repaired.'

Kristin waited at the foot of the ladder leading up to the deck. 'Andrews says there's no lead available. Anyway, she's not going anywhere until this lot is over.'

Jamie went to her. 'Do you reckon he knows we come here?'

'He has eyes, even if he's not here all the time' She kicked off her shoes, and rested her hand on his shoulder to stand on one leg and take off her socks, which today she was wearing under her slacks in preference to stockings: the rungs of the ladder were inclined to be slippery. Then she climbed up. Jamie followed; he was wearing deck shoes with non-slip soles. He looked up at the long legs immediately above him; even when encased in slacks they could turn him on. The thought that in a few moments they would be his to possess was overwhelming. If only he could understand her mood; he had never known it before.

Kristin reached the top, threw one leg over the rail, and followed with the other. She unlocked the padlock on the hatch, pushed the wooden cover back, and slid down the companion into the cabin. 'My feet are freezing.' She sat on the mattress covering the starboard settee berth, and put her legs up.

Jamie immediately sat at her feet and began massaging her toes. But . . . 'Where did the mattress come from?'

'I brought it down a couple of weeks ago. Just after we got back from Guernsey. I was tired of bruising my bottom on bare boards. Getting it up that ladder on my own was quite a job.'

'I can imagine. What have you done with the picture?'

The reason she had been in Guernsey at all, and thus trapped by the unexpected arrival of the Germans at the end of June, had been to regain possession of the full length and rather risque nude of herself, painted when she had been a girl, before anyone else got it.

'It's been reframed and is hanging above my bed. I'll leave it to you in my Will, if you're good. Ummm, that feels good. But the rest of me is just as frozen. Look, I brought a blanket as well.' She lifted her jumper over her head. She never wore a brassiere, and in the chill her nipples were enormous. 'These also need attention.'

He moved up the bunk gently to massage the soft flesh. 'I could do this all day.'

'And I could have it done, all day, by you.' Her arms went round him and their mouths became locked for several seconds.

'Do you think his lordship will go back to racing when this lot is over?' he asked when they paused for breath.

'Of course he will. And he'll want you to crew him again.'

'I don't know that I'll be able to.'

She had been unfastening his pants. Now she pulled her head back. 'What?'

'I mean, I don't think I could ever sleep in this cabin again without wishing you were here with me.'

'I'm here with you now,' she pointed out. 'That's all that matters. Here and now, Jamie. Tomorrow is a bonus.' She lay back so that he could remove her pants in turn.

'Mr Carling!' Duncan said. 'Good to see you again. You're not . . .?'

'Yes, sir.' Carling was a heavy-set man on whom the blue uniform sat like a glove. 'I'm your new PO. If you'll have me.'

'Have you? My dear fellow, it's an honour.' He shook hands and turned to Cooper standing patiently to one side of the little bridge. 'Petty Officer Carling, Sub-Lieutenant Cooper. Petty Officer Carling took me out on my first ever trip on an MTB.'

'Mr Carling.' Cooper followed the example of his captain and shook hands, although it was easy to see that he did not altogether approve of such fraternity.

'That was quite an occasion,' Duncan said. 'I all but wrecked the harbour. Poor Mr Leeming nearly had a fit.'

'Very sad about Mr Leeming, sir.'

'Yes,' Duncan agreed. 'Well . . .'

'But this is something quite different to the old *Seventeen*,' Carling hurried on, as he saw that his new skipper did not wish to go into Leeming's death. 'What's she like at sea?'

'I haven't found out yet. But now you're here, we have a full complement, so we are going to try her out right now. This is Leading Seaman Rawlings.'

Rawlings, lean and hatchet-faced, had sailed with Duncan from the day he had taken command of his first ship. He stood to attention.

'Petty Officer Carling,' Duncan explained. 'Rawlings is my senior crew member. He's been acting PO for the past month. You may regard him as bo'sun. Show Mr Carling below, will you, Rawlings, and stow his gear, then make ready for sea in half an hour.'

'Aye-aye, sir.' Both men spoke together, but Carling checked as he turned to the hatch and saw Jamie emerging.

'Ah,' Duncan said. 'This is Jamie Goring. Our engineer.'

'Petty Officer!' Jamie acknowledged.

'Goring.' As with most people, Carling was clearly taken aback by Jamie's youth.

'All well below?' Duncan asked.

'Aye-aye, sir,' Jamie said. 'She's in perfect nick.'

'Bilges clean?'

This was a rhetorical question, as Jamie was as likely to forget to pump the bilges before any voyage as he was to forget to put his shoes on when getting out of his bunk. But it was also an essential part of the drill when preparing for sea, as Cooper needed to understand.

'All clean, sir,' Jamie acknowledged.

'Very good. Carry on, Petty Officer.'

'Aye-aye, sir.'

'Do you mean she makes water?' Cooper asked.

'Not unless she opens a seam,' Duncan said. 'But we have a petrol engine, remember? Petrol gives off fumes, and these are apt to accumulate in the bilges. They can't be seen, and with all the other smells in the engine room, they can't be smelt very easily, either. But they are highly explosive. That is the main reason smoking on board is forbidden. But equally dangerous, when I turn on the engine, which relies on internal combustion, there is the chance of a spark which could cause an explosion. Thus the bilges must be pumped, before starting up, whether there is water down there or not. The pump will extract petrol fumes as well. You with me?'

Cooper gulped. 'Yes, sir.'

Jamie had already ducked down the hatch, and the petty officer and Rawlings followed him.

'I've been meaning to ask,' Cooper ventured. 'How on earth did an inexperienced lad like that find himself on board a boat like this with such a responsible job?'

'Jamie Goring,' Duncan said, 'has more sea experience than the entire rest of the crew put together, including me. He has been sailing ever since he could stand, he knows the Channel better than you know the back of your hand and he has the guts of a lion.'

'Oh. I didn't mean to speak out of turn.'

'You didn't. Most people make the same mistake about Jamie. But just for the record, he's been recommended for the DCM for his part in our raid on Guernsey in September.'

'Oh,' Cooper said again. 'Then I apologize again. That must have been some show.'

'It was a pointless propaganda exercise that cost the lives of three Commandos and put several others in hospital, including three of my crew, all for no visible gain.' Save for the rescuing of my mother, he thought. But that was a very private, and indeed, confidential matter.

'Oh. This seems to be my day for putting my foot in my mouth. The papers—'

'If you ever believe anything you read in the newspapers, you need your head examined. Now, are we ready for sea?'

'I believe so, sir.'

'Mr Cooper, as you are my executive officer, I require you to know, not believe.' He looked at his watch. 'You have ten minutes to make sure.'

'Aye-aye, sir.' Cooper went down the ladder.

Duncan looked up at the Command Building, while he wondered if he was being hard on the boy. But it was essential to set a standard from the beginning, or it would become more difficult later on. He knew he was being overlooked from the many windows above him. Fitzsimmons, certainly. Alison, almost certainly. And even Lonsdale, perhaps. But in such strong contrast to fourteen months previously, he was totally confident.

He watched his crew file on deck to take up their positions for casting off. Four were members of the crew of *Seventy-Two* as were the two not on deck, Jamie in the engine room and Wilson in the galley. That the other three were not here was because, as he had reminded Cooper, they were in hospital. Of the four newcomers, apart from Carling, in whom he had every confidence, and Cooper, the other two were gunners to handle the quick-firer. As he had admitted to Cooper, here he was again the tyro; he had not had anything larger than a machine-gun on either of his previous boats. But again he was totally confident.

Cooper arrived on the bridge, somewhat breathless. 'The ship is ready for sea, sir.'

'Thank you, Mr Cooper. Prepare to cast off, Mr Carling.'

The Petty Office was also on deck. 'Aye-aye, sir.'

Duncan pulled the throttle lever sideways to disengage the gears, turned the ignition key and the Packard engine growled into life. Jamie would be checking gauges and making sure everything was operating properly. 'Cast off aft, cast off forward. Bear away.'

The warps were jerked off their bollards and reeled in, the crew took in the fenders. Duncan clicked the throttle lever back in and immediately the engine noise changed from a rumble to a low purr, and the MTB moved away from the pontoon. The next pontoon, filled with boats of various shapes, sizes and functions, was about a hundred yards away. As soon as his stern was clear of the end of the floating wharf Duncan spun the wheel to port while easing the throttle forward half-an-inch. The purr slightly increased in volume, and the boat came neatly round to head for the harbour exit, while Duncan spun the wheel amidships.

'Does she always require this much helm?' Cooper asked.

'At anything over a thousand revs she reacts like a dream,' Duncan said. 'But at low speed she's very sluggish. We only have three feet in the water, you see.'

'So when can we open her up?'

'Not till we're clear of land and other shipping; she also

has quite a wake.' He negotiated the harbour mouth and turned into the Solent, opening the throttle to a thousand revs. Now the boat moved smoothly and quickly to the east and the passage between the barrier forts, the wind already whistling past their ears. The crew abandoned the foredeck and moved either aft or below, although as yet there was no spray.

'How fast would you say we're going?' Cooper asked.

'Fifteen knots.'

Carling had joined them on the bridge. 'Oilskins, sir?'

'Thank you, Mr Carling.'

The petty officer went below.

'And you'll want to secure your cap,' Duncan recommended. Cooper brought the strap down from the brim to fasten under his chin, while the boat passed between the forts. 'Now take her.'

'Me?' the sub-lieutenant asked.

'That's why you're here, Mr Cooper. Starboard your helm and we'll pass inside the Nab. Remember, you don't require too much helm at this speed.'

'Aye-aye.'

Cautiously Cooper grasped the wooden spokes while Duncan secured his own cap, and put on the oilskin jacket being offered by Carling. Cooper put the helm down, and the boat came round and headed south, the coast of the Isle of Wight falling away to starboard, as did the huge Nab Tower, marking the start of the deep-water channel, to port.

'How does she feel?'

'Like nothing I've ever handled before.'

'The conditions are ideal. It'll be a little more brisk in the Channel.' The wind was westerly about Force Four, but for the moment the bulk of the island was acting as a breakwater and the sea was calm. 'Let Mr Carling get the feel of her,' Duncan said.

Cooper stepped back and Carling took the helm.

'And you put your oilskins on, Mr Cooper.'

Cooper obeyed, while Duncan looked around him. The clouds were still low and grey, as they had been all week, but it was not actually raining at the moment. The Isle of Wight was now astern of them and they were into the Channel. As he had observed, the wind was westerly fresh, and the sea was lumpy over a long swell; there was only the occasional whitecap. Away to the south he could make out a patrolling destroyer, and to the west there was a freighter, proceeding as close to the shore as was safe. It was a peaceful scene, and could have been at any time before the war; it was difficult to accept that only sixty miles away to the south there was an enemy, busily dreaming up ways of bringing death and destruction to these domestic waters. But then, no doubt, he reflected, the Germans were thinking the same thing as they looked north.

Cooper was properly cocooned. Duncan thumbed the intercom. 'How are things down there, Jamie?'

'Couldn't be better, sir. She's purring like a cat.'

'Very good. We're going to give here a run now.'

'Aye-aye, sir.'

'All hands stand by.' Duncan closed the mike. 'Mr Cooper will take her, Petty Officer.'

Carling handed back the helm, and Cooper grasped the spokes again, now looking grimly determined, but also apprehensive.

'Concentration is the name of the game,' Duncan said. 'You must retain total control at all times.'

'Aye-aye, sir.'

'Very good. Starboard your helm, course two seven oh. Take her up to two thousand revs.'

Cooper swallowed and obeyed, first of all lining up the boat to run parallel to the Isle of Wight, and then cautiously pushing the throttle forward. *Forty-One* slowly gathered speed, first of all slapping the shallow waves, sending spray clouding away to either side, as she passed twenty knots, and then seeming to disappear in flying water as she topped thirty. Now the spray shot straight up over the bows as well as to either side, clouded on to the glass windshield of the bridge, and over the top on to the heads and shoulders of the three men.

'Manoeuvre,' Duncan commanded. 'Port your helm. Easy now, or you'll have us over.'

Teeth clenched, Cooper cautiously put the helm down, and the boat came round in a wide circle, until she was steering east, up-Channel, with the wind and the sea behind her. The spray settled into a surge, and the roar of the engine seemed to increase. Behind them the wake spread away to either side, out of sight.

'What do you reckon?' Duncan asked.

'Tremendous,' Cooper said. 'I've never known anything like it.'

'Excellent. And you handled her well. Now, take us home.'

'Well?' inquired Rear-Admiral Lonsdale. He was a stockily built man with strong features and thick iron-grey hair brushed straight back from his forehead. Duncan had known him for some time, before, in fact, he had been called up, and since then had become very much a protégé of the commanding admiral. This was certainly in part because Jimmy Lonsdale and Kristin Eversham were close friends. Some would say that the word friends was wide of the mark. Duncan had no evidence that this was so – he had long made it a rule never to inquire, or even think, about his mother's peccadilloes – but he did know that when Mother desperately wanted something to happen, it invariably did, as exemplified both by the strange appointment of Jamie Goring to be his engineer before the boy had even completed his basic training, simply because she apparently considered that Jamie was his lucky charm, and even more by the way she had engineered the removal of Alison from the wilds of Scapa Flow to the comparative civilization of Portsmouth, to be the Admiral's private secretary. She was here now, sitting at her desk just beyond the open door.

But when they were both in uniform Lonsdale never failed to reveal his true metier, which was commanding ships and men. 'Captain Fitzsimmons seems satisfied. And you've had enough time. Four weeks, is it?'

'Just on five, sir. I would say we're ready,' Duncan said.

'All six?'

'Yes, sir. I have been out with each of them, individually, more than once, and we have been out as a flotilla, several times. They're practised, and they're keen.'

'And you're happy with your commanders?'

'They're human beings, sir. And they've volunteered to command MTBs. That also makes them individuals.'

'But on your wavelength, as they also volunteered.'

Duncan permitted himself a brief smile. 'With respect, sir. I did not volunteer. I was appointed. By you.'

'Ah, well, yes. That was before the war started, and even when it did, we had no idea it was going to come to this. We assumed, everyone assumed, that it would be fought in France, just like the last one, and that we would retain absolute control of the Channel, save perhaps for the odd U-boat.'

And you did it for Mother's sake, Duncan thought, on the assumption that rushing about in a fast motor boat in an area where hostilities would be at a minimum would be the best way to keep me out of danger.

'That we might wind up having to share our own Channel with an enemy who outnumbers us in the water never crossed anyone's mind,' the Admiral went on. 'You have twice been offered a post on a larger ship.'

'I would not dream of it, sir.'

'I didn't think you would. And I congratulate you. But these individualists among your commanders—'

'Are all keen to do their jobs to the best of their ability. Just give us the word.'

'The word is two days' time.'

'Not tomorrow? Didn't the Jerries get in amongst a convoy last week?'

'Yes, they did. And sank three coasters. The destroyers on patrol only got there in time to chase them off, not to engage them. But, as you seem to have forgotten, tomorrow is Christmas Day. Your people have been working very hard and are about to undertake a most dangerous operation. I think they should be allowed Christmas with their families before putting to sea.'

'Thank you, sir. I know that will be much appreciated.'

'There are just two more points before you go. You will be operating, normally, in two flotillas. I need to know the name of your second flotilla leader.'

'Lieutenant Cooley, sir.'

'That was quick.'

'I had already selected him, sir. He skippered the *Seventy-Three* boat when I commanded that flotilla, and did it very well.'

'Hm. He's a regular, isn't he?' Lonsdale was well aware of the rivalry that could exist between regulars and reservists.

'He is, sir. But that doesn't interfere with his competence.'

The admiral gazed at him for several seconds, also aware that his protégé was taking the mickey. Then he nodded. 'It's your choice. The other point is, your commanders, and their crews, need to bear in mind at all times that the S-boats are bigger and more heavily armed than our MTBs.' He pushed a file across his desk. 'Study that, and then make sure your commanders do also. I'm not suggesting that this should inhibit them in any way, but we will have accomplished very little if you were to lose your entire command in your first action, or at all.' He held up a finger as Duncan would have spoken. 'I know, in September you sank one S-boat and caused another to strand. That was local knowledge and, if I may say so, superior skill. I doubt any of your commanders have quite reached that level as yet.'

'Thank you, sir. I intend to see that they do, as quickly as possible.'

'I'm sure you do. The other point is that Captain Fitzsimmons gave you to understand that you would be operating in two shifts, one on and one off. Right this moment that is not possible. I have wangled you Christmas Day off, but as from Friday that's it. The Navy is becoming increasingly stretched trying to cope with the convoy situation. Thus the Channel is going to be yours. You will have support from Coastal Command if you need it and if they can provide it at the time. But you need to be at sea, all of you, twelve hours a day, and on standby every night. The situation will improve. There are new boats coming off the production line every week. But we are talking about the next month, at least. Understood?'

'Aye-aye, sir.'

'Very good. Now, I assume that boy Goring is again sailing with you?'

'Indeed, sir.'

Lonsdale nodded. 'He is going to get his medal. It's been confirmed. Perhaps you'd like to tell him. I have no idea when the investiture will be, but the knowledge that he is going to get it will be a Christmas present.'

'Thank you, sir. He'll be delighted.'

'Very good. Dismissed, Lieutenant.'

Duncan stood up, put on his cap, and saluted.

'Oh, by the way, Duncan,' the Admiral added. 'Your mother has very kindly invited me to Christmas lunch. So I shall see you there.'

'I'll look forward to that, sir.' Duncan went into the outer office. The door was still open and he had not been invited to close it, so he jerked his head, and Alison, after a bright smile at the other two secretaries, got up and followed him into the lobby. 'You heard all of that,' he suggested.

'Yes. Tres intime.'

'I don't know why she doesn't marry him. I'm sure he's been in love with her for the past couple of years.'

'I don't think,' Alison said, choosing her words with care, 'that your mother is actually in the mood to marry anyone, right now.'

Duncan frowned. 'I have a feeling that you know something I don't. You and she are very close, aren't you? Girl chat. What exactly has she been telling you?'

'It's more girl intuition,' Alison lied, skilfully evading an answer. 'I hope you won't mind my saying it, but I have a feeling that marriage to your father has put her off the institution.'

'You could be right. But listen, I . . . um . . . well . . .'

Alison raised her eyebrows. Her husband was not normally a diffident speaker.

'This chap Cooper,' Duncan said.

'Your exec.'

'Yes. Well, he doesn't seem to have any folk except some distant uncle, who paid for his education. Epsom or somewhere . . .' Duncan, an old Etonian, could not avoid a certain snobbishness when it came to other schools. 'And, well, I couldn't accept the idea of him sitting all alone on the boat while we're wassailing . . .'

'Have you told Kristin?'

'Well, not yet. It's your house. The thing is, when I asked Cooper I had no idea she'd invited his nibs. Do you think it'll go down all right?'

'I think you need to get your facts straight,' Alison suggested. 'In the first place, it is not my house; it is Kristin's. In the second, will it go down all right with whom? I don't think it'll bother Kristin, although I think she should know about it as soon as possible, like right now. As for what the boss may think of it, if he does have designs on some nookie over the holiday, I wouldn't care to offer an opinion.'

'Oh, come now, darling. I was thinking of his feelings about having to sit down to lunch with about the most junior lieutenant in the Navy. I mean to say, Cooper is eighteen years old. He's still wet behind the ears. Lonsdale couldn't possibly see him as a possible rival. Not for Mother.'

'Amorous men do form some strange ideas,' she suggested. And even more, amorous women she thought. 'Well, anyway, you can't take back the invitation. Tell you what, I'll call her now and bring her up to date.'

'Would you? You're the best wife a man could have.'

'Just remember that.' She stood on tiptoe to kiss him. 'See you this evening.'

'There's just one thing more.'

'Yes?' she asked cautiously.

'I've told Jamie we'll give him a lift out.'

'You mean along with Cooper.'

'Well, yes. It'll be a bit cramped, but they're both part of the crew.'

'Shit!'

'Eh?'

'My phone is ringing,' she explained, and hurried off.

'Going to a party tonight, Jamie?' Duncan asked over his shoulder. He was driving, with Alison alongside him. Cooper and Jamie were in the narrow back of the Bugatti, and the sub-lieutenant was sitting rather stiffly at finding himself in such close proximity to a rating.

'Well, no, sir,' Jamie said. 'I'm looking forward to a quiet night.'

'But you are going to celebrate Christmas?' Alison suggested. 'And your medal.'

'My mum will have a turkey for us tomorrow, ma'am. And we'll drink a couple of toasts.'

'And then it's off to Lymington with your girlfriend.'

'Well, I may go into Lymington for an hour or so.'

'Jamie doesn't have a girlfriend,' Duncan asserted. 'Ships and engines, eh Jamie?'

'What else, sir?'

'Ah!' Alison commented.

'Merry Christmas! You're down early,' Alison remarked. She was herself down early, because, although she had no doubt everything in the kitchen was under total control, she was still a little nervous. After all she had spent the first month of her

married life as an invalid with a broken shoulder, and she and
Duncan were engaged in fighting a war, and this, however
small, would be her first lunch party as Lady Eversham. Thus
she had left Duncan still in bed, as apparently was Cooper.
And her remark was made with meaning.

'I have to go out for a little while.' Kristrin was eating toast
and marmalade and drinking coffee. She was also wearing
slacks and a jumper and low-heeled shoes, the exact garb she
had worn the last time she had set off early in the morning.
'Don't get uptight. Lucia and Harry have everything in hand,
and I shall be back by eleven. Bags of time to bathe and
change before Jimmy gets here. Here's your present.' She indicated the gift-wrapped box on the table.

'Oh,' Alison said. 'Thank you. I didn't bring yours down.
I thought we were going to open them when we were all
together, before lunch.'

'Well, then, you can leave it there until the right time. Now
I have to rush.'

'Of course,' Alison agreed. 'He is a nice boy, isn't he?'

Kristin wiped her mouth on her napkin. 'Of whom are we
speaking?' As if it could possibly be Jimmy Lonsdale.

'Lieutenant Cooper.'

'Oh. Yes, indeed. A bit tongue-tied. But I suppose he feels
a little out of his depth.'

Alison sat opposite her, poured coffee for herself.
'Absolutely. I think you're being perfectly splendid, accepting
him at such short notice, and with . . . well . . .'

'I have always believed in saying exactly what I believe to
be true,' Kristin pointed out. 'That habit has made me quite
a few enemies, but at least I have known that they were
enemies, and not ersatz friends. You are now my closest and
dearest friend. So?'

'I was just wondering if Admiral Lonsdale might be put
out at having five at the table.'

Kristin regarded her for several seconds. 'Jimmy knows me
well enough to understand that I do not let other people dictate
how I should live my life. Anyway, you don't seriously suppose
that he would be jealous of an eighteen-year-old boy, who is
also his subordinate.'

'Of course I do not,' Alison lied.

'That would be supposing I were the least bit interested in

Mr Cooper, which I am not.' She got up. 'I will be back soon after ten.' She smiled. 'Ready to open presents. I am expecting Jimmy about twelve. Hasta la vista.'

'Kristin,' Alison said.

Kristin, already at the breakfast room door, turned back.

Alison licked her lips. 'You do realize that the day after tomorrow . . . well . . .'

'Duncan commences patrolling the Channel. Jimmy told me. But he's been doing that for weeks.'

'This is different. Did he tell you what is involved?'

'Seeking out and destroying enemy shipping wherever possible.'

'Which means . . .'

'I have lived with the daily possibility of Duncan's death for well over a year. As you have for several months. You have even shared in it.'

'Dunkirk was different too. We were there. If he went, we went. And then, anti-submarine patrols . . . one never feels that the pursuing surface vessel is itself in any danger. I wish I could have been with him on the Guernsey raid, like you, but somehow, well, a midnight dash across the Channel and back did not seem a terrible risk. None of us had any idea he was going to have to take on those S-boats. But even then, he had the home advantage, you could say, especially as they did not know it.'

'He also had Jamie,' Kristin pointed out. 'As he will have Jamie again this time.'

'And that gives you confidence.'

'Yes. Yes, it does. Not because of Jamie, per se. But because the pair of them give each other strength.'

'Do you love him? I mean, love, as opposed to, well . . .'

'As opposed to wanting him inside me? Don't look so shocked. That is what matters between a man and a woman, at the beginning of their relationship. What you call love develops out of that, if it ever does. It never did with my husband, so when fucking became a bore we drifted apart.' She came back into the room, laid her hand on Alison's cheek. 'It will happen for you, because you are not me, and Duncan is not his father. But as to whether you get that far . . .' she sighed. 'If they go up, well, you will only have one life to mourn. Now I must rush. He'll be waiting.'

'For you to pick him up and take him to Lymington.'

Kristin frowned. 'Why, yes. How did you know that? He didn't tell you, did he?'

'Only that he might go into Lymington this morning, to see a friend. Do you go to a hotel, or something?'

'No, we do not go to a hotel. And you ask too many questions.'

'Are you angry with me? I suppose I'm just fascinated by the whole scenario. It's not something I ever expected to encounter, in real life.'

'You are too well brought up. Real life is the only life worth living. But if you are unlucky, you will never have to find that out. Just keep loving my son for as long as possible.' She closed the door.

'That was a magnificent lunch, Kristin,' Rear-Admiral Lonsdale said, swaying slightly as he left the table.

'You're not leaving?' Kristin protested, also getting up and taking his arm.

'Duty calls. And . . . well . . .' he glanced at Cooper. 'Yes. Duty calls. I will see you gentlemen tomorrow. And you, Alison. Merry Christmas.'

'Lucifer behave,' Kristin commanded. 'Knocking admirals over is strictly against the law.'

'Take care of her, old fellow,' Lonsdale recommended, massaging the great head before ambling through the door.

Duncan waited until it had closed before remarking, 'Do you think he's fit to drive?'

'Legally, no,' Kristin said. 'But then, I'm not sure he's fit for anything else, either, right this minute. Admirals have a lot on their minds.'

'Well,' Duncan said, also getting up, only a trifle more steadily than the admiral. 'I'm for bed. *We* are for bed,' he added meaningfully.

'I don't think we should abandon Kristin,' Alison protested.

'Oh, go ahead,' Kristin said. 'If everything I understand is correct, you need to spend as much time in bed, together, as possible while you can. And I have Mr Cooper to keep me company.'

The young man sat bolt upright, and Kristin smiled at him and then at Alison's expression; she could at least interpret what was going through the girl's mind. 'I do promise to try to be good, or if that's not possible, I definitely promise to be careful.'

Duncan had reached the door and was holding out his hand. Alison hesitated a last moment, then she said, 'Well, we'll see you at tea, Mr Cooper,' and followed him from the room.

Cooper had also risen, and was standing uncertainly.

'Some more port?' Kristin invited.

'I think I've had sufficient, milady.'

'Very wise. I would hate you to pass out. Shall we go upstairs?'

'Eh?'

'To my sitting room,' she explained, and led the way. For Christmas lunch she had changed into a silk dress and rustled enchantingly. 'Sit beside me,' she commanded, patting the settee. Cautiously he obeyed. 'I had planned an afternoon of unrestricted nookie,' she pointed out.

'Milady?'

'With the admiral. But he's defaulted.'

'Oh, milady. I hope I didn't . . .'

'Your behaviour has been impeccable. And actually, I have had my ration for today. The Admiral was to have been a bonus. And this milady business is becoming tiresome. Call me Kristin. How old are you?'

'Eighteen, mi— Kristin.'

'Good heavens! And how many girls have you had?'

'Girls, milady? I mean, Kristin?'

'Don't tell me! You're a virgin. By the time I was sixteen, I was a mother. Duncan's mother. Mind you, I must admit that Eversham was a good deal older than that. I suppose I could have had him sent to gaol,' she added thoughtfully. 'They're very heavy on things like that in Spain. Even heavier back in 1913. But I married him instead. On the whole, I think that was probably the right choice. Don't you agree?'

Cooper had been staring at her as if he were a rabbit and she a snake. Now his head jerked. 'Oh, absolutely. I mean, if you'd charged him with . . . well . . .'

'Oh, it wasn't rape,' Kristin said. 'I wanted it. It was on a yacht at sea. I always get very randy when I'm at sea in a small boat. And it was his yacht. But I was still under age the first time he had me. You were saying?'

'I . . . ah . . . just that, well, he left you all this.'

'Douglas,' Kristin said, 'did not leave me a goddamned thing. Nor did he ever pay me a penny in alimony. The fault was entirely mine. Adultery,' she growled. 'Adultery, and adultery, and adultery. Well, what was a woman to do? I had to get it somewhere.'

Cooper produced a handkerchief to wipe his neck.

'Not that he had a lot to leave, anyway,' Kristin went on. 'A couple of houses. These went to Duncan. I even paid the death duties on them. My father was Spanish, you see. He was very wealthy, and I was his only heir. I'm boring you.'

Cooper had got his brain back into gear. 'You could never do that, milady.'

Kristin regarded him for several seconds. Then she said, as if speaking to herself, 'But I am not promiscuous. Not that promiscuous, anyway. I think you and I should play a game of Bagatelle.'

'Milady?'

The table had been moved against the wall. Kristin got up and went to it. 'Have you never played Bagatelle? It's great fun. You place the little ball here, you see, and you pull the trigger. The secret is how hard to pull it. Whether to give it an almighty whack and trust to luck, or just enough to move it up the board so that it may trickle back slowly. You're trying to get it into one of these little half-cages, see? You have first go. Then we shall go for a walk to burn off our excess energy.'

Salvage

'Gentlemen.' Duncan surveyed the six officers – the five commanders and Cooper – seated in the mess cabin of *Forty-One*. At twenty-six he was at least three years older than any of them, and the only two of them who had actually seen action had been under his command. 'I hope you all had a good Christmas. Now we get to work. As you know, we are going to operate in two flotillas of three boats each. One will patrol from the Solent to the Dover Strait, the other from the Solent to the Scillies. Lieutenant Cooley, you will command B Flotilla.'

Cooley, lean and hatchet-faced, stiffened. 'Thank you, sir.' As Duncan had reminded the Admiral, they had served together already.

'Starting tomorrow, it will be A Flotilla West, B Flotilla East. We will alternate territory day by day.'

'Will we patrol every day, sir?'

'For the time being, yes. And I'm afraid that we are on standby every night, so there will be no shore leave for the next few weeks. More boats are coming off the production line every week, but their crews have to be trained, and while by the summer we should have sufficient in service to control the Channel, that is six months away. Now, the enemy is installed in just about every French Channel port. I am told that in a short while our new RDF equipment will be able to monitor the French coast just as efficiently as it monitored the sky during the Battle of Britain, but of course the sky remains the priority for this equipment. So right now, Jerry can move up and down the French coast unseen by us, and choose his moment, and his place, to come out. He relies on observation by the Luftwaffe to inform him of vulnerable shipping in the narrow seas. Now obviously, Coastal Command is doing what it can about that, but it simply does not have the aircraft to be everywhere all the time. And the S-boat, with its tremendous speed, can be in and out long before adequate conventional forces can be assembled to deal with it, while ditto, it's not exactly an easy target from the air. So it all comes down to us, and our motto is very simple, Attack!

'Now, a word as to the enemy, because if you underestimate him, you're done. Remember that, like us, he knows he's vulnerable to a hit, so, again like us –' he swept their tense faces with his gaze – 'he is a man of immense courage and determination, a man who is not afraid to take risks because every time he leaves harbour he is at risk. More important, he has the more powerful boat.' This time there was a rustle of movement. 'I'm afraid this is true,' Duncan said, and indicated the file he had placed on the table. 'I want all of you to read this, and memorize what is in it, but I will summarize it for you. Schnell means quick, fast, rapid, hence Schnell-boat. Well, you can say, our MTBs are also fast, rapid, quick, in fact, faster, rapider, quicker, just. The difference is in design. The average S-boat is more than a hundred feet long, as opposed to our seventy-odd, and displaces around a hundred tons, full load. Yet he can make well over thirty knots. How does he travel so fast? Well, unlike us, he is actually powered by a Mercedes-Benz four thousand bhp Diesel. You all know that a diesel engine is about twice the size and weight of its petrol equivalent, but he can cope with that and get the speed because of his size. And of course, because of their larger size they have a larger crew than us, sixteen. For all of these reasons he is a useful substitute for a U-boat, in waters which may be too shallow or too cluttered for submarines, that is, the coastal waters of Great Britain.

'Now, when it comes to engagement, while we will have slightly the greater speed, he will have the greater armament. He has two torpedo tubes, like us, but he also has two quick-firing twenty-millimetre cannon, as opposed to our one. They are both in a single turret, forward, but he will still pack twice the punch. So, no heroics. Our business is to destroy the bastards, not get our names in the newspapers. You attack as a flotilla. Identify your enemy, and fix on him, ignoring his mates. Go in, fire, using your tubes if possible, and get back out. If you stay in close and try to match him in a shoot-out, with your cannon, you will lose. I want this clearly understood. And you must also use everything we possess, every means we have to discourage him. Remember that a merchant ship laden with goodies for our people is more valuable than an S-boat, therefore if he can be discouraged from attacking in the first place you will have gained a more important victory than if you manage to sink him after he has sunk the merchantman. So, when you have a target, announce to the world in clear on the Shipping Channel that you are attacking, with your position. This will bring any Coastal Command Sunderland within range to your assistance, and also it will bring up any destroyers that happen to be around. Jerry will undoubtedly be monitoring your wavelength and he may well be put off. That's about the size of it. So, any questions?'

'Didn't you engage three S-boats single-handedly last September, sir? And sink two of them?' someone asked.

Duncan grinned at him. 'You don't want to believe everything you read in the newspapers, Mr Longridge. I got mixed up with three S-boats, yes, but I had everything going for me. I was in a piece of water I knew very well, and they did not. And I did not sink two of them. One hit a rock and blew up. The second stopped to see what he could do about survivors. The third, well, I suspect he was shaken by what had happened to his sister. We were still in close waters, and he seemed to get the idea that I was going to ram him, so he turned away and allowed me to get in a torpedo strike. As I say, it was a lucky job. Thank you, gentlemen. Dismissed. We cast off at first light.'

Alison did not go home that night, but slept in the Wren quarters, and dined in their Mess. She knew better than either to visit the boat or to expect Duncan to come ashore; he had too much to do and he would have too much on his mind. Nor did she feel like Kristin's company tonight. Kristin was simply too mentally strong, and thus too overwhelming, for an occasion like this.

An occasion like what? she asked herself. They were simply going out on patrol, as they had done so often in the past. But unlike most of the others they were actually going to seek combat, in their frail wooden cockleshells. She had only had this experience once before, that unforgettable day when the fleet had sailed to mine the Norwegian coastal waters so as to deprive the Germans of the safe havens they had used so profitably. But even then, the Navy had not sought combat. No one had known that at that very moment the Germans had been sending an invasion force across the Kattegat to occupy Norway.

Yet she had known a peculiar sense of mortality. The MTB flotilla had been given the most dangerous task of all, to get right into the Kattegat itself before dropping their mines. It had been supposed, she felt correctly, that with their speed they could be in and out again before anyone knew they were there. At that time she had known none of the crews at all well, had met the officers only in the mess ashore, from time to time. She had marked Duncan Morant as an attractive and essentially nice man, with whom she had thought she would like to get together, at some time, and suddenly the time had come . . . and gone again. She had stood with him on the headland immediately before he had left. He had hardly remembered her name, and had indeed been not altogether pleased to have his reverie interrupted as he had considered the sea and the sky and what lay ahead. And she had suddenly thought, I am standing next to the most attractive man I have ever met, and in a couple of hours time he may well be dead! Spending most of her time locked away in the cipher office with her clerks, it was the first time she had come face to face with the realities of war.

Thus when, unlike his two fellow officers, he had come back, she had felt that life could never be the same, had given him her all . . . and it had been her all in every sense, as up to that moment she had never got close to a man. So now she was his wife. Despite having stopped a bullet during the Dunkirk evacuation, the last six months had been the happiest of her life. And now, almost without warning, she felt that perhaps the clock might have completed a full circle.

She was up at five, dressed, breakfasted, and went across to the Command Building; in December it was still very dark and very cold. She went through the outer office to the Admiral's, where the windows looked directly down at the pontoons, and found Lonsdale already there, standing at the window and looking out. 'Good morning, sir,' she ventured, as brightly as she could.

He did not turn. 'Couldn't you sleep?'

'Cat naps.'

Now he did turn. 'We are both being ridiculous, you know.'

'He's my husband, sir.'

'Oh, quite. And I have some hopes that he may one day be my stepson. Which would make you my stepdaughter.'

'I'd like that,' Alison said, truthfully, even if she had to feel that it was extremely unlikely to happen.

She thought he might be going to say something more, and braced herself to tell the appropriate lies if necessary, but instead he turned back as the engines roared into life, and the six sleek motor boats took in their mooring warps and slipped into the dawn.

The flotilla moved quietly through the Needles Channel beneath the cliffs of the western end of the Isle of Wight and the red and white painted Needles light tower, with Hurst Castle close on the starboard hand. It was a clear, cold late December morning, at eight o'clock only just light, with little wind; only the ships' wakes, still small, were breaking on the shingle bank on the inner side of the passage. 'Flotilla will maintain fifteen hundred revs,' Duncan said into the VHF mike. 'Course two six five. Line ahead.'

He waited for the other two boats to take up their stations, corrected his own speed, then said, 'Like a spell, Petty Officer?'

'Aye-aye, sir.' Carling took the helm, and Duncan retired to the rear of the bridge. He was wearing greatcoat and heavy gloves but it was still extremely cold.

Cooper joined him. 'One almost expects to see ice.'

'Could be.' Duncan agreed.

Cooper licked his lips, then passed the back of his glove across his mouth before the moisture could settle and freeze. 'I never had the opportunity to thank you, sir, for having me to that splendid Christmas lunch. I've never been that close to an admiral before.'

'He's all right, when you get to know him. And as long as you always remember who and what he is.'

'So I gathered. You've known him for some time.'

'Since before I was called up. He's a friend of the family.'

'I gathered that too.'

Duncan glanced at him. 'You didn't mind my wife and I abandoning you to my mother, did you?'

'Good heavens no, sir. Your mother is a delightful lady. Most stimulating company.'

'Yes,' Duncan said thoughtfully. 'You mean you enjoyed being taken for a five-mile tramp on a winter afternoon.'

'I think it was a good idea, after such a lunch.'

'Hm.' Duncan considered. 'She does like to shock people, you understand.'

'I have an idea that she would say that she likes to speak her mind.'

'Yes,' Duncan agreed, more thoughtfully yet.

The radio was crackling. 'Portland is reporting an unidentified vessel twenty miles south of the Bill, sir,' Carling said.

Duncan moved forward to stand beside him. Even at half speed they had already crossed Christchurch Bay. St Albans Head was on their starboard beam and Portland Bill, guarding the naval base at Portland and the seaport of Weymouth inside it, was the next major headland, but on a grey morning was still not in sight. 'Signal that we'll investigate,' Duncan said, and took the helm. 'Flotilla will alter course two one oh, speed two thousand revs.'

'Aye-aye, sir.' Cooper issued the orders. 'What do you reckon?'

'Could be laying mines. Get Rawlings up here, will you, Petty Officer.'

'Aye-aye, sir.'

Rawlings appeared a few moments later, and Duncan gave him the binoculars. 'Sweep south-west,' he said.

Rawlings, as he remembered from their previous operations together, possessed exceptional eyesight. Now he focussed the glasses, and peered at the horizon. Duncan waited. The land to starboard was dropping away behind them, but it was only sixty-odd miles from Portland to Alderney, which was now a German base. 'Have all hands prepare for action stations, Petty Officer. Life jackets and steel helmets.'

'Aye-aye, sir.' Carling rang the bell.

'I have a single object, stationary,' Rawlings said, and glanced down at the compass. 'Green ten.'

Duncan made the alteration of their course to starboard. 'Course two-two-oh, Mr Cooper. Relay to Flotilla.'

'Aye-aye, sir.'

'Identification?'

'I would say it's a trawler, sir,' Rawlings said.

'Out here? Action stations, Mr Carling. Well done, Rawlings. Thank you.'

The seaman understood that he had been dismissed, touched his cap, and went down the ladder to join his shipmates manning the machine-guns and the quick-firer.

'If it's a trawler . . .' Cooper said.

'Could still be a mine-layer. Or a decoy. We can't take the risk. Keep your eyes on her.'

'Aye-aye.'

The sub-lieutenant levelled the glasses, while Duncan surveyed the deck below him; every man was at his post, and now Jamie came up the hatch. 'Have we got a fight, sir?'

'Probably not. But you can keep your fingers crossed.'

'Red ensign,' Cooper remarked.

'Not conclusive.'

'Nothing on deck to suggest mines.'

'They could have finished laying.'

'Three men on deck, waving. And here's a flare.'

The Very pistol cartridge burst high above the drifting vessel.

'For God's sake,' Duncan commented. 'They must know we've seen them. What are they trying to do, announce their presence to the world?' He picked up the mike. 'Flotilla will reduce speed. One thousand revolutions, and keep your eyes open. Study the water. You too, Jamie. Anything floating.'

'Aye-aye, sir.'

The three boats had slowed right down, still some four hundred yards away from the ship. Duncan thumbed the mike on 2182, the Shipping Channel. 'I am the MTB approaching you. What is your problem?'

There was no reply.

'Doesn't he have a radio?' Jamie wondered.

'Presumably that's why Portland couldn't raise him,' Duncan said.

'There's an aerial,' Cooper commented, still studying the trawler through the glasses.

'Jamie, fetch up the loud hailer,' Duncan commanded, and

thumbed his mike again. '*Forty-Two* and *Forty-Three*, keep your distance, but also keep your guns trained on him. I'm going in. Take command of our gun, Mr Cooper.'

'Aye-aye, sir.' Cooper slid down the ladder and joined the men on the foredeck.

Forty-One had been steadily moving closer, now at dead slow. The other two boats promptly turned off, every man ready for action.

Jamie returned with the loud hailer; they were within a hundred yards. Now there were five men on the trawler's deck.

'Take the helm, Jamie.' Duncan held the trumpet to his mouth. 'What is your problem?'

The trawler skipper had also equipped himself with a speaking trumpet. 'Explosion in the engine room,' he shouted. 'Knocked out all power. There was a fire, but we put that out.'

'Are you making water?'

'Some. But our pumps can cope.'

'And what are you doing out here?'

'We've been drifting since midnight. Couldn't call for help, and I didn't want to put up any distress signals in the dark in case they were spotted by Jerry.'

'Is your engine repairable?'

'Not out here.'

Duncan turned to Jamie. 'What do you reckon?'

'I'll have a look if you wish, sir. But if he's had a major explosion I'd say he needs a dockyard.'

'Hm.' He lifted the trumpet. 'Very good. Prepare a line, and we'll tow you into Portland.' He handed Jamie the trumpet, took the helm, and thumbed the mike. 'Mr Beattie, *Forty-Two* will take this vessel in tow for Portland. You can rejoin us later probably on our way back.'

There was a moment's hesitation, then the sub-lieutenant said, reluctantly, 'Aye-aye, sir.'

'Call them and let them know what you are doing,' Duncan recommended. 'And Mr Beattie, endeavour not to pull the bows out of the poor thing. Good luck. *Forty-One* and *Forty-Three* will resume course two seven oh. Fifteen hundred revs.'

'Come in, Duncan,' invited Captain Fitzsimmons. 'How's it going?'

Duncan entered the office. 'We're burning a great deal of petrol with very little to show for it. After a month!'

'But Jerry is out,' said the third man in the room. 'He attacked a convoy off Newhaven only two days ago.'

Duncan had noted the two-and-a-half stripes of a lieutenant-commander. 'Yes, sir. We just didn't get there in time.'

'Lieutenant-Commander Bruton, Lieutenant Lord Eversham,' Fitzsimmons said, a trifle wickedly.

'Sir.' Duncan saluted and shook hands. He had a sinking feeling in the pit of his stomach. Bruton was a good head the shorter, but was heavily built, with a pronounced jaw.

His apprehensions were well founded. 'Lieutenant-Commander Bruton is taking over command of the MTB Channel Squadron,' Fitzsimmons said. 'You'll have noticed the new boats?'

'Yes, indeed, sir. Am I being transferred?'

'Not unless you put in for one. But now that your strength is up to twelve boats, the MTB fleet requires a more senior officer. Do you wish a transfer?'

Duncan considered, briefly. No one, and that included Lonsdale, had given him the slightest indication that he was being replaced as commanding officer of the flotilla. He had every reason to be annoyed. But MTBs were still what he did best and what he liked best. 'No, sir.'

'Excellent. Lieutenant-Commander Bruton will be very happy to have your experience at his disposal.'

'Thank you, sir.' Duncan looked at Bruton. 'You know MTBs, sir.'

'I have not yet served on one,' Bruton said. 'But I have read a great deal about them.'

'Ah,' Duncan commented.

'Lieutenant-Commander Bruton has been executive officer on a cruiser,' Fitzsimmons explained.

'I'm afraid, sir, that you'll find MTBs a little crowded.'

'Well, Lieutenant,' Bruton said, 'shall we go and find out?'

They walked along the pontoon. 'We were at Scapa together,' Bruton remarked.

'Oh? I do apologize, sir. I didn't recognize you.'

'No reason why you should. We never actually met. But you had a fairly high profile. Which I understand has become higher yet.'

'Sir?'

'You're wearing the DSC.'

'Ah. But that was before I ever went to Scapa.'

Bruton frowned. 'I don't recollect your wearing the ribbon there.'

'The investiture didn't take place until June, owing to one thing and another.'

'And since then you have carried out a raid on Guernsey.'

'Not exactly, sir. I ferried a troop of Commandos to Guernsey so that they could carry out a raid.'

'But you sank an S-boat.'

'Pure luck.'

Bruton digested this. 'But you have not been tempted to carry out another such raid. With the flotilla.'

'No, sir. My brief, and I assume that has not been changed, is the protection of coastal convoys.'

'At which you have not been totally successful.'

Duncan suppressed the urgent desire to reply in kind. 'Sadly, no, sir.'

They had reached the end of the pontoon, and he turned to look up at the Command Building, and salute.

'Why did you do that?' Bruton inquired.

'I was greeting my wife, sir.' He hadn't actually identified Alison at any of the windows, but she might have been there, and in any event he was determined to take this character down a peg.

'Your wife?'

'Yes, sir. She's at the window up there.'

'Your wife? Who is she?'

'Her name is Second Officer Lady Eversham.'

'Good lord! What on earth is she doing in the Command Building?'

'She's Rear-Admiral Lonsdale's secretary, sir.' Duncan left him considering this and called, 'Ship's crew, attention for inspection.'

Men appeared from their various tasks, assembling on the after deck. Cooper stood on the bridge, straightening his tie. Jamie emerged from below, wiping his hands on an oily rag.

'Lieutenant-Commander Bruton is our new commanding officer,' Duncan explained. 'He wishes to familiarize himself with the lay-out and function of the boat. If you will, sir.'

He indicated the gangway, and Bruton, having given him a dirty look for the implied put down, stepped on board.

Duncan followed. 'Petty Officer Carling, sir. He has forgotten more about MTBs than you or I will ever know.'

Carling saluted. 'Sir.'

'Petty Officer.'

'Sub-Lieutenant Cooper, sir.'

Cooper saluted.

'Like you, sir, Mr Cooper had no previous experience of MTBs when he came to us, but he has learned very quickly.'

Another dirty look, then the frown was transferred to Jamie.

'Engineer-Artificer James Goring, sir,' Duncan explained. 'He keeps us going.'

'You're very young, to be an artificer,' Bruton commented.

Jamie looked at Duncan.

'Goring was practically born with a spanner in one hand and an oil can in the other,' Duncan explained. 'Now, sir. I assume you'd like to see below. But as you know, we are about to commence our morning patrol.'

'I am accompanying you.'

Oh, God Almighty! Duncan thought. But he said, 'Of course, sir. What I meant was, we should cast off now. So if you will permit Mr Cooper to show you over the ship . . . Mr Cooper.'

'Sir! If you will come with me, sir.' Cooper indicated the door into the Mess cabin, and after a moment's hesitation Bruton stepped inside.

'Very good,' Duncan said. 'Stations for sea.' He went up to the bridge, accompanied by Carling.

'Is it going to be all right, sir?' the petty officer asked in a low voice.

'That, Mr Carling, we shall have to wait and find out.' Jamie having already returned below, he picked up the intercom mike. 'All correct, Jamie?'

'Ready when you are, sir.'

'Very good.' He thumbed the VHF, well aware that the past ten minutes had been watched by the skippers of the other two boats. '*Forty-Two, Forty-Three*, we are putting to sea. Acknowledge.'

'Aye-aye, sir,' they both replied.

'Very good. Mr Cooley, you will take your flotilla east-about. Acknowledge.'

'Aye-aye, sir.'

'Good hunting.' He put down the mike, turned the ignition key.

The growl of the engine brought Bruton up from below, followed by Cooper. 'I'm told these craft are difficult to handle,' the new CO remarked.

'They need nursing at slow speeds,' Duncan acknowledged. 'Would you like to take her?'

'I'd like you to show me how it's done.'

'Of course, sir.' Duncan negotiated his way out of the harbour, the other two boats in line astern.

'You were married before the war, were you?' Bruton asked.

'No, sir.' Duncan turned west into the Solent. 'My wife and I only met last year when we were both stationed at Scapa.'

'Scapa? Then I should know the young lady.'

'Her name was Alison Brunel.'

'Brunel? The cipher section?'

'That is correct, sir.'

'But wasn't there . . . ah . . .' Bruton looked embarrassed.

Duncan refused to be. 'I suppose there was. Second-Officer Brunel was posted AWOL last May. But that was because, before her leave had expired, she happened to be on board my boat when we were called to assist at Dunkirk, and she couldn't get off.'

'Good lord. So, did you get married before or after your heroics with that German cruiser?'

Duncan eased the throttle forward and the boat gathered speed, but in the calm, sheltered water it was hardly perceptible. 'Neither, sir. We got married in hospital, after Dunkirk.'

'Good lord! You mean you were wounded during the evacuation?'

'No, sir. My wife . . . well, she was my fiancée then . . . was wounded during the evacuation. As I explained, she was with me on board, and we were strafed.'

Bruton lapsed into silence while he considered this. They slipped into the Needles Channel and could see the open sea beyond. 'I've been told these things can make forty knots.'

'Yes, they can. But we normally operate at thirty except when there's an emergency.'

'In what conditions? There's a bit of a chop on out there today.'

'Well, there's a fresh westerly. It'll be easier coming back. But for the time being, I think we had better have oilskins up, Mr Carling.'

'Aye-aye, sir.'

Carling left the bridge, and Duncan flipped the tannoy switch. 'Two thousand revs,' he remarked. 'All correct down there, Jamie?'

'Raring to go, sir.'

'Very good.' He picked up the VHF mike. '*Forty-Two, Forty-Three*, cruising speed.'

'Aye-aye, sir.' As always, Beattie and Phillips answered together.

'You seem to have a great deal of intimacy on this ship,' Bruton remarked. 'In fact, in this flotilla.'

'Well, sir, in a boat this small, a certain amount of intimacy is inevitable. And besides, most of these fellows have been with me since the war began. I know their worth, and I believe they know mine.'

'I accept that. But still, to address your engineer by his Christian name when on duty . . .'

'Jamie Goring has been with me longer than anyone, and is a personal friend. Thank you, Mr Carling. Will you take her, Mr Cooper? Two thousand revs.'

'Aye-aye, sir.' Cooper, who had already donned his oilskin top, took the helm, and Duncan pulled on his.

Bruton did so as well. 'You expect to have spray back here?'

'At least.'

Bruton looked forward and instinctively half ducked as the first sheets of water came over the bow. 'I see what you mean. Do you maintain this throughout the patrol?'

'We've a long way to go.'

'Hm.'

The radio was crackling, and Carling listened. 'We have a Mayday, sir.'

'Not another bloody trawler broken down?'

'No, sir.' Carling's voice took on a note of excitement. 'This is a trawler, but an armed escort. She and six merchantmen are being approached by what she estimates to be a flotilla of five S-boats. She will do what she can, but considers that the convoy is in danger of destruction.'

'Get their position, and tell them that we're on our way.

Then plot me a course.' He smiled at Bruton. 'I would say that you have brought us good luck, sir.'

'Let me get this straight,' Bruton said. 'You intend to attack five superior enemy craft with your three?'

'That's our job, sir. At least to see if we can't distract them from the convoy.' He looked at the pad on which Cooper had scribbled the trawler's position. 'Thank you, Mr Cooper. Two and a half thousand revs. Mr Carling, it'll take us at least an hour to get there, but inform all hands that we are going into action and have them stand by. Every man in a life jacket and steel helmet.' He flipped the switch. 'Jamie? We'll be up to maximum revs for the next hour.'

'Aye-aye, sir. Action?'

'Hopefully.' He turned to the VHF. '*Forty-Two, Forty-Three* did you hear that information?'

'Yes, sir,' they both agreed, voices filled with excitement.

'Then you'll understand that full speed is required. Course two four oh.'

'Aye-aye, sir.'

Carling returned to the bridge with the hard hats and the life jackets.

'Thank you, Mr Carling. Now, will you call both Portland and Plymouth and request any assistance, either air or sea, that they can supply. Give them the estimated position of the convoy, and tell them we hope to engage within ninety minutes. Use 2182 and be specific.'

'Aye-aye, sir.' Carling got busy with the radio.

'Aren't you telling the world what you're doing?' Bruton asked. 'Including the enemy?'

'That's the idea,' Duncan said. 'To convince him the whole world is on its way to attack him.'

'Ninety minutes,' Cooper muttered, having been calculating time and distance. 'It'll be over by the time we get there.'

'The report was that the S-boats had been sighted not that they were actually attacking, as yet,' Duncan pointed out. 'We can still save some of those ships. And maybe bag a Jerry as well.'

Forty-One and her sisters were now bounding along, seeming to leap from crest to crest of the shallow swell with bone-shattering violence, displacing clouds of spray to either side and bringing it flying over the bows to splatter across the bridge.

Bruton was hanging on to the grab rail beside the helm. 'Can your hull stand this?' he shouted.

'She's designed to,' Duncan replied.

Bruton digested this. Then he asked, 'What is your tactical plan?'

'They are larger and more heavily armed than us,' Duncan said. 'But we are faster and more manoeuvrable. Therefore we pick a target and go in together. The theory is that having three attackers will distract their fire. Only one boat, in the first instance, us, will use torpedoes. The others will support with gunfire. Then we regroup and make another run at a fresh target. This time *Forty-Two* will use her torpedoes. Then the procedure is repeated a third time.'

'You seem to have it all worked out. And after the third time?'

'We'll have either made it too costly for them to hang around, or we'll all be sunk.'

Bruton swallowed.

The next half hour seemed to last forever. But then Cooper, using the binoculars as best he could with the boat bouncing beneath him like a runaway horse, said, 'Smoke, dead ahead.'

'Action stations!' Duncan said. 'You'll take the gun, Mr Cooper.'

Carling rang the bell, and the men swarmed on deck to take up their positions in the midst of the flying spray. Cooper slid down the ladder and made his way forward with the two gunners.

'Range six miles,' Carling said.

'One of those looks like a fire,' Bruton remarked.

'Yes,' Duncan agreed, grimly, and cast a glance at the sky, which was, sadly, still empty. 'Mr Carling, tell the other boats that we are going straight in. I will pick the first target. Then call Portland and tell them we are attacking.'

'Aye-aye, sir.'

'There they are,' Bruton said.

Duncan squinted through the spray. That apart, the morning was clear with excellent visibility, and he could make out seven ships in the convoy, two of them quite large. Around them there circled the five S-boats. One of the ships was in a sinking condition, and another was on fire. He estimated that the doomed vessel had been hit by a torpedo, as he did not believe the Germans could have sunk one so rapidly purely by the fire of their quite small cannon. This was good news, from a purely tactical point of view, if it meant that at least one of the enemy and probably more had expended his torpedoes.

'They've seen us,' Bruton muttered.

'And are cocksure,' Duncan observed.

Only two of the S-boats had turned away to confront the onrushing MTBs.

'Well, that sorts out our first target,' he said, and throttled back. 'Take your position, Mr Carling. Send Rawlings to me.'

Carling left the bridge and went forward to the torpedo tubes as the boat lost way. It was still travelling very fast, but while spray continued to fly to either side, less came over the bow to distract either the torpedo crew or the gunners.

Rawlings arrived on the bridge. 'Sir?'

'Are those German tubes loaded?' Duncan asked.

Rawlings refocused the glasses. 'I would say not, sir. There is no one standing by.'

'Good enough.' Duncan was now steering directly at the approaching enemy, and the gap between them was closing rapidly; it was down to just over a mile. Now the guns on the German foredecks exploded, but the shots were wide. 'Reply, Mr Cooper,' Duncan bellowed, and *Forty-One*'s own gun barked. But with the two boats travelling at a combined speed of sixty knots hitting a target with a single shell was next to impossible.

Now they were right up to each other, passing broadside to broadside at a distance of no more than a hundred yards. The machine guns chattered, and the air became filled with flying lead. 'Holy Jesus Christ!' Bruton muttered, and Duncan knew he was awaiting the eternal bang when a bullet penetrated the hull and struck a fuel tank. But the combined speed was too fast even for machine-gun bullets, which had in any event been aimed at clearing the decks.

'The torpedoes!' Bruton shouted. 'Use the torpedoes!'

'They'd be wasted, head on,' Duncan told him. 'And we only

have two.' He was more concerned to see one of his men lying prone on the deck. 'Jamie!' he bellowed down the hatch.

'Aye-aye, sir.' Jamie had already come up to the Mess, and he and Wilson now dashed outside to drag the stricken man below.

Duncan cast a hasty glance right and left, and saw that both of the other boats were still with him. He grabbed the VHF mike. 'Forget those two. Follow me.'

He increased speed again, and headed straight for the remaining three S-boats, and their victims, still some distance away. Another of the merchantmen was burning, men jumping into the sea. But now, too, the Germans had seen that the British boats were still coming, and were turning to meet them, at necessarily reduced speed. Turning! 'Range, Mr Carling'

Carling peered into the range-finder. 'Four thousand.'

That was maximum, but they'd never have a better opportunity. 'Fire torpedoes!' Duncan bellowed.

There was a gigantic hiss as the steel fish plunged into the sea. As soon as they were gone, Duncan turned away so as not to get too close to the hoped for explosion; he was himself presenting a target, but as he had estimated the Germans had exhausted their torpedoes on the merchantmen. However, the quick-firer was still banging away, and one shell landed only just astern.

'Rawlings!' Duncan shouted. 'Jettison those charges.'

He realized that the order should have been given before the engagement commenced. A single shot landing on the depth charges would blow them out of the water.

'Aye-aye, sir,' Rawlings responded from the after deck, and a moment later the metal containers plunged into the sea.

'We've missed the bugger,' Cooper shouted, as the S-boat, apparently unharmed, turned back to resume the fight.

'Look there!' Bruton shouted.

The noise of the explosion reached them, and they saw a great plume of red-tinged smoke rising into the air.

'That wasn't ours,' Cooper complained.

'*Forty-Two*,' Duncan said. 'Well done, Beattie! Oh, shit!'

For now he saw that *Forty-Three* was on fire.

'Extinguishers, Mr Carling,' he shouted.

'And here comes support.' Cooper cried.

Two Coastal Command Sunderlands were dropping from

the sky, and the remaining four S-boats were turning for home; they would have to be lucky to escape the planes.

'All hands to rescue stations!' Duncan said into the tannoy, reducing speed as he brought the boat round.

'You're not going up to him?' Bruton asked. 'He'll explode at any minute.'

'We're not going to abandon our people, sir.'

Bruton bit his lip.

Speed reduced to dead slow, Duncan approached the blazing vessel, having to plough through the drifting wreckage of the sunk S-boat to do so. He picked up the loud hailer. 'Abandon ship!' he bawled. 'Abandon ship!'

Several men were already in the water, now they were joined by some more, but as the last man dived overboard the MTB exploded.

'Jesus Christ!' Bruton shouted.

The flash was so bright, the noise so enormous, that for a moment Duncan suspected he lost consciousness; he certainly lost vision. But it returned a moment later, and he found himself surrounded by showers of burning debris. 'Mr Carling!' he shouted. 'Soak the decks. Mr Cooper, check casualties.'

'Aye-aye, sir.' Several men, including the sub-lieutenant, had been blown off their feet. Cooper scrambled up and started checking them for injuries. Although it had been strapped under his chin, he had lost his steel helmet. Duncan put his hand up and realized that his had also gone and that his hair was standing on end, while there was a continuous ringing in his ears.

Bruton was panting. 'We have to get out of here.'

'Not till we have picked up those men, sir. That water is freezing.'

The MTB was still nosing gently forward, and now she was surrounded by the swimming, gasping men. They were hauled on board one after the other . . . but there were only six. Jamie and Wilson assisted them below for blankets and hot drinks. Meanwhile Carling and his crew continued to flood the deck with water, but by now the debris had all settled.

Cooper arrived on the bridge. 'I'm afraid that's it, sir. There are two more, but they're dead.'

'Sub-Lieutenant Phillips?'

'No, sir.'

'Damn, damn, damn.'

'You did your best,' Bruton said. 'And took an enormous risk. And you got one of the bastards, between you. We can go home with pride.'

'Go home?' Duncan demanded. 'What about that lot?' He pointed at the stricken merchantmen.

Duncan thumbed the VHF mike. 'That was good shooting, Mr Beattie.'

'Thank you, sir. *Forty-Three* . . .?'

'Only six survivors. Phillips didn't make it.' He knew that Beattie and Phillips had been good friends. 'Are you damaged?'

'A couple of bullet holes.'

'Very good. Let's see what we can do about those civilians.' He put down the mike. 'Jamie,' he called, 'check for damage below.'

'Aye-aye, sir.'

'Anything up here, Mr Carling?'

'Lots of paint missing.'

'Your windshield is cracked,' Bruton pointed out.

'So it is, sir. It'll be downwind going home.'

He eased the throttle forward, and the MTB slipped through the water. The trawler had disappeared, apparently with all hands; their gallant delaying action had not been in vain. One of the stricken merchantmen had also gone, the other was still afloat, but burning fiercely and clearly had only minutes to live. The remaining four vessels, as would have been their sailing instructions, were hurrying on their way, and were already a mile away, although a voice came over the radio, 'Thank God for the Navy!'

Duncan was concentrating on the scene in front of him. There were quite a few people, some seeking a precarious salvation by clinging to an upturned lifeboat, most still in the water, sustained by their life jackets. Several of these were waving and shouting, but others were drifting inertly, already overcome by the cold.

'What can we do?' Bruton asked.

'Pick those people up and take them into Plymouth.'

'Pick them up? There must be fifty of them.'

'Well, sir, I took twenty-five heavily armed Commandos into Guernsey in September, and brought them back again. And I took sixty men at a time off the beach at Dunkirk. We have two boats, so we should be able to manage fifty between us. It won't be comfortable, but we're less than an hour away from Plymouth. Rescue procedure, Mr Carling.'

'Aye-aye, sir.'

'You'd better give a hand, Mr Cooper.'

'Aye-aye, sir.'

'Report, Jamie.'

Jamie had appeared in the hatch. 'We're making water forward, sir. Just a trickle at the moment. I think that bang opened a seam.'

'Well, you'd better get the pump going.'

'Aye-aye, sir.'

'We won't do those people much good if we sink,' Bruton complained.

'We're not going to sink, sir. I've got home with opened seams before.'

He closed the throttle as they were amidst the bodies, a hundred yards away *Forty-Two* was also cautiously nosing into the throng. He thumbed the VHF. 'Everyone you can, Mr Beattie. You should make twenty-five, at least.'

'Aye-aye, sir.'

The boat was now stopped, and Carling, Cooper and their men were dragging people on to the deck. Jamie, having started the main pump to send a steady flow of water over the side, was on deck with Wilson, equipped with blankets, to which, Duncan knew, they would add mugs of hot cocoa the moment everyone possible was on board. The rescued sailors and passengers were shivering and some were vomiting sea water; others lay still on the deck. And . . .

'My God!' Bruton said. 'That's a woman.'

It was certainly someone in a dress, her yellow hair matted to her head and her legs shuddering uncontrollably.

'Jamie!' Duncan shouted. 'Take the lady below. Put her in my bunk and see what you can do.'

'Aye-aye, sir. Able Seaman Lambert is in you bunk, sir.'

He'd forgotten about Lambert. 'Then use Mr Cooper's.'

'Aye-aye, sir.' Jamie heaved the woman to her feet, and held her against him to get her through the saloon door.

'Can that boy cope?' Bruton inquired.

'He's done it before.'

'What?'

'We had a wounded woman with us when we left Guernsey,' Duncan explained, 'and Jamie coped very well.'

'Good lord! A woman? In Guernsey?'

'Oddly, sir, they do have women in Guernsey.' He saw no reason to inform the lieutenant-commander that the woman in question had been his mother.

PART TWO
The River

'Fly, Honesty, fly! Seek some safer retreat;
For there's craft in the river, and craft in the street.'

James Smith

Flotsam

Jamie got the cabin door open and half-carried, half-dragged the woman inside, while water drained out of her hair and clothes, her teeth chattered and she moaned incoherently; she did not seem to know where she was. Several of the men sitting or lying in the cabin made comments, but he ignored them and carried her down the companion and through to the two officers' staterooms. The doors of these, as always at sea, were opened and hooked back against the bulkheads. Lambert was lying on Duncan's bunk; he had been hit in the thigh and was bandaged as well as Jamie had been able, and although he had been given a sedative, was fully awake, and a trifle agitated. 'What's happening? What's happening? Did we get the buggers?'

'We got one of them,' Jamie told him. 'But they got one of us. Now we're off to Plymouth. You'll be in hospital in a couple of hours.'

'Can't be too soon. I think I'm dying. What've you got there?'

'It's a who, not a what. Go back to sleep.'

He carried the woman into Cooper's cabin, spread an extra blanket on the bunk, and laid her on it, then unhooked and closed the door, before turning back to look at her. She was certainly worth looking at, with crisp features, even if presently distorted with cold and her chattering teeth, shoulder length yellow hair, presently in a tangled, sodden mess, and as far as he could make out, an excellent figure; certainly she had good legs. She wasn't all that old, either. He put her age down as about thirty. But then, he had put Kristin's age down at about thirty as well, when he had first met her and before he had discovered who she was. And she wore a gold wedding band and an expensive-looking engagement ring.

And he was required to do something about her, because Duncan, however much he might value him as an engineer and pilot, still regarded him as a virtually sexless youth. Well, now was the time to act that role, however much he might be looking forward to it. And she certainly needed help

She seemed to be recovering her senses. 'Help me,' she muttered. 'I'm so cold. Please help me.' Her voice had a very pleasant nasal twang.

'I am going to do that,' he assured her, surveying the situation. Her shoes had come off, and her stockings were torn. She wore a skirt and blouse, both wrapped around her like a second skin, although for the moment partly concealed by the heavy, hip-length life jacket. 'This first, I think.' The cords were too sodden to be untied; he drew his seaman's knife and cut them.

Her eyes, which had remained shut until now, opened; they were pale blue. 'What . . . what are you doing?' Her teeth began to chatter again.

'Helping you.' He put his arm round her shoulders to raise her while he pulled off the jacket.

'God,' she muttered. 'I'm freezing. I'm going to die.'

'That's what they all say.' He dropped the jacket on the deck, released the waistband for her skirt and pulled it down.

'What are you *doing*?' she cried.

'Undressing you. It's to stop you freezing,' he explained.

She stared at him as he pulled the skirt off and dropped it also on the floor. 'What's your name?'

'Jamie Goring. Let's get you up.'

He pulled her forward to raise her jumper.

'Are you a doctor?'

She lifted her arms to help as he pulled the jumper over her head. 'I'm an engineer. This too?' He fumbled at the brassiere.

'Ow!'

'I'm sorry. I've never seen one of these before.'

He freed it and she seemed to understand what he was doing.

'No,' she protested, trying to hold the sodden material to her breasts. 'You'll want my knickers next.'

'Of course. I'm trying to get you warm.'

'I am going to scream,' she threatened.

'I think they're all too busy up there to hear you.' And at that moment the engine roared into life and the boat surged ahead. The woman gave a little shriek and fell back, leaving the brassiere in his hands.

'Are you married?' she gasped.

'Sadly, I'm too young.' He took advantage of her position to pull down her knickers, and had a sudden surge of guilt, not at what he was doing, but at the thought of what Kristin might say: this woman, with almost translucently pale skin – probably appearing so because of the cold – the slender hips and legs, combined with the surprisingly large breasts and now the delicious pale patch of hair at her groin, was the second most evocative sight he had ever seen.

'I am going to have you arrested,' she said.

'For saving your life?' He removed the suspender belt and the remains of her stockings, then took a towel from the heads and began massaging her shoulders and breasts.

'Oh,' she said. 'Oh!'

He switched his attention to her legs, sliding the towel up and down her thighs before reaching her feet.

'Oh,' she gasped again. 'That feels so good. Have I got frostbite?'

He looked more closely; they were lovely feet. 'I don't think so. It may hurt a bit as they warm up.'

The blanket on which she was lying was now soaked. He raised her torso and held her against him while he dragged it out from beneath her, then wrapped her in a dry blanket, laid her down again, and began massaging her hair.

'Why are you doing this?' she asked, her teeth still chattering.

'I'm obeying orders. Listen. Just lie here, and I'll get you something to drink.'

Wilson had a kettle on the go and he made cocoa. 'Is she all right?'

'A little disgruntled at the moment.'

'I hope you've behaved yourself.'

'I am either going to wind up in prison, or I have made a friend for life. I'll let you know.'

He returned to the cabin. She hadn't moved, and the hump beneath the blanket was still shuddering, but less violently. 'Get this inside you,' he told her, 'and you'll start to warm up.'

Her eyes had closed again. Now they opened, as he thrust his arm under her shoulders to raise her up; the blanket slipped past her breasts but she didn't seem to notice. He held the mug to her lips, and her head jerked. 'Ow!'

'You should drink it as soon as you can. You need the warmth inside you.'

She breathed deeply for several seconds, then took a sip. 'How old are you?'

'Nineteen, ma'am.'

'Nineteen! You seem to know a lot about women.'

I know a lot about one woman, he thought. But then, once one had known Kristin, all other women had to be pale imitations, although he wasn't sure about this one; he didn't think he would ever forget her still frozen nipples or the smooth sheen of her legs. Or what lay between. 'Just doing what comes naturally, ma'am. How are you feeling?'

She drank the cocoa. 'Cold. But better for that. I need to go.'

'Eh?'

'The bathroom. I need the bathroom. Desperately.'

'Ah.' This was something he had never done for, or with, Kristin.

'There is a bathroom on board this thing, isn't there?'

'We have heads, yes.'

'What?'

'On a boat, the bathroom is called the heads.'

'Why?'

'It would take too long to explain. Can you walk?'

He helped her swing her legs out of the bunk and placed them on the deck. She gasped, and her knees gave way. 'I'm in agony.'

'Um.' He held her up and got her into the heads Duncan shared with Cooper, carefully averting his eyes; there were some intimacies that were a shade too intimate. Then he put her back to bed, wrapped her in the blanket, and left her while he used the pump.

'That feels a whole hell of a lot better,' she acknowledged when he returned. 'Thank you.'

'Just doing my job, ma'am. Now, I have to get back to duty. You rest up. We'll be there in half an hour.' He went to the door. 'I'm going to have to hook this open. Regulations. If anything were to happen and it was closed, it could jam and trap you in here.'

'Is anything else going to happen, Jamie Goring? I don't think I could stand that.'

'I don't think anything is going to happen, ma'am. But it pays to obey the rules. Tell you what, though: if anything does happen, I'll come and get you.'

'I'd like that, Jamie Goring. Don't you want to know my name?'

'That might be an idea.'

'Rebecca.'

'Rebecca. And you're an American.'

'I'm an American citizen, yes. How did you know that?'

'The accent, ma'am. Now I have to go. You just lie there until the ambulance people come for you.' He left before she could continue the conversation. The incident had left him quite turned on, and he did not feel that he should allow himself to be turned on by any woman save Kristin. But then, he had never seen, much less touched, any naked woman save Kristin.

He checked the engine room first. The pump was still humming reassuringly, but when he lifted a board there was over an inch of water in the usually dry bilges. He went up to the saloon, which was crowded with men lying about, wrapped in blankets and being served hot drinks by Wilson and a couple of other ratings. 'That took you awhile,' the cook grumbled.

'There was a lot to do,' Jamie said, enigmatically, and went on deck. This was also crowded, but now the Plymouth break water was on the port beam. The *Forty-Two* boat was on their starboard beam, her decks also crowded with men. He climbed to the bridge.

'All well below?' Duncan was on the helm.

'We're still making water, sir.'

'Serious?'

'Once we get this load off, I'd say we can get her home, sir. But she'll have to come out.'

'Shit!' Duncan commented.

'Happens often, does it?' Bruton inquired.

'It has happened before,' Duncan acknowledged. 'And the lady?'

'I think she's all right, sir. A little shaken up.'

'Any idea who she is?'

'Not really, sir. I know that her name is Rebecca, and that she's an American, and that she's married.'

'An American?' Bruton demanded. 'On a small ship in the English Channel?'

'We know that one of the sunk vessels was out of Lisbon, sir,' Cooper suggested, having chatted with the rescued Portuguese skipper. 'Would you like me to have a word with her?'

'You?'

'Well, sir, I believe she's in my bunk.' He looked at Jamie for confirmation.

'There was nowhere else, sir.'

'I'll interview her,' Duncan determined. 'When we dock.'

'Stations for entering harbour, Mr Carling.'

'Aye-aye, sir.'

Ten minutes later both boats were alongside, and were being overrun by ambulance men, doctors and WVS ladies. Duncan left Cooper to cope and slipped below, to stand in the cabin doorway. He did not think he had ever seen a more evocative sight, even if she was totally concealed from the neck down. 'Mrs . . . ah . . . Rebecca . . .?'

She opened her eyes. 'Strong.'

'Ah. Right. Mrs Strong . . .' He looked for her left hand to make sure that Jamie had been correct, but it was hidden beneath the blanket.

'I am Mrs Rebecca Strong,' she confirmed.

'I see. Mr Strong, was he . . . well . . . Is he . . .?'

'He wasn't on board, if that's what's bothering you.'

'Thank God for that. I mean, well . . .'

'You wouldn't have liked me to be an instant widow.'

'Of course not. Now, Mrs Strong, in a few minutes some men will be down here to take you to hospital.'

'I have no clothes.'

Duncan looked at the still sodden heap on the deck. 'Not to worry. They'll wrap you in a blanket, another blanket, and carry you out on a stretcher. Or can you walk?'

'I'm not sure. I couldn't just now.'

'And it probably wouldn't be a good idea without clothes,' he pointed out. 'Now, Mrs Strong, I understand that you are an American.'

'I am an American citizen,' she agreed, as with Jamie, stressing the word citizen.

'Of course. Therefore, well, I assume that you have a passport? Some form of identification?'

'I do have a passport. And several other forms of identification. Unfortunately, right now they, along with my purse and all my travel funds, and all my clothes, are at the bottom of the English Channel. Although I suppose they could be floating about.'

'I understand. But you must understand that as you are not a British citizen, and as you were a passenger on a ship out of Lisbon . . . you were on the Portuguese vessel?'

'Yes, I was.'

'May I ask why? I mean, the quickest way to get from the United States to Great Britain is New York–Liverpool. Or any British port. To arrive via Lisbon seems rather a roundabout route.'

'You mean that I'm an illegal immigrant coming from the wrong direction without identification, and thus I am probably a spy.'

'Well, I wouldn't say that.'

'But you're suggesting it.'

'I'm just trying to warn you that there will be people who wish to interview you, and who will require answers.'

'I'll bear that in mind. Now let me ask you something: who are you?'

'I am the captain of this ship,' Duncan said, feeling rather foolish.

'But you have a name as well.'

'Eversham. Duncan Eversham.'

'Eversham,' she said, thoughtfully 'And that nice young guy who took off my clothes is one of your people?'

'Jamie Goring. Yes, he's my engineer.'

'I'd like to see him again before I'm carted off to gaol.'

'My dear Mrs Strong, you won't be going to gaol. I hope. But . . . did you say, he took off your clothes?'

'How do you suppose they got on the floor?'

'The deck,' he said absently.

'And they had to come off,' she explained. 'They were sopping wet.'

'Yes. But . . . couldn't you take them off yourself?'

'At that time, I couldn't do anything for myself. Anything,' she repeated meaningfully. 'So I reckon this Jamie knows me better than any man in the world, save maybe my husband.'

'I see. And you mean you want to see him again.'

'Yes, I do.'

'To . . . ah . . .?'

'To thank him, you great oaf. Oh, I do apologize. You being a captain and all.'

'Accepted. Well, I have to get on. I'll arrange for Jamie to see you before you go.'

He had gone to the door when she said, 'Hold on a minute.'

He waited.

'Eversham! That's been buzzing about my brain like an angry bee. Eversham! You wouldn't happen to know anyone named Kristin Eversham? She's a lady. I mean, that's her title.'

Duncan turned back. 'Kristin Eversham is my mother.'

'You don't say? Holy Shit! Now I have to apologize again. I didn't mean to imply . . . well . . . but if you're her son, then . . .'

'In civilian life, I am Lord Eversham. My father was killed at Dunkirk. You mean, you've heard of my mother?'

'I used to know her. Well, a few years back.'

Duncan returned to stand by the bunk. 'Would you like to explain that? My mother was born in Spain.'

'But her mother was Swedish, right? So was mine. They were friends, oh, before the last War. Then she got married to this Spanish tycoon. But she took your mom home to see her grandparents . . . must have been 1912. I met her then. Of course she was a bit older than me. Ten years. I was five. But I still remember her. And then . . . well . . .'

'There was enough scandal to keep her name in the gossip columns.'

'I am sorry, Lord—'

'Lieutenant.'

'OK, Lieutenant. I didn't mean to drag up anything that might embarrass you.'

'You didn't. I long ago stopped being embarrassed by my mother. I'll tell her I fished you out of the sea. She'll be amused.'

'Now you're peeved. I have apologized. And here I was, hoping that you might be able to help me.'

'Help you to do what?'

'Well, these people who are going to interview me . . . I guess they'll be from Scotland Yard, right?'

'Good lord, no. Unless you *were* suspected of being a spy. It'll be the local people here in Plymouth. I'm sure you'll be able to explain everything to them.'

'It's just possible that I may not be able to do that.'

'You have a casualty down here,' someone said from the corridor.

'Take the other fellow first,' Duncan said. 'He's next door. Just what were you trying to say, Mrs Strong?'

'That I need your help.'

'I'm sorry. I don't see what I can do. I mean, I can't even ask Mother to give you a reference, if she hasn't seen you for something like twenty-nine years.'

'All I would like you to do is make a telephone call for me.'

'You mean you'd like me to telephone the American Embassy in London? The police here will be quite happy to do that.'

'Not the American Embassy. Do you have a piece of paper, and something to write with?'

Duncan raised his eyebrows, but unbuttoned his tunic and took out his notebook, which had a pencil attached. Rebecca extracted two long white arms from beneath the blanket – Duncan was at last able to ascertain that at least part of her story was true: she was wearing a wedding band – flipped it open, and wrote. 'Call that number,' she said.

Duncan frowned. 'Who is it?'

'I can't tell you that.'

'Sorry. No can do.'

'Please,' she begged. 'I will be eternally grateful if you'll telephone that number, ask to speak to Robert, and tell him what has happened to me and where I am. That's all. Then you can hang up and forget you ever saw me.'

That is going to be difficult to do, he thought, as she put her arms back beneath the blanket. But that simple reflection meant that he was lost, however dangerous a situation he was getting himself into. A damsel in distress! An increasingly suspicious damsel. 'If you are going to be eternally grateful,' he pointed out, with an enormous sense of helpless guilt, 'you will have to see me again.'

'Good point. Tell you what: when I get out of the calaboose

and find some clothes, I'll come and visit your mother. She's still around, isn't she?'

'Very much so. And I'm sure she'd love to see someone from her girlhood.'

'Then you'll make that call?'

'Well,' he said. 'I suppose I could do that.'

'Can you call right away?'

'Well, no, I'm afraid not. I must look after the boat first, get her back to Portsmouth. Technically, we're sinking.'

'What?' She looked over the side of the bunk, as if expecting to see water coming over the floorboards.

'Only technically. We should be back in Portsmouth in a couple of hours, and I'll make the call as soon as I can after that.'

'A couple of hours,' she muttered. 'Oh, well, thanks anyway.'

The stretcher bearers were back, and Duncan left them to it.

'Quite a lady,' Bruton remarked as he watched Rebecca Strong being carried ashore, her clothes neatly piled at the foot of the stretcher. He also watched her squeeze an embarrassed Jamie's hand as she said goodbye. 'I hope that boy behaved properly throughout.'

'She says he did,' Duncan assured him. But he couldn't be certain he was telling the truth. And he was stuck with his promise to make that telephone call for her, without the faintest idea what he might be getting himself into. He dearly wished he could discuss the matter with Kristin, but there was no hope of getting home for a couple of days. And he did not feel he would obtain any unbiased advice from Alison. But there were precautions he could take.

As he had estimated, they were back in Portsmouth in the middle of the afternoon. He had called ahead and there was another large reception committee waiting, to take the boat out and to find out what had happened. Duncan let Bruton do the talking while he saw to the boat. Hawkins the yard superintendent wore his usual long expression. 'We're talking about a week, Lord Eversham, at the very least. What did you hit?'

'I didn't hit anything,' Duncan retorted. 'Something hit me. A week. Bugger it. Well, do the best you can.' He turned to Carling and Cooper, who had followed him, together with Beattie. 'Stand the crew down, Mr Carling. They've had a long day. Same goes for you, Mr Beattie. Although you'll be on patrol again tomorrow, I imagine.'

'Aye-aye, sir.'

'A message from Captain Fitzsimmons, sir,' Cooper said. 'He wishes you to report immediately.'

'Very good, Mr Cooper. I just need to go to the Mess first.'

He found a vacant telephone booth, first of all called Inquiries. 'I'd like to know who this number belongs to,' he told the girl, and gave her the number.

'One moment, please.' She was back even quicker than that. 'I'm sorry, sir. That number is unlisted.'

'Thank you.' He hung up and considered. Commonsense told him now was the time to drop the whole matter, and let Rebecca Strong sort out her problems on her own. But she had suggested that she might not be able to do that, and he had given her his word. And she was such an attractive woman . . .

He picked up the phone again, gave the number. Several seconds passed, then a man's voice repeated the number.

'Would I be speaking to Robert?' Duncan asked.

'You could be.'

Which was exactly the sort of answer he had anticipated. 'Well, if you are Robert, or can get in touch with him, I'm sorry to bother you, but I am calling on behalf of Mrs Rebecca Strong.'

There was a brief silence, then the man asked, 'Who is speaking, please?' At least he used a rather upper crust English accent.

'Who I am is not relevant. Do you wish to receive the message?'

There was another brief silence. 'Yes,' the man said. 'Will you give me the message?'

'Mrs Strong was on a Portuguese freighter which this morning was torpedoed and sunk off the Scillies.'

There was a startled exclamation from the other end of the line.

'Mrs Strong is all right,' Duncan added. 'Apart from perhaps a touch of hypothermia. But as she lost her passport and any kind of identification, not to mention all her clothes and money, and she is an alien, she seemed to feel her position might be uncertain. She is certainly under restraint. She felt that this would be important to you, and to tell you that she needs your assistance. Does this make sense to you?'

'Yes,' the man said, 'We will attend to the lady. She told you nothing else? About what the purpose of her visit to this country might be?'

'No. Is it important?'

'Everything is important, Mr . . . ah?'

'Smith,' Duncan said, and hung up.

Before he reached Fitzsimmons' office he encountered Alison. 'Duncan!' Despite the fact that they were both in uniform and there were people about, she threw her arms round him for a hug. 'I've been so worried.'

'Now you know they always miss me.'

'Always isn't the same thing as forever. But you got one of them.'

'Beattie did that. We lost *Forty-Three*. Now I'd better rush. Fitzsimmons wants a blow-by-blow.'

'I know. He's going spare. Where have you been?'

'Trying to put a bomb under Hawkins to get the old girl back in the water as soon as possible.' He frowned. 'How do you know Fitzsimmons' mood?'

'Because he's with the boss. That's why I was sent to find you. You're to go straight up.'

'Hm.' They went up the stairs together. 'I suppose Bruton is there too?'

'He was, but he's left. Duncan! There wasn't trouble, was there?'

'I wouldn't call it trouble. It's just that I don't think the lieutenant-commander is entirely suited to MTBs.'

'And you told him so. Oh, lord!'

'I did not tell him anything. But I think the entire crew got the message.'

They had arrived at the door to the outer office, and she opened it for him. 'Good luck.' She led him past the other secretaries, knocked, and opened the door. 'Lieutenant Eversham, sir.'

'Thank you, Lady Eversham. Come in, Lieutenant.'

Duncan entered the room, stood to attention, and saluted. Alison closed the door behind herself as she left.

Lonsdale sat behind his desk, Fitzsimmons seated to one

side. 'Sit down, Duncan,' the Admiral invited. 'In the wars again, I understand.'

Duncan took off his cap and sat down, the cap on his knees. 'Aren't we all, sir?'

Lonsdale cleared his throat. 'Of course. How bad is *Forty-One*?'

'Not bad at all, sir. A few strained seams.'

'But she will be out of action for a while.'

'If Hawkins gets his finger out, she could be back in the water in a week.'

'I understand that the damage was caused by approaching too close to a ship that was on fire and clearly about to explode. You would not concur with the opinion that you were hazarding your command?'

'No, sir, I would not. The stricken vessel was under my command, and was crewed by my people. Not to have attempted to take them off I would have considered a dereliction of duty As it was, six were lost, including the commanding officer.'

Lonsdale regarded him for a few moments, then glanced at Fitzsimmons, but the captain made no comment. 'Very good, Lieutenant. Now I would like a brief description of the entire action.'

'We were on routine patrol along the south coast when we received a Mayday from the armed trawler escorting a small convoy that he had sighted five S-boats approaching him and was of the opinion that he was about to be attacked. I therefore proceeded to the scene with all speed, but unfortunately arrived too late to prevent the sinking of two of the merchantmen and the trawler. I immediately attacked the enemy, and succeeded in sinking one of them, and driving the others off. Unfortunately we also suffered a casualty.'

'You say, you made the decision to attack. But you had a superior officer on board. Wasn't the decision his to make?'

'I suppose it was, sir. But he didn't seem to be prepared to make it. He gave me to understand that he was on board in the capacity of observer only.'

Again Lonsdale and Fitzsimmons exchanged glances. 'So you took matters into your own hands,' the Admiral commented. 'You are, of course, aware that a German S-boat is larger and more powerfully armed than any MTB we possess?'

'I read the file you gave me, sir. So did my commanders.'

'And in addition, you were outnumbered by five to three. Yet you went straight in. You would not call that hazarding your command? Your entire command? Wasn't it possible for you to manoeuvre your boats so as to distract the enemy from their attack on the convoy until help arrived? You did request help?'

'I did, sir. But it did not arrive very promptly. And I could see no evidence that the enemy were going to cease their attack just because we turned up. Another ten minutes and the whole convoy would have gone down. Besides sir, if I remember my naval history, did not Lord Nelson tell his officers, no captain can do wrong if he lays his ship alongside one of the enemy?'

Again Lonsdale regarded him for some seconds, then he nodded. 'Very good, Lieutenant. There is another point. This familiarity you have with your crew, the use of Christian names when on duty, is not proper procedure.' He allowed himself a brief smile. 'I don't think even Lord Nelson permitted that.'

'With respect, sir, where twelve men spend their time in each other's pockets, and are aware that their survival depends entirely upon every one of them doing his duty at all times and with total confidence in his fellows, including his officers, and also knows that were we to receive a fatal hit we would all go up together, a certain degree of intimacy is inevitable. I understand that anyone coming, shall I say, straight from the more traditional discipline of a cruiser or a battleship, where officers and men live totally separate existences, would find this hard to accept.'

'You should be a lawyer,' Lonsdale remarked. 'Very good, Lieutenant. Tell us about this woman.'

'Woman, sir?'

'You fished a woman out of the sea, did you not?'

'Ah,' Duncan said. 'Yes. An American lady, or so she claimed. I may say, sir, that I 'fished', as you put it, twenty-five people out of the sea, as did Lieutenant Beattie.'

'Point taken. But did you not send this woman down to your cabin with a member of your crew?'

'I sent her to Mr Cooper's cabin, sir, with a crew member, yes. She was incapable of walking, and had to be carried. She was also suffering severely from hypothermia and I realized that she needed to be put to bed and warmed up as rapidly as possible.'

'When you say put to bed . . .?'

'Yes, sir. Her clothes had to be removed. They were sopping wet and were contributing to her condition.'

'And this crew member was your nineteen-year-old engineer. Do you think that was either wise, or proper?'

'It was a problem. In the circumstances, I could not leave the bridge myself, and whoever I chose would have been open to question by any prurient observer. I chose Goring because I knew that of all my crew he is the most innocent, and indeed, he has never shown the least interest in the female sex.'

'And how did he take it?'

'He was embarrassed, of course. But he had been given an order, and he obeyed that order, as I expected him to. I may say that when I spoke with Mrs Strong later, she assured me that Goring had been a perfect gentleman.'

'Where is this Mrs Strong now?'

'I would suppose in hospital in Plymouth. When last I saw her she was in the hands of the WVS and an ambulance crew.'

Lonsdale considered for a few moments, then turned to Fitzsimmons. 'Would you like to comment, Captain?'

'With your permission, sir, I would like to recommend Lieutenant Eversham for a bar to his DSC, for a very courageous and gallant action, which saved fifty lives and resulted in the sinking of an S-boat, for the loss of one of his own command.'

'Thank you, sir,' Duncan said, feeling quite dumbfounded by the unexpected support.

'You have my permission to do so, Captain,' Lonsdale agreed. 'There are some matters I would like to discuss with you. Shall we say, nine o'clock tomorrow morning?'

'Of course, sir.' Fitzsimmons stood up and glanced at Duncan, but as he had clearly not been dismissed, he saluted and left the office.

Lonsdale waited for the door to close. Then he said, 'You do set me some problems, Duncan.'

'Not intentionally, sir.'

'Accepted. But there you are. Don't misunderstand me. I entirely agree with Fitzsimmons that you behaved splendidly and deserve to be rewarded. I shall endorse his recommendation.'

'Thank you, sir. I would like to recommend Lieutenants Beattie and Phillips also for an award.'

'They shall be. However, the fact remains that you are the subject of a highly critical report made by a superior officer who was present and who was technically in command of the operation.' He paused.

'Had I not gone to the rescue of those people, sir, I would have deserved to be cashiered.'

'Are you suggesting that Lieutenant-Commander Bruton should be cashiered?'

'Of course not, sir,' Duncan lied. 'But the fact is, as I have said, that when he joined the flotilla I asked him if he wished to take command and he told me to carry on until he got the hang of things. I may say, sir, that at the conclusion of the action, Lieutenant-Commander Bruton congratulated me, and my crew, on our behaviour and our achievement.'

'Good point. However, he seems to have had second thoughts on reflection. And in your implied criticism of the lieutenant-commander, you need to remember, as you yourself have pointed out, that his previous experience had been in large craft. Were the captain of, say, a cruiser, to engage an enemy squadron far superior in every way to himself, except as a desperate measure, he would certainly be court-martialled, at least.'

'And I contend that this was a desperate measure, sir. To save as many lives as I could.'

'You're a difficult man to argue with, Duncan. But however much I may agree with your point of view, I cannot alter the fact that I have received this report and that it must go into your file. Despite this, I have no doubt that their Lords of the Admiralty will accept Captain Fitzsimmons' recommendation, especially, as I say, as I intend to endorse it. But this will put Lieutenant-Commander Bruton in a most invidious situation. He will be given the opportunity to apply for a transfer back to a larger unit, but if he decides not to do so, he must, for the foreseeable future, remain in command of the Channel MTB flotilla, as he volunteered for the post and was accepted.'

'I understand that, sir.'

'Which raises the question, will he wish you to continue serving under him, or indeed, will you wish to do so yourself?' Again he paused.

'I will serve in whatever capacity I am required, sir.'

'But you still wish to remain with MTBs.'

'Yes, sir. I believe that they are suited to my talents, such as those are. And I know that I have accumulated a great deal of practical experience which I think it would be a shame to waste.'

'I happen to agree with you. If that is your decision, then it comes down to Lieutenant-Commander Bruton's take on the situation. Fortunately, the matter does not call for an immediate resolution, as your boat is going to be out of action for the next week or two. By the end of that time, feelings may have eased. Dismissed, Lieutenant. And congratulations.'

'Mrs Strong is here, sir,' said the woman secretary.

'Then show her in.' The tall, thin, strong-featured man behind the desk stood up, to peer at the woman entering his office. 'Mrs Strong?'

'So I look like a drowned rat,' Rebecca agreed. 'That is because I *am* a drowned rat. And a penniless rat. These rather battered clothes are all that I possess in the world, until I can contact New York.'

'Do sit down.'

She sank into a chair before his desk.

'I appreciate that you have every right to be upset. You've had a horrifying experience . . .'

'I'm alive,' Rebecca pointed out. 'Quite a few people aren't. That I'm here is courtesy of your Navy.' Two in particular, she remembered; she had thought a lot about that pair over the past twenty-four hours. 'So right now I'm on your side. You're Chadwick, right?'

'Robert Chadwick, yes. I am so very pleased to make your acquaintance.' He leaned across the desk, hand extended.

Rebecca regarded it, and him, for a few seconds, then took it. 'Pleasure, I'm sure.'

'My surprise at seeing you was because, well . . . I had expected someone older.'

'I left school fifteen years ago, Mr Chadwick. You don't want to base your estimates on my parents; they tried for a long time before coming up with me. Or on my husband. It would be charitable to say that he likes cradles. Or he did. So now you have the entire story of my life. When do I get to see Dad?'

'Ah,' Chadwick said.

'Say again?'

'It's something we have to discuss. Shall we go out and have some lunch?'

Rebecca had a peculiarly piercing gaze, on which Chadwick now found himself impaled. 'Mr Chadwick,' she said, 'you contacted me, through your Washington Embassy, and told me that it was a matter of life and death that I come across to see my dad before it was too late. Whatever the risks. Frankly, I didn't even know the old buzzard was in England, but then, we haven't been real close since my mother died. But I took the risk, and travelled the way you wanted, to be inconspicuous, you said. And I damn near got drowned. So, please, no prevarication. A little straight talk will be appreciated.'

'Of course. You understand that anything I say to you is in the strictest confidence?'

'I got that message from your letter. I had to tell George I was coming over to see Dad before he died, but even that didn't please him too much.'

'George being your husband?'

'Who else? So what's happened to Dad? Or is it still happening?'

'Are you acquainted with your father's line of work?'

'God, no. It's always been too complicated for me. All those bottles and Bunsen burners and ghastly smells. I always approximated his laboratory with hell.'

'You could have been closer than you supposed,' Chadwick remarked.

'Say again?'

'Professor Hallstrom has been working on the ultimate scientific goal. Quite a few scientists are after that goal, but he is perhaps the most far advanced in his researches. It is concerned with splitting the atom.'

'Why should anyone want to split an atom?'

'Because splitting the atom, the right atom, of course, would release an unimaginable source of energy. Something akin to the power of the sun.'

'You're putting me on.'

Chadwick looked puzzled for a moment, then realized it had to be an Americanism. 'I assure you that I'm not. I'm not going to bore you with endless scientific data, but the facts are there. Now, as I said, a lot of people are working on this project, with some success. But we believe that your father's work is the most advanced in this field. We want, we need, we have to have, that research in this country.'

'Because . . . holy shit! You guys think you can make that technology into a bomb!'

'We know that it can be made into a bomb, Mrs Strong. And whoever has that bomb will rule the world. Our scientists tell us that a single atomic bomb could wipe out an entire city the size of London.'

'Some deal. And Daddy is working for you to accomplish this? I'm not sure where I come in. I'm not sure I'm in favour of the whole idea.'

Chadwick decided not to go into her ethics right then. He said, 'Your father is not working for us, at this moment.'

'You've lost me.'

'Professor Hallstrom is at his home in Sweden. He is not working for anybody, at this moment, except the university that employs him. He appears to regard his researches into the possibility of harnessing atomic power as purely academic, and equally, the possibility of it being used to make a bomb as unthinkable.'

'Well, good for Daddy. I always knew he'd turn up trumps.'

'Mrs Strong, as I said, we have to have that expertise working for us.'

'So that you can blow up Berlin or whatever? We're talking about a couple of a million people, right?'

'I should point out, again in the strictest confidence, that your government scientists in the States are working with us on this, and would also like to have your father on our side.'

'They're not my government. I vote Republican.'

'You're an American.'

'I'm an American citizen,' she corrected, with her usual exactitude. 'So who is Roosevelt aiming to blow up? He doesn't have a target right this minute.'

'Hopefully, he, and we, are not going to blow up anybody. But we, and they, feel that such an enormous power is better off in our hands than somewhere else.'

'Oh, come now, Mr Chadwick. I was born thirty-three years ago, come August. Not yesterday. Governments that obtain special weapons mean to use those weapons. That's history.'

Chadwick sighed. 'You may be right, Mrs Strong, but just consider this point: a few months ago your father published a paper on his researches. That paper was undoubtedly read in Berlin as well as in London and Washington. Now, can you suppose that if Hitler got hold of the necessary technology he wouldn't make an atomic bomb, and then use it?'

Rebecca stared at him for several seconds. Then she said, 'Daddy would never work for the Nazis. He hates the very idea of them.'

'Mrs Strong, if, and it is more likely to be when, the Nazis determine that your father is essential to their war effort, they will kidnap him and he would have no choice *but* to work for them, as the alternative would be a slow and unpleasant death in a concentration camp.'

'You mean you guys actually believe there are such camps?'

'We have irrefutable documentary evidence that they exist, and about what happens to the inmates. It is not considered useful to publish it at this time, but it is there.'

Another long stare. Then she asked, 'So what am I supposed to do?'

'Obviously, our people in Stockholm have spoken with your father and tried to persuade him to come to England, where we would provide him with every facility to continue and hopefully complete his work. But he has always refused to consider playing any part in creating a weapon of such mass destruction. You are our only remaining hope. You are his only daughter. He may not have kept in very close contact with you in recent years, but the evidence we have, as for instance, the number of photographs of you he keeps all around him in his home and his laboratory, leads us to believe that since your mother died you are the most important person in the world to him. Certainly you are the only person who could alter his point of view.'

'You'll have me in tears in a moment. I haven't seen my father for five years.'

'That doesn't mean he doesn't love you, or that he wouldn't have had it differently if he could.'

Rebecca continued to stare him, remembering how Dad had asked her to come and see him twice in that time, and George had refused to let her go. Only the fact that the British Government had suggested that the old man was dying, in

England, and while working for them, had got her this leave of absence, as it were. 'So you want me to go to Sweden,' she muttered. Well, she certainly wanted to see him again. 'How?'

'We'd fly you in.'

'You can do that?'

'Certainly. I'm not saying there isn't a certain element of risk, but it is far smaller than attempting to get there by sea.'

Rebecca considered. 'And you'd bring Daddy out the same way?'

'Of course.'

'You'll have a problem.'

Chadwick raised his eyebrows.

'Daddy does not like flying.'

'Lots of people don't like flying, but in this day and age it is often the only practical way to get about. Your father is a sensible man. After all, he's a genius, isn't he?'

'The connection between common sense and genius is a tenuous one, Mr Chadwick. Many people would say that it doesn't exist. Geniuses are actually more likely to have hang-ups and phobias than ordinary people. Daddy does not merely dislike flying. He has never flown in his life, and he never will. He's terrified of it, and he simply will not do it.'

'Oh, come now, Mrs Strong. You can surely talk some . . . well, persuade him . . .'

'First of all, to confide his secrets to your care, then to leave Sweden, and thirdly to fly in an airplane? I'm not a magician, Mr Chadwick.'

'I have explained how desperate the situation is, and how much in danger your father may be, without even knowing it. Won't you at least try?'

Rebecca brooded for a few moments, then sighed. 'When you put it like that, I suppose I have to.'

'Then you'll go to Sweden and see your father?'

'That's what I said I'd do. When I can get a decent wardrobe together.'

'We'll look after that. We will also arrange for you to receive a new passport.'

'An American passport.'

'Of course. It will only take a few days.'

'So how, and where, do I live for those few days?'

'We'll arrange for funds to be provided, pending a transfer from your bank in New York.'

Rebecca shook her head. 'Not a good idea. To do that would be to put George in the picture, at least that I've been torpedoed. He'll go spare, and demand my return, immediately.'

'And you don't feel that you have rights of your own?'

'Sure I have rights of my own. But none that outweigh the advantages of being married to George. He may be a dirty old man, but billionaires are thin on the ground, and he keeps me in the style to which I have become accustomed, and to which I have no desire to become unaccustomed, if you're still with me.'

'Ah. You're being very frank, which I appreciate. All right, then, we will advance you whatever funds you require until this operation is completed. Then we can discuss repayment.'

'You sure must want Daddy badly. I have extravagant tastes. Well, the first thing you can do is find me a decent hotel. When last I was over here we stayed at the Dorchester.'

'I'm afraid that won't be possible this time.'

'Don't tell me it's been blown up?'

'No, no. But it would be too risky.'

'You mean you're expecting it to be blown up.'

'No, Mrs Strong. But we cannot take the risk that German agents might discover that you are in this country. That's why we arranged for such a roundabout route to get you here.'

'You mean the Nazis have agents staying at the Dorchester? Why don't you lock them up?'

'I very much doubt there are Nazi agents in the hotel, Mrs Strong.' Chadwick spoke with great patience. 'But we do know that they are in this country. And as I have said, it is essential that no one knows that *you* are in this country.'

'Ah,' Rebecca said.

'Mrs Strong?'

Rebecca decided against landing that nice young man, who had also been so helpful, in the soup. Besides, various ideas were knocking about her brain. So she ignored the implied question. 'If I can't stay in a decent hotel, where can I stay?'

'We will put you in one of our houses, where you will be absolutely safe until all arrangements have been made.'

'You are saying that you haven't made any arrangements yet?'

'Well, we didn't know that you were actually coming . . .'

'And I damn near actually didn't get here,' Rebecca put in.

'Quite. Nor did we know if you would be prepared to help us.'

'And I'm still not sure I don't need my head examined. OK, so how long will these arrangements take?'

'Not more than a couple of weeks, I'm sure.'

'A couple of weeks. So what do I tell George? My husband,' she reminded him as he raised his eyebrows. 'He's going to expect to hear from me, that I've arrived safely, that I've seen Daddy, etc., etc.'

'Ah. I'm afraid we are going to have to ask you to, how do you Americans put it? String him along for a while.'

'You are asking me to lie to my husband.'

Chadwick looked at her down his nose. 'Are you saying that you have never lied to your husband, Mrs Strong?'

'I ought to lean across this desk and slap your face. But I suppose you'd lock me up. OK, I'll see if I can keep him happy. So what happens now?'

'Mrs Bainbridge will see to everything.'

'You mean the dragon outside?' Rebecca stood up. 'I won't say this has been a pleasure, Mr Chadwick, but it's been interesting.'

'There's just one more thing, Mrs Strong.'

Rebecca waited.

'That we were able to find you, and extricate you from the clutches of the immigration authorities was because we received a phone call from a mysterious man who seemed to know all about you. Would you explain who this man was, and how he came to know all about you?'

'Didn't he give you his name?'

'Smith.'

'Of course. Roger.'

'Who?'

'Roger Smith. He was on that boat with me, and we found ourselves in the water together. Well, when we were fished out, he had no problems; he had an English passport in his pocket. So when it was obvious that I was going to be held, I gave him this number and asked him to call and tell you I needed help.'

'Tell me.'

'I only said to ask for Robert.'

'I see. And you are sure his name was Smith?'

'Shouldn't it be?'

'And you told him nothing of your purpose in visiting Britain?'

'Of course not.'

Chadwick regarded her for several seconds. Then he nodded. 'As I said, Mrs Bainbridge will take care of anything you need. Good morning, Mrs Strong.' He had obviously changed his mind about taking her out to lunch.

Orders To Die

'Well, Admiral?' the Sea Lord asked. 'What do you think?' Jimmy Lonsdale was never one to mince his words. 'Frankly, Sea Lord, I think it stinks.'

'Oh, come now.'

'You are asking me to send my people to almost certain death, or at least, captivity.'

The Sea Lord examined his fingernails. 'I don't know how familiar you are with the figures, Admiral Lonsdale. Obviously we do not broadcast them. But the fact is that for every three bombers we send over Germany, one goes down. The other fact is that for every hundred bombs we drop, only one finds its target. We are told by the 'experts' that things will improve, that they will supply us with long-range fighters able to afford protection from the Luftwaffe, that superior navigational equipment is in the pipeline that will enable our bombers to find their targets more readily, and that a new bombsight is being developed which will give our people pinpoint accuracy. However, none of these things has as yet turned up. Right now, our attempts to carry the war to Germany have been a total and bloody failure.'

He raised his head to stare at the Admiral. 'Yet we must continue the bombing raids, because we must keep reminding the enemy that we are alive and kicking, because the people of this country demand some measure of retaliation for the death and destruction they have themselves suffered, and perhaps most important of all, because we have to convince the presently neutral world that we are a long way from being beaten, no matter what Herr Goebbels may be saying. Now, your boats are as capable of penetrating enemy waters as our aircraft are of penetrating his air space. More important, when your people see a target, they can hit it with almost that pinpoint accuracy we need. Certainly if it is a stationary target. Tell me if I am wrong.'

'No, Sea Lord, you are not wrong. But there is one factor you have not taken into account. I accept that the RAF is suffering severe casualties. But they still have the whole sky in which to manoeuvre, and the Germans have to scour the whole sky to find them. Once a boat is discovered in an enclosed stretch of water, however fast she may be, and however skilful her crew, the enemy still know that she has only two options, one is to keep on going forward on a known track, the other is to turn and go back along the same track. But whatever she does, it has to be over the same stretch of water. Nor does she have any clouds into which she can duck.'

'Actually,' the Sea Lord argued, 'in this instance there is cover. Apart from the long empty stretches, am I not correct is saying that there is thick fog on the Gironde up till at least ten o'clock every morning, and sometimes longer than that?'

'Which of course prevents the boats from using their speed. And they still have to get back out.'

The Sea Lord sighed. 'I am not saying that there won't be casualties, Admiral Lonsdale. The point is that casualties have to be weighed against possible results. We send a hundred bombers over Germany, knowing full well that something like thirty are not going to come back. That is, thirty pieces of very expensive equipment, and a hundred and fifty very highly trained men. And we also know that we have very little concrete results to show for that very heavy loss of life and equipment. Now you have the opportunity to strike a very heavy blow at the enemy. The Canal du Midi is the vital lifeline across the south of France. It may not be able to carry any large vessels, but there is a constant stream of heavily laden barges, coming and going, transferring materiel from the Mediterranean to the Atlantic and vice versa, for loading on to ocean-going vessels in Bordeaux Harbour, materiel which, if Bordeaux were not available, would have to go through the Straits of Gibraltar and up the Atlantic coast, and thus be vulnerable to our submarines and planes. If your people can put Bordeaux out of action, for even a couple of months, it would rank as a great victory.'

'And if none of them come back,' Lonsdale remarked, 'they would all be posthumous heroes.'

'Well, heroes, certainly. Can you do it?'

'It can be done.'

'*Will* you do it?'

'If that is what is required, Sea Lord, I will do it. You wish an entire flotilla?'

'We feel that is the best way to go about it. One boat can easily have an accident, and besides, each boat has limited fire power. Do you agree?'

'I seem to have no choice,' Lonsdale reminded him. 'So all I have to do is select three of my crews to send to hell.'

'You'll call for volunteers, of course,' the Secretary put in. 'This has to be a volunteer mission.'

'Of course. And do you know what will happen when I ask for volunteers? Every man in my command will step forward. So the choice will still have to be mine.'

'But there are some men in your command who are more suited to an assault of this nature than others, are there not?' the Sea Lord suggested.

'I'm not sure what you mean.'

'Don't you have an officer who has already led an assault on the enemy. Who has a most distinguished record against them? Lieutenant Lord Eversham.'

Oh, my God! Lonsdale thought.

'And isn't he also,' the Sea Lord continued, 'something of a maverick, who has proved and is proving, difficult to command? This mission is best suited to an independent command.'

'However briefly,' Lonsdale remarked.

'I would have thought,' the Sea Lord said, 'going on his record, that of all the junior officers in the Royal Navy, Lieutenant Eversham is the most likely to be able to carry out an assignment like this successfully.'

'Lieutenant-Commander Eversham.'

'Ah . . . just what do you mean by that? Lieutenant-Commander? Isn't he RNVR?'

'That is correct.'

'And he has only been on full service for eighteen months?'

'He has been on regular service from the day war broke out, yes.'

'And he has a most irregular service record. Didn't he go to Dunkirk with his wife on board?'

And even more, Lonsdale reflected, his mother! 'She was not actually his wife at the time.'

'My God!'

'She happened to be on board when he was ordered to assist in the evacuation, and he determined that getting to the beaches was more important than pausing to set her ashore. I had assumed that sort of élan and dedication to duty was what you were looking for.'

'Yes, of course. But to promote such a character ahead of more senior officers . . .'

'If I instruct Lord Eversham to take his flotilla a hundred miles up the Gironde, torpedo every ship he finds in Bordeaux Harbour, lay as many mines as he can, and blow up the docks themselves, he is going as a lieutenant-commander.'

The two men stared at each other for a few moments. Then the Sea Lord inclined his head. 'As you wish. You may gazette Lieutenant Lord Eversham as lieutenant-commander, effective immediately.'

The marine sentry presented arms, the staff inside the building hurriedly stood to attention, as their admiral strode past them. Lonsdale's responses were perfunctory. His secretaries seemed to coagulate as he passed them as well, but Alison followed him into the inner office. 'I hope the meeting went well, sir.'

Lonsdale peered at her as if he had never seen her before. Then he said, 'Alison, I would like to have dinner at your house tonight. Will you invite me?'

'Of course, sir. Do you wish it to be a surprise, or may I telephone them to let them know?'

'Oh, let them know. Duncan will be there?'

'Oh, yes, sir. He's still on leave.'

'Good.'

Alison retreated to the door, and there paused. 'There's nothing wrong, is there, sir?'

'He's just been promoted lieutenant-commander.'

'Duncan? Oh, that's marvellous. Can I tell him now?'

'It hasn't been gazetted yet. We'll tell him together, shall we?'

'Of course, sir. I'll just telephone Kristin and tell her you're coming to dinner. She'll be so pleased.'

She frowned as she sat at her desk and picked up the phone.

She couldn't fault the Admiral for wishing to be present when Duncan learned the good news – but she had a gut feeling that Lonsdale was not a happy man at that moment, and that his mood was connected with Duncan's promotion.

'Excuse me, Mr Chadwick.' Mrs Bainbridge stood in the doorway looking like the messenger from hell.

Chadwick raised his head. 'Yes, Mrs Bainbridge?'

'I have just had a telephone call from Maynard, sir.'

'Oh, my God! Don't tell me she's gone down sick or something.'

'No, sir. She's just gone.'

'Gone? What do you mean, gone?'

'Gone, sir. Disappeared.'

Chadwick leaned back in his chair. 'No jokes, please, Mrs Bainbridge. Not at ten o'clock in the morning. How can she have disappeared?'

'Well, sir, you said she was to be allowed out, if she wished.'

'With a minder.'

'Yes, sir. But she gave Miss Luckin the slip.'

'I'll have that girl's guts for garters. What is Maynard doing about it?'

'That is what he wants you to tell him, sir. As he understands it, the last thing you wish is any publicity about Mrs Strong's presence in England. Therefore, he does not feel that he can go to the police, without your say so.'

'He cannot go to the police,' Chadwick confirmed.

'Yes, sir. So . . .?'

'Let's not lose our heads. She can't have gone far.'

'She can have gone anywhere in the country, sir.'

'Oh, really, Mrs Bainbridge. What with?'

'You opened a bank account for her, sir, with virtually unlimited credit. You also, at her request, replaced her driving licence as well as her passport.

'Well, her husband is a millionaire, don't you know. I believe he comes into the multi bracket.' He snapped his fingers. 'But that's it. To hire a car or go anywhere outside London, she'd need money. Get on to the bank and find out if she made a withdrawal this morning.'

'They'll need authorization, sir.'

'Refer them to me.'

'Yes, sir.' She hesitated. 'This woman is safe, isn't she?'

'What do you mean?'

'Well . . . if she wasn't, isn't, I mean, she need not have left London at all. She could have gone to some contact right here.'

'What contact? She knows no one in London.'

'Well, sir, obviously, if she did have a London contact, a subversive contact, she wouldn't broadcast it.'

'Mrs Bainbridge, you are seeing spies under the bed. Mrs Strong knew nothing about the situation with her father until I told her, a week ago. And since then she has been under the constant surveillance of our team. She has not been allowed to make any telephone calls, or any appointments to meet people, save for a dressmaker, who is known to us. In any event, her meetings with Mrs Compton have always been in the presence of Miss Luckin. Have they not?'

'Yes, sir. But it is a little coincidental, isn't it, that, as you say, she knew nothing about the situation until you told her. Then she behaves herself perfectly, for a week . . . while her wardrobe is at least partially restored. But as soon as she has some decent clothes to wear, her identification documents have been replaced and her credit has been set up, she drops Luckin and disappears. While we only have her unsubstantiated claim that she is Rebecca Strong. And she came to us via Lisbon. I know that is the route we chose for her, but if she, I mean the real Mrs Strong, had been indiscreet, well . . . aren't there more Nazi spies in Portugal than stray cats?'

Chadwick stared at her for several seconds. Then he said, 'You traced that telephone call, didn't you?'

'Yes, sir. It came from the Naval Officers' Mess, Portsmouth.'

'And have you followed that up?'

'There didn't seem much point, sir. There must be well over a hundred officers using that mess every day, as well as staff.'

'Agreed, Mrs Bainbridge. But the call had to have been made by someone who recently, very recently, had encountered Mrs Strong. Now, earlier that day she was torpedoed. Ergo, the only naval officers she would have come into contact with were those on the MTBs that fished her out of the drink. Now, as far as I know, those small craft only have one officer each. That narrows it down a bit, wouldn't you say? Get me the names of those three officers.'

'I'll need authorization.'

'Refer them to me.'

'Yes, sir. Will this man be able to help us?'

'As you have just reminded me, it is essential that we regain control of this woman just as rapidly as possible. Therefore we need every possible lead as to who she knows in this country and where she might have gone.'

'Yes, sir.' Mrs Bainbridge went to the door, hesitated. 'What if it was one of the seamen, and not an officer, who agreed to help her?'

'Mrs Bainbridge,' Chadwick said, with great patience. 'Seamen do not use the officers mess.'

'Ah,' Mrs Bainbridge commented, and closed the door.

Kristin pulled into the bus stop just short of Goring's Garage, and squeezed Jamie's hand. They had hardly spoken on the drive out from Lymington. But then, they seldom did. She had been in a pleasant daydream, as she usually was after an hour in Jamie's company. Her body still tingled, as if she had just had a massage. Well, she had just had a massage, everywhere that mattered.

'So,' she said as he opened his door. 'Tomorrow?'

'No, milady.'

She raised her eyebrows. 'Are you going somewhere?'

'*Forty-One* goes back in the water tomorrow.'

And Duncan hadn't mentioned it, the beast. 'So when will you have leave again?'

'I don't know, milady. But I imagine, as we've had this time off, that they'll keep us at it awhile.'

'Fuck it. But as you've already done that, you'd better give me a kiss.'

He leaned across the seat to close his mouth on hers, resting his hand on her breast to give it a last gentle squeeze.

'I adore you, Jamie,' she whispered. 'Come back to me.'

'I have that in mind, milady,' he agreed, and closed the door.

It really was a farce, dropping him here, as she needed to stop at the garage anyway for petrol. But he was terrified of his parents ever finding out. And now they were going to be separated, at least for a while. On the other hand, he had always come back, so he would come back again. And as he always came back, so would Duncan.

She pulled into the forecourt. 'Good afternoon, Mr Probert. Fill her up, will you.' She held the book of coupons out of the window.

'Pleasure, milady.' He got busy with the nozzle, and another car pulled in on the other side of the pump; the small saloon was dwarfed by the Bentley.

'Good afternoon,' said the rather striking blonde woman, rolling down her window. 'I am looking for Eversham House. I believe it's somewhere around here. Can you direct me?'

She had been addressing Probert, but instead of replying, he looked at Kristin.

'Are they expecting you?' Kristin asked. She could only suppose the woman was a friend of Alison's, although how Alison came to know an obvious American she had no idea.

'No, they're not. Is that important?'

'Well,' Kristin said. 'It might be, to them.'

'I assure you that they'll be pleased to see me.'

'Is that so,' Kristin said. 'Well . . .'

But Rebecca had looked in her rear view mirror and seen Jamie just coming into view round the bend. 'Good lord!' She opened her door and got out. 'Jamie Goring!' she cried.

Jamie halted, and looked from her to Kristin, who had also got out of her car.

'There you are, Lady Eversham,' Probert said, with unusual emphasis. 'Full to the brim.'

'Thank you, Mr Probert.'

Rebecca, starting forward to greet Jamie, checked and turned back. 'You are Lady Eversham?'

'Actually,' Kristin said, 'I am now the Dowager Lady Eversham.'

'Your name is Kristin?'

'That is correct.'

'But it's you who I've come to see! Excuse me one moment. I just have to speak with this young man.' She turned back to Jamie, who had come up to them and was looking somewhat apprehensive. 'Mr Goring! Jamie! What a magnificent surprise. I had not expected to see you again.'

'Neither had I, Mrs Strong. To see you, I mean.'

'But what are you doing here? And not in uniform.'

'I live here,' Jamie explained, and indicated the sign above the office. 'And I'm on leave.'

'How splendid. I am so happy to see you again.' To Jamie's obvious embarrassment, she seized his hand to squeeze it.

'You've been keeping secrets from me, Jamie,' Kristin said, her voice, rather sinisterly, lower than usual.

'Ah . . .'

'You mean you two know each other?' Rebecca asked.

'Well, we should,' Kristin pointed out. 'This is my garage. Just how long have you known him?'

'Only a week. Ever since he pulled me out of the sea.'

Kristin looked at Jamie, eyebrows arched.

'It was after that engagement with the S-boats, milady.'

'They torpedoed the ship I was on,' Rebecca explained. 'And I was rescued by Jamie and . . . Good lord! Your son!'

'It's a small world,' Kristin agreed, some of the ice leaving both her tone and her eyes. 'Well, I won't keep you, Jamie. Thank you, Mr Probert. It's been nice meeting you, Mrs . . .?'

'Rebecca Strong. May I come with you?'

'Why?'

'Because I've come to see you.'

'Why?'

'Because we're old friends.'

'Are we?' Kristin's tone was redolent of disbelief.

'I'll explain it.' Rebecca turned back to Jamie. 'I am so glad to have run into you again. I'll never forget . . . well . . . what you did for me.'

Jamie's cheeks were flaming.

'You said he pulled you out of the water,' Kristin reminded her. 'That was very gallant of you, Jamie.'

'It was in the line of duty, milady.'

'And then he had to put me to bed.' Rebecca believed in dotting I's and crossing T's. 'And . . . assist me in various directions.'

'Was that also in the line of duty, Jamie?'

'Well, I was ordered to do it, milady. By Lord Eversham.'

'I'll tell you all about it,' Rebecca volunteered. 'You were going to explain to me what the heads were, remember?'

'Ah. Well . . .'

'I will explain that to you,' Kristin said. 'After you have told me why they are important to you.' The glacier was back in place. 'Well, goodbye, Jamie. Perhaps I'll see you again, when next you have leave. You'd better follow me, Mrs . . . ah . . .'

'Strong,' Rebecca said, understanding that she had got into something that could just be above her head.

'Strong. I must try to remember.' Kristin got behind the wheel and exited the forecourt at full speed, which she maintained for the short drive home. But a glance in the rear view mirror assured her that Rebecca was immediately behind here.

She braked at the front door, and Rebecca pulled in beside her. 'What a lovely old pile. We don't have antiques like this in the States.'

'I thought you had to be from somewhere odd. And you say we know each other?'

'We did, as children.'

'Ah.' Kristin went to the door, made sure that Rebecca was immediately behind her, and opened it, at the same time stepping smartly to one side.

'Aaagh!' Rebecca screamed, as she was struck by a white mountain. She went flat on her back on the gravel. 'Help me!'

'He won't harm you. He likes you.'

'God Almighty!' Rebecca made an unsuccessful attempt to push the dog away. 'What is it?'

'A Pyrenean Mountain Dog,' Kristin explained. 'Do get off the lady, Lucifer. You've torn her dress. Such a pretty dress.'

Lucifer stopped licking Rebecca's face and ceased straddling her. Slowly she sat up. 'Is that his name? Lucifer?'

'Well, what would you call him? Are you hurt?' Kristin inquired, solicitously.

'Yes,' Rebecca said, peering at herself. 'You knew he was going to do that.'

'I knew he was going to fall in love with you at first sight,' Kristin acknowledged. 'He can't keep his paws off pretty women. Can you, you naughty boy?'

Lucifer panted.

'This was a new dress,' Rebecca remarked.

'I'll buy you another one. Let me help you up.' Kristin held her arm. 'What you need is a stiff drink. I assume you're staying for tea? Or even dinner?'

'Well . . .' Rebecca allowed herself to be set on her feet.

'As you've come all this way just to see me. You were going to explain that. And about your acquaintance with young Goring. And you want to know about heads, remember?'

'Well . . . oh!'

'Mother?' Duncan emerged from the house. 'What was the racket? Oh, hello, Mrs Strong.'

'Of course,' Kristin remembered. 'You two have met. That racket was merely Lucifer being boisterous.'

'Don't tell me, he knocked you down.' He held Rebecca's hands and then looked at her dress. 'And tore your dress. You really are a shocker, Lucifer. Come inside and have a drink, Mrs Strong.'

'I am trying to have her do that,' Kristin said. 'And stay to dinner. You have an awful lot to tell us, haven't you, Mrs Strong?'

'I think you should call me Rebecca,' Rebecca decided.

'So,' Kristin said, sipping tea. 'We met when I was fourteen. I'm terribly sorry, but I can't remember you.'

'It was a long time ago,' Rebecca said, magnanimously, putting down her cup. She would have preferred the drink she had been offered, but it hadn't materialized yet.

'Don't remind me.'

'You were fourteen, I was five.'

Kristin regarded her as if she were a beetle.

'My mother, Margo Hallstrom, and yours were good friends.'

'Hallstrom,' Kristin said thoughtfully. 'I remember the name. Wasn't your father some kind of scientist?'

'He still is.'

'Good heavens!'

'But my mother is dead.'

'So is mine. And you were on your way to see him? Your father? What a disaster.'

'Oh,' Rebecca said, 'I am still hoping to get there. Sweden, I mean.'

'Unless you are torpedoed again,' Kristin remarked, her tone indicating that in her opinion that would be no bad thing.

Rebecca gave Duncan, leaning against the sideboard, a bright smile. 'When perhaps your gallant son will be there to rescue me again.'

'Oh, he pops up all over the place,' Kristin acknowledged. 'So you're dragged out of the water . . .'

'Along with twenty-four others,' Duncan put in.

'But Rebecca was the only woman.'

'Well, yes.'

'So you felt obliged to have young Jamie put her to bed.'

'He was the only one I could immediately spare from the deck.'

'And as you had spent some time in the sea, you were sopping wet.'

'And very cold. I thought I was going to die.'

'But you didn't,' Kristin pointed out, regretfully. 'It must have been very uncomfortable, and difficult to get warm, in those wet clothes.'

'Oh, Jamie . . . Mr Goring . . . took off my clothes.'

Beetles no longer came into it. Cockroaches were paramount. 'You cannot possibly stop now.'

Pink spots had arrived in Rebecca's cheeks. 'Well, he dried me, and then he wrapped me in a blanket . . . two blankets, and put me to bed.'

'And you didn't object to any of this, somewhat intimate behaviour?'

'Do you know, I felt I should. But he was so kind, so gentle, and he seemed to know what he was doing. I actually thought that he was the ship's doctor.'

'Did he tell you he was the doctor?'

'He told me that boats so small did not have a doctor. That he was the engineer.'

'By which time it was too late for you to do anything about it.'

'By which time I did not want to do anything about it.'

'Of course. He was massaging you with a towel.' Kristin looked at Duncan.

'It was a difficult situation for all of us,' Duncan explained. 'I mean, someone had to look after Mrs Strong: she was suffering from hypothermia. I couldn't leave the bridge, and it seemed to me that Jamie was my best bet. I mean, Mother, you know Jamie. He has absolutely no interest in women. To him, Mrs Strong was a job of work, just as looking after his engine is a job of work.'

'He was a perfect gentleman throughout,' Rebecca insisted. 'He even took me to the heads.'

Kristin's gaze would have frozen a blazing fire.

'I couldn't walk, you see,' Rebecca explained.

'But you didn't know what they were.'

'Well, obviously I knew what they were.' Rebecca said. 'I just didn't know why they were so called.'

'I think Rebecca needs a drink,' Kristin announced, finishing her tea. 'In fact, we all do. We'll have some sherry to begin with. Heads are so called because in the old sailing ships there were no toilets for the crew. Instead, in the head of the ship, just forward of the forecastle but behind the bowsprit, there was a grating, which was constantly being washed by the sea breaking over the bow. When a sailor needed to go, he squatted on the heads and hoped not to get swept away by the next wave. Which, of course washed everything else away. Hence, going to the heads.'

'Ugh! The one Jamie took me to was nothing like that.'

'I hope not. I assume it was Duncan's.'

Duncan poured.

'You still haven't told us why you're here,' Kristin said. 'I mean here, in Lymington. Or is it merely to use my heads?'

'I thought I had.' Rebecca accepted her glass from Duncan. 'I was looking for you.'

'Because you had known me, briefly, twenty-nine years ago.'

'Well, no, not exactly. I wanted to tell you how grateful I am for your son's help.'

'In getting you out of the water.'

'That, of course. But even more, afterwards.'

'Don't tell me he helped you dress when you decided to get up. Or perhaps you needed to use the heads again.'

'Now, Mother, please,' Duncan protested.

'No, no,' Rebecca said. 'He made a very important telephone call for me. You did, didn't you, Lord Eversham? I was rescued quickly enough.'

'Well, of course I did,' Duncan agreed, astonished that she should have doubted. 'I said I would.'

'I'm so glad you're staying to dinner,' Kristin said. 'You'll be able to meet Duncan's wife, and tell her all about it.'

'Ah,' Duncan said. 'I should have mentioned it before, Mother, but while you were out, Alison telephoned to say that the admiral is coming to dinner tonight. Apparently he requested the invitation. Said he had something important to tell me. She sounded quite excited. Don't worry,' he added, misinterpreting Kristin's expression. 'I told Lucia we'd be four for dinner.'

'Well, now you can go and tell her we'll be five,' Kristin suggested.

'Mrs Strong!' Jimmy Lonsdale was obviously pleased with what he was looking at.

'Why, Admiral, it's a pleasure. I must apologize for my appearance.'

She had had a wash and a brush-up in Kristin's bathroom, refraining from any comment on the huge and somewhat explicit nude of her hostess hanging above the bed, but her clothes remained crushed and her skirt was still torn.

'I'm afraid,' Kristin explained, 'that Lucifer fell in love with her at first sight.'

'One of these days, Kristin, you are going to have to do something about that dog.'

'Certainly not,' Kristin said. 'He protects me,' she pointed out, with some emphasis.

'I'm sure he didn't mean any harm,' Rebecca said, anxious to keep the evening light and fluffy.

'He's a menace,' Lonsdale insisted. 'And it is very difficult to suppose that Kristin has ever needed protection in her life.'

'I am a very vulnerable old woman,' Kristin insisted. 'Now, come and sit down and have a drink before dinner.' She led the way into the drawing room. 'And Rebecca will tell you all about how she had to be put to bed by Duncan.'

Alison looked at Duncan, who raised his eyes to indicate that this was just Mother being Mother.

'But first,' Kristin said, 'you can tell us this important news you have.'

This time Alison looked at the Admiral, who gave a quick nod. She drew a deep breath. 'Today Duncan was gazetted lieutenant-commander.'

'Magnificent!' Kristin cried. 'Let me give you a hug and a kiss.' She did so, and then turned to Lonsdale. 'I had better give you a hug and a kiss as well. I assume you had something to do with it?'

'Well . . .' But he submitted to her embrace.

'Have I that kind of seniority, sir?' Duncan asked. 'And after that business with Lieutenant-Commander Bruton . . .'

'There are wheels within wheels,' Lonsdale said. 'In fact, Kristin, before we settle down to an evening's wassailing, I would like to have a chat with Duncan, in private.'

'Of course, sir,' Duncan agreed. 'We'll go into the study.'

'So if you girls will excuse us for half an hour,' Lonsdale said. 'I'm sure you have a lot to talk about.'

'You'll miss the story of Rebecca's adventures,' Kristin pointed out.

'I already know it,' the admiral assured her.

'This is one of those occasions when one wishes one smoked,' Lonsdale remarked, settling himself into a leather armchair.

'Bad as that, sir?' Duncan also sat down, after carefully closing the door.

'It couldn't be worse. What I have to say is in the strictest confidence.'

'Of course, sir.'

'In that I have to include both Alison and your mother.'

'Yes, sir.' Even if he was totally mystified: Alison was this man's secretary.

'Well, then . . .' Lonsdale outlined what he had that morning discussed with the Sea Lord.

When he had finished, Duncan whistled. 'Sounds quite a show.'

'You have to volunteer.'

Duncan grinned. 'Does volunteering have anything to do with my new rank?'

'Your new rank has been gazetted.'

Because, Duncan thought, you knew I would volunteer. 'And I assume it means that I will be leading the assault? With what and with whom?'

'They want three boats. Who mans them is up to you, but they also must be volunteers. However, before we go any further, can it be done?'

'I think so. Coming out might be a bit tricky.'

'We would of course provide you with the very best pilotage available. The Gironde is a tidal river.'

'I have a pilot, sir.'

'Explain.'

'The boy Goring.'

'He knows the Gironde?'

'He's been up and down it a couple of times, with his dad, before the war.'

'Good Heavens! And you think he'll volunteer?'

'He'll volunteer, sir.'

'Very good. How soon can you be ready?'

'Well, sir, obviously the sooner it's done the better. Before the nights start to shorten.'

'In February, the weather in the Bay is likely to be severe.'

'There are fine spells. We'll have to rely on the Met boys to set us up.'

'Then I'll leave that in your hands.'

'Very good, sir. There's just one thing: am I allowed to find my crews wherever I wish? What I mean is, I would obviously most like to have the members of my old flotilla, who are now members of Lieutenant-Commander Bruton's enlarged flotilla.'

Lonsdale nodded. 'You are permitted to recruit as and where you choose. You now hold the same rank as Bruton, but I don't want any unpleasantness. If he objects, refer him to me.'

'Thank you, sir. What am I allowed to tell the men?'

'Nothing.'

Duncan raised his eyebrows.

'I have said, this is absolutely top secret, and can be known to no one except you and me. The merest suspicion of what we are up to would alarm Jerry and have his every seaport on red alert. The only thing you have going for you is that right now he must be feeling pretty secure, especially in such far off places as Bordeaux. You will ask for volunteers for a most hazardous mission. Nothing more until you are actually at sea. Then you can alert your commanders and issue concrete orders. You will not, of course, use your radios at any time: all messages between your boats must be conveyed by lamp, loud hailer or flag.'

'Aye-aye, sir.'

Lonsdale leaned forward. 'I want you to know, Duncan,

that I am fully aware that this is a shitty assignment, and I feel a shit for having to put it to you.'

'I understand that, sir.'

'So, any further questions?'

'No, sir.'

'Well, then, shall we rejoin the ladies?' He turned his head. 'What on earth is that racket?'

'They are taking a very long time over their chat,' Kristin remarked, somewhat morosely, peering into her third whisky and water.

'Must be something big,' Alison suggested. 'They'll tell us about it when they come in.'

'When,' Kristin growled. 'Lucia's dinner will be spoiled. What's that noise?'

'It sounds like an automobile,' Rebecca suggested.

'Oh, really. You didn't invite anyone else to dinner, Alison?'

'No, I did not.' Alison went to the window. 'Good heavens! It's a police car.'

'Oh, lord!' Rebecca said.

'Don't tell me you're wanted by the police as well?' Kristin inquired.

Lucifer was barking, and a moment later Harry appeared in the drawing room doorway, hanging on to the dog's collar. 'There's a police officer here, milady.' He looked from one to the other, as usual completely baffled when confronted with both of them. 'Asking to speak with Lady Eversham.' Another eye-roll from face to face.

'I'd better see him off.' Kristin got up. 'And do let go of Lucifer. You know how he hates being dragged about.'

'But milady, if I let go of him . . .'

'Brrr,' Kristin said, and went to the front door. 'Can I help you?' And frowned at the man in the lounge suit waiting there. 'You're a policeman?'

'Inspector Burden, Special Branch, ma'am.'

'Then what are you doing here?'

'I'm trying to locate Lady Eversham. Would you be her?'

'No.'

'Oh! Well . . .'

'She is.' Kristin indicated Alison, who had joined them.

'Ah.' Burden took her in; coming straight from the office,

with Lonsdale in tow, Alison was still in uniform, although she had removed her hat and freed her hair. 'Well . . .'

'Actually,' Alison said, 'She is too.'

The inspector looked ready to scratch his head.

'I,' Kristin announced, 'am the Dowager Lady Eversham. This is the current one. Which of us do you require?'

'Well . . .'

'Gosh, look out,' Alison cried.

Harry had finally released Lucifer, who came bounding down the hall, tail wagging furiously. Alison tried to stop him by throwing both arms round his neck, but was merely dragged along as an appendage.

'Is that dog safe?' Burden inquired, anxiously.

'Not when it comes to policemen,' Kristin said. 'Lucifer, behave.'

As usual, her admonition was ineffective, but with Alison round his neck Lucifer ran out of steam before he could get up on his hind legs and kiss the inspector.

'Are you all right, ma'am?' Burden inquired. 'Milady?'

'He's very affectionate, really,' Alison panted.

The two men emerged from the study. 'Alison?' Duncan demanded. 'What are you doing on the floor?'

She had released Lucifer, who was sitting beside her, panting and licking her face.

'Who is this man?' Lonsdale demanded.

'He is a Special Branch officer,' Kristin explained. 'Who has come to arrest either Alison or me. But he won't tell us which one.'

'No, no, no,' Burden protested, feebly, and took what he apparently hoped would be the safest route. 'Am I addressing Lord Eversham?'

'No.'

'Oh. Ah . . .' This time his hand actually went up to his head.

'This gentleman is Lord Eversham,' the admiral explained. 'I am only an admiral.'

Burden looked at Duncan, who was lifting Alison to her feet. 'May I, we, assist you?' Duncan asked, carefully restraining himself from adding, 'my good fellow'.

Burden squared his shoulders. If he obviously felt that he had inadvertently strayed into a madhouse, he was prepared to go down with all guns blazing. 'Based on information received, my lord, I have come here in search of a woman named Rebecca Strong.'

'Oh, lord,' Rebecca muttered again.

'A dangerous criminal, is she?' Kristin inquired, hopefully.

'Well, no, milady. She is an American lady.'

'Same thing.'

'I beg your pardon,' Rebecca said, aggressively. 'I am Mrs Strong.'

'Ah.' Burden exuded relief. 'Well, madam, I will have to ask you to come with me.'

'Just hold on one moment,' Duncan said. 'Suppose she doesn't want to go with you? Do you have a warrant?'

'Well, no my lord, but . . .'

'She hasn't had dinner yet,' Kristin put in, changing sides. 'Although I suppose we could fit you in. Harry!' she bawled.

'I'm sorry, milady,' Burden said. 'My instructions are to locate Mrs Strong and then return her to protective custody without delay.'

'I suppose those orders came from Chadwick,' Rebecca said.

'Yes, madam. They did.'

'Are we allowed to ask why Mrs Strong is the object of so much official interference?' Lonsdale inquired.

'I'm afraid I do not know, sir. I am simply carrying out orders.'

'In that case I would like the rank and telephone number of this fellow . . . Chadwick, is it? . . . who is responsible for this furore.'

'I cannot give you that, sir.'

'I think I had better go with the inspector,' Rebecca said. 'This isn't his fault. I'm sorry to have caused so much trouble. All I wanted was a bit of fresh air and a chance to talk with some friends. I'm grateful, believe me.'

'But if you're in some kind of trouble,' Duncan said, 'at least you can tell us what it is. We may be able to help you.'

'I'm sorry, Lord Eversham. I can't tell you what the problem is. And I'm not really in trouble, just important to a lot of people. Thanks for everything. Shall we go, Inspector? I presume your people can take care of the hire car.'

'But when are you going to eat?' Alison asked.

'We'll be in London in an hour or so,' Burden assured them. 'Good night, my lord, milady, milady, Admiral.' He regarded the still sitting Lucifer, but thought better of addressing him, stepped back, and waited for Rebecca to join him.

Duncan closed the door.

'Well,' Kristin remarked. 'I'm not sure whether that has made or ruined the evening. I feel like a glass of champagne.'

'I think, in all the circumstances, that might be a very good idea,' Lonsdale agreed, and looked at Duncan.

Tactics

Nancy Luckin opened the bedroom door, somewhat apprehensively. 'Mr Chadwick is here, Mrs Strong.'

Rebecca was sitting up, drinking coffee. 'Is that supposed to interest me?'

'He wants to see you. When you're dressed.'

'I am not getting dressed, this morning. He can see me here.'

Miss Luckin looked more apprehensive yet. Included in Rebecca's new wardrobe, courtesy of HM Government, was the satin nightdress she was at that moment wearing, and which was the reverse of modest. She turned to the door, took the dressing gown from its hook, and advanced to the bed.

'What's that for?' Rebecca inquired. 'I told you that I am not getting up, at least until lunch.'

'But you must put this on, before, well . . .'

'Entertaining a man in my nightie? Forget it.'

Miss Luckin hesitated, uncertainly, then turned back towards the hallway, holding the door open. 'Mrs Strong will see you, sir. But . . . she's still in bed.'

'I can wait.'

'It could be a long wait,' Rebecca called. 'Either come in or go away.'

Another hesitation, then Chadwick entered the bedroom, as apprehensively as Miss Luckin had done. 'Good morning,' he said brightly. 'And how are we today?'

Rebecca's stare could be almost as devastating as Kristin's. 'I am not a schoolgirl,' she reminded him. 'Nor am I a convicted criminal. I do not like being treated like either.'

'It was necessary. I mean—'

'That you regard me as your prisoner. I am not that, either. What you seem to have forgotten is that one day, and it could be soon if George doesn't give up smoking, I am going to be one of the six richest women in America.'

Chadwick did not look impressed. 'You must understand, Mrs Strong, that if you were to fall into the wrong hands . . .'

'They would pull out my toenails or whatever to get me to tell them about Daddy's work? It wouldn't do them too much good. I told you, I don't have a clue as to what Daddy does, nor do I really believe this atom business.'

Chadwick advanced to the bedside, cautiously, having checked to make sure that Miss Luckin was still standing in the doorway. 'Yes, but don't you see, they could use possession of you to make him work for them?'

'Isn't that what you're doing, Mr Chadwick? Oh, do sit down. You're making me nervous, quivering like that. Aren't you married?'

Chadwick picked up the straight chair on the far side of the room and set it beside the bed before cautiously lowering himself on to it. 'Actually, no, I'm not.'

'Good grief! Then you have something to look forward to. Maybe,' she added thoughtfully.

'And you did agree to work for us, without coercion.'

'Your powers of self-deception amaze me. You got me over here on the pretext that I would be meeting my sick father. Now I discover that not only is he not sick, but he's not even here. OK, I still want to see the old gink, so I'm playing ball. But there's a limit. I have to breathe. Four walls are things I can do without. As for being in danger, the Evershams are old friends.'

'And would I be correct in assuming that Lieutenant Lord Eversham was the man who telephoned me as to your whereabouts?'

'Forget it.'

'We have just about identified the caller.'

'OK. What you want to remember is that if he hadn't called you I'd probably still be sitting in a cell in Plymouth awaiting deportation back to the States. You'll forgive me for wondering if that would be so much worse than being locked up in this pile.'

'Well, you'll be pleased to know that that is over.'

'You don't say?'

'We have received a reply from our Stockholm Embassy. They have contacted your father, and he is delighted to know that you are on your way to see him. You fly out tonight.'

'Tonight? Fly?'

'I told you, it's the safest way. Don't worry. Our people do it all the time. You'll be met by our Stockholm people when you land, and you'll be with your father for breakfast tomorrow. Then as soon as you, and your father, are ready to leave, all you have to do is contact our Embassy, and they'll arrange everything.' He beamed at her, endeavouring to keep his gaze above the level of her plunging décolletage.

'You guys really live in cloud-cuckoo land.'

'I beg your pardon.'

'Do you really think it's a business of hello Dad, nice to see you, now pack your bags, we're off after lunch to England, so that you can share your secrets with the Brits?'

'We understand,' Chadwick said stiffly, 'that it may take a day or two. We are quite prepared to allow you that much time.'

'A day or two. That is bullshit, if you'll pardon my French, Mr Chadwick.'

He frowned. 'Am I to understand that you wish to renege on your promise to help us?'

'I'm not reneging on anything. I'm just reminding you that Dad has a mind of his own. I'll do everything I can, but I can't promise a miracle.'

'I'm sure you'll do very well,' he agreed, mollified.

'There is also the business of getting him back.'

'Haven't we discussed that?'

'On your unrealistic level, yes. But supposing he says no way to flying?'

'That could be difficult. But I imagine we could bring him out by submarine.'

'That is even less likely to be acceptable than an aircraft. He suffers from claustrophobia.'

Chadwick regarded her for several seconds. 'With respect, Mrs Strong, you are painting a picture of a somewhat, shall I say, unstable character.'

'What did you expect? He's a genius.'

'Yes, of course. But he's also your father.'

'Just what do you mean by that?'

'That you strike me as being a very sensible and strong-minded young woman.'

'Well, what do you know? There may be hope for us yet.

As friends, I mean. Trouble is, I take after my mother. Look, Robert, I don't want you to get your knickers in a twist. I understand and appreciate everything you have told me, and as you keep reminding me, I have promised to do everything I can to bring Daddy out. I'm not in the habit of breaking my promises. But also I am not in the habit of making promises I may not be able to keep.'

'I have every confidence in you, Mrs Strong. A car will pick you up at four this afternoon. Enjoy your day.'

Because it may be my last, Rebecca thought, as the door closed. She lay back, closed her eyes, and thought of Jamie.

'There you go, Lord Eversham,' Hawkins said enthusiastically. 'Good as new.'

Duncan walked slowly round the boat, peering up at the hull. Out of the water she always looked enormous. But the hull certainly appeared to be intact.

'Big job, is it?' Hawkins asked.

'What makes you think that, Mr Hawkins?'

'Well . . . the rush. I was told to drop everything and concentrate on getting you ready for sea.'

'Everything's in a rush nowadays, Mr Hawkins. We need every boat we have in the water all of the time. When will she go in?'

'The crane will be along in an hour.'

Duncan nodded. 'I'll be back. Now, there's something else I want you to do for me, right away.'

'Well . . .'

'It's not difficult. I wish you to make me up a green net, large enough to drape over the entire boat. Can you do that?'

'I reckon so. How soon do you want it?'

'I said, right away. By the day after tomorrow, at the outside.'

Hawkins stroked his chin. 'I think we can make that.'

'Jolly good. I want three of them.'

'Three? Now look here, Lieutenant . . .' Duncan had not yet had the thin stripe inserted between his two broad bands.

'I'm afraid it is urgent, Mr Hawkins.'

'That's all very well, but all this work is urgent too.' He swung his arm to include the entire dockyard.

'Then what I suggest you do is telephone Captain Fitzsimmons and receive a direct order.' Duncan slapped him on the shoulder. 'I know you'll do your best, Mr Hawkins. You always do.'

He went up to the Command Building, very aware of a growing sense of excitement, mingled with the knowledge that he had been asked to carry out the most dangerous assignment of his life. He was sure he could do it, at least as regards getting up to Bordeaux and creating mayhem . . . but as to getting back out . . .

In the admiral's outer office, Alison held up a large parcel. 'There we go.'

'Another rush job?'

'I think they've done a very good piece of work. Now, if you'd like to take that tunic off, and put this one on, I'll have that one sent to the tailors and you'll have it back by tomorrow. Will that be in time?'

'In time for what?'

'For whatever you're setting off to do.'

They gazed at each other.

'You know I'd tell you if I could,' Duncan said.

'Of course I do, silly. I'd just like you to tell me that you'll be coming back. And that it's nothing to do with that woman.'

'Didn't you like her?'

'I'm sure she's absolutely charming. I'm also sure I'm not unique among wives in feeling a certain hostility towards women who have been put to bed by their husband, especially when they are most attractive.'

'Point taken and accepted. But I'd like to remind you that I did not put Mrs Strong to bed, Jamie did. And I did not get her out of bed; the stretcher bearers did that. But just to put your mind at rest, I have absolutely no idea what has happened to her or what she is doing now. Nor can I envisage any circumstances in which we can possibly meet again.'

'The admiral is waiting for you,' she said, preferring not to comment.

Duncan went into the inner office, saluted.

'Oh, good morning, Duncan, sit down.'

Duncan took off his cap and obeyed.

'The mines are earmarked and waiting,' Lonsdale said. 'But I assume you do not wish to load until you're ready to go.'

'Yes, sir.'

'Which will be?'

'I hope, by the weekend.'

'Questions?'

'None I couldn't handle.'

'Very good.' Lonsdale pushed a file across his desk. 'Here are the charts and plans you required.'

'Thank you, sir.'

'Have you assembled your crews yet?'

'No, sir.'

Lonsdale raised his eyebrows.

'I am seeing the commanders this evening when they return from patrol. Those who are prepared to volunteer will be required to put it to their crews tomorrow. I will have my crew by Friday. However . . .'

'I told you, refer Bruton to me, if you have to. So you'll be ready by Monday.'

'As long as the nets are ready.'

'And the weather?'

'There seems to be a front coming up towards the beginning of next week. It should be fast moving, and maybe around only a couple of days, but the Met people are very insistent that I remember that weather forecasting is an inexact art. Anyway, they've promised me a full report tomorrow.'

'If it's fast moving, wouldn't it make sense to wait until it's through?'

'No.'

Another raise of eyebrows.

'If I can get in before the weather breaks, I've an idea that bad weather might assist us in getting back out.'

'Into the Bay. Hm. Of course we'll have a heavy unit standing by, but you'll have to get to it.'

'I understand that.'

'Now tell me, how is Alison taking it?'

'Well, sir, if she wasn't curious she wouldn't be a woman. But she is also a naval officer, and is satisfied that I'll tell her all about it when I get back.'

'And your mother?'

'I don't think Mother is aware that anything special is going on. The appearance of that odd woman Rebecca Strong distracted her from wondering what our private chat was about the other night. Anyway, she seems to have something on her mind. We'll find out what it is, eventually.'

'Hm. Talking about the Strong woman, have you heard anything of what happened to her?'

'No, sir. I have not. And frankly, for the sake of my domestic peace, I have no wish to.'

'Attractive little thing, though, wasn't she? I can't help feeling that perhaps we could have done more to help her.'

'I suspect she is quite capable of taking care of herself.'

'I'm sure you're right. Thank you, Duncan. I'd like you to keep me right up to date until you're actually ready to sail.'

'Aye-aye, sir.' Duncan stood up, put on his cap, and saluted.

He had requisitioned a private room in the Mess, and having made his request for a meeting of the flotilla commanders, waited for them. Not altogether to his surprise, Bruton was the first to arrive. 'I see your boat's in the water. But you haven't reported.'

'That's because I am not rejoining the flotilla at this time.'

'What?' Bruton was taken aback by the absence of the obligatory 'sir', and then looked at Duncan's sleeve: he was wearing the tunic Alison had had altered for him. 'Good God!'

'Thank you.'

'Just what has happened?'

'I am to command a special op. Which means that I have to recruit from amongst your commanders and their boats.'

'The devil you will. What special op?'

'I'm not at liberty to tell you that.'

'And you think you can just walk off with my crews . . . how many?'

'I require three boats. One is my own, obviously. The others have to be volunteers.'

At that moment there was a knock on the door, and the other skippers filed in. Their strength had now grown to fifteen, and they looked suitably anticipatory. Bruton glared at them, and then turned back to Duncan, who smiled at him. 'You are welcome to stay, Mr Bruton. In fact, you are welcome to volunteer.'

'I am also welcome, I presume, to find out what this is all about. That I intend to do.' Bruton left the room.

Duncan surveyed the commanders; several of them were strangers to him. But they included such of his veterans as Longridge, and above all Beattie, who had immediately identified the thin stripe separating the two broad on each of Duncan's sleeves. 'Welcome back, sir. May we offer you our congratulations?'

'Thank you, Mr Beattie. As to the welcome, I think you should wait until you hear what I have to say. Will you close the door, please, Mr Longridge?'

Longridge obeyed.

'And sit down, please.'

Chairs scraped. Duncan waited until everyone was seated, then stood up. 'I apologize for bringing you here this evening, when I know that you have all had exhausting days. Unfortunately, tempus fugit. I am required to carry out a mission which our Lords of the Admiralty seem to feel may be of considerable importance to our future success in this war. Needless to say, I cannot at this stage tell you what the mission is, but I can tell you that it will involve a very high degree of danger. Therefore I must ask for volunteers. Anyone who is willing to undertake this mission, please raise his hand.'

As he had anticipated, every hand went up.

'Thank you, gentlemen. However, I cannot accept any of you without your crews, and these also have to volunteer. I know that quite a few of your people are married men. What I require you to do, is find out how many of your men are prepared to undertake what may turn out, as I have said, to be a considerable risk. This must be done over the next two days. In the case of each boat, I require a list of those men willing to volunteer. Please make it clear to them all, that a decision not to volunteer will not be entered in their records, and will not in any way ever be held against them. Are there any questions?'

'Will we be away for long, sir?' someone asked.

'Not more than a week.' He looked over their faces. 'Thank you, gentlemen. We shall meet again in two days' time.'

Next morning he spoke to his own crew, in the Mess cabin of *Forty-One*, repeating what he had said to the commanders. 'I expect no man to make a decision now,' he told them. 'Or to make it in public. I shall be in my cabin, and any man who wishes to see me, for whatever reason, may do so.'

Cooper followed him down. 'Is there anything I can do, sir?'

'That depends on what you wish to do, Mr Cooper.'

'I wish to take part in the raid, sir. It is a raid?'

'I'm sorry. I cannot put you in the picture until we are on our way. This is no reflection on you or anyone else. I am simply obeying orders. But I'll be glad to have you along.'

'Thank you, sir. Can you tell me when the operation will commence?'

'It will commence as soon as the crews are selected, and one or two vital pieces of equipment have been delivered.'

'Yes, sir. It's just that I, well, um . . .'

'You have got yourself a girl, to whom you would like to say goodbye.'

'No, sir. I have been invited out to dinner, on Sunday night.'

'Hm. I was intending to leave on Monday morning, so you will have to sleep on board. Is it an important invitation?'

'Well, sir, I . . .' He flushed. 'I don't really know. But won't you be there?'

Duncan, seated at his tiny desk, leaned back. 'I'm afraid that you have lost me, Mr Cooper. Why on earth should I be there, or you wish me to be there, if you are having dinner with some young lady, and, I presume, her family?'

'Ah, it is not a young lady, sir. Well, I mean, she is a most lovely lady. Your mother.'

'My mother has invited you to dinner, Mr Cooper?'

'Yes, sir.'

'When did she do this?'

'The invitation arrived yesterday. Handwritten. Would you like to see it?'

'I think that would come under the heading of prying. Would you like to accept?'

'I accepted immediately, sir. I thought, well, that you and Lady Eversham, young Lady Eversham, would be there. Like at Christmas, sir. I did so enjoy that meal.'

'Thank you, Mr Cooper. Well, as you have accepted the invitation, you must go. As to whether my wife and I will be there, I should think we will be, again providing nothing untoward has cropped up.'

'I understand that, sir. And thank you.'

'For what?'

'For giving me permission to dine at your house.'

'You're a grown man, Mr Cooper. However, if I may give you a word of advice . . .' he paused, looking for words.

'Sir?'

'As I think I mentioned once before, my mother has a weakness for shocking people. It would be very unwise of you to take anything she says, or does, too seriously.'

'Yes, sir.'

He left the cabin and Duncan remained staring at the door. Oh, Mother, Mother, he thought. What game are you playing now? But he knew that trying to come over heavy with her would be a waste of time. Kristin made up the rules of life, her rules, as she went along, and seemed to have the ability to survive any self-inflicted disasters. He remembered that he had once compared her, to Lonsdale, with the Pelasgian Mother Goddess Eurynome, the Creator of all Things, who danced carelessly through space and time, creating and destroying as the mood took her. Lucky for some. Certainly for Lonsdale himself. But what on earth had caused Mother to introduce this new complication into an already complicated life? And involve him in it as well?

There was a tap on the door. Here we go, he thought; someone's dropping out. 'Come,' he called, and blinked as the door opened. 'Jamie?' He couldn't believe it.

'I'm sorry to bother you, sir, but I was concerned about something you said at the briefing.'

Duncan sighed. 'Yes. I'm afraid that it is likely to be a very hazardous operation. I couldn't possibly blame you for opting out. Except . . .' he decided not to say it: Jamie was to have been his navigator.

'Oh, I'm not worried about that, sir. Goes with the job. But you said something about the op taking several days. If we're going to be using any sort of speed throughout that time, we could have a fuel problem.'

Duncan sighed with relief. 'I was allowing for possible delays, Jamie. As far as I have been able to make out, we shall be covering approximately fourteen hundred nautical miles, there and back. That's well within our range, isn't it?'

'Oh, yes, sir. Seven hundred miles out . . . that sounds like the Gironde.'

'What?' Duncan shouted. 'How do you know that?'

'That was the distance my Dad and I worked out for our trip down to Biscay in 1938.'

'Of course,' Duncan said.

'Mind you,' Jamie said, 'we went right up the river to Bordeaux. That's another hundred-odd miles. Now that was quite a trip. They have a mascaret, you see, sir. What we call a bore.'

Duncan frowned. He knew very little about rivers, although he had heard both names before. 'Which is what, exactly?'

'It's caused by the river flowing out coming into contact with the tide flowing in. The Gironde, and the Garonne, are actually tidal right up to Castets. That is, the first lock of the Canal du Midi. But normally, the tide diminishes considerably in the upper reaches, and when rising does no more than slow the river flow rather than check it. But on a spring tide, and especially after recent rain, the flood tide not only checks the river flow but pushes it back on itself. The level rises several feet, and the speed is tremendous. Whole areas within fifty yards of the bank are inundated, and most boats are torn from their moorings and wrecked.'

'And you've experienced this, have you?'

'Yes, sir. We caught the flood at Royan, that's the little port at the mouth of the river, and rode it up for six hours. It was at once the hairiest and the most exhilarating ride of my life. Even old *Tamara*, with a designed maximum speed of eight knots, was making something like twelve. By the time the tide turned we were all but there. In Bordeaux, I mean.'

'Sit down, Jamie.'

'Sir?' Jamie looked left and right; there was only the one chair.

'Use the bed. And tell me, have you discussed this deduction of yours as to our possible destination with anyone else?'

'Well, no, sir. You only just told me the mileage.'

'Of course. Well, under no circumstances are you to mention this conversation to anyone.'

'Aye-aye, sir. But you mean, that's where we're going. To the Gironde?'

'If you're prepared to navigate us, we're going to raid Bordeaux, shoot up and torpedo everything in sight, and lay a carpet of mines.'

'Great stuff.'

'So, will you do it?'

'Of course, sir.'

'Let me put that another way. *Can* you do it?'

'One boat?'

'Their lordships want three.'

'Hm.'

'Not so good?'

'Well, sir, obviously, we need to get up there as quickly as possible, and before Jerry wakes up and starts taking action. Three boats are more likely to excite him than just one. But even that is going to be tricky.'

'I've thought about that,' Duncan said. 'Is the river navigable in fog?'

Jamie snapped his fingers. 'But not at any speed.'

'Obviously. But as I understand it, the fog commences an hour or two after dawn. Correct?'

'Yes, sir. It's convection fog. The river gets very cold at night, but the moment the sun rises in those latitudes the air becomes very warm. The combination of the suddenly warm air and the cold water throws up the fog. At this time of year it generally settles in about eight, and gets thicker as the morning goes on.'

'And lasts until when?'

'Again, at this time of year, oh, it won't lift much before eleven. That's when the air and water temperatures tend to equalize.'

'So, if we arrived off Royan about six . . . Is the river lit?'

'The mouth, yes. The rest, poorly. But that was before the war, sir. I don't think there'll be any lights now.'

'But you can take us in? It's pretty broad at the mouth, isn't it?'

'I can take us in.'

'We go in at speed. My information is that, as the war hasn't really got down there yet, the river is not fortified and only scantily patrolled. We should whizz past Royan before anyone can identify us, and we stand a fair chance of being mistaken for S-boats. When the fog sets in, we creep up river as far as we can, and then halt for the rest of the day. Is that practical?'

'Stopping is quite practical, sir. Remaining all day unobserved, well, that's asking a lot.'

'The dockyard is preparing camouflage nets. They should disguise us from the air, or even from the river unless someone gets very close.'

'And if someone comes by on shore? There's a road runs along the south bank. That's the side we will have to shelter.'

'If that happens, Jamie, they will have to be taken out.'

'They'll be French people sir.'

'I know. But we have been given a job to do.'

Jamie swallowed. 'Yes, sir. And afterwards?'

'We come out just as fast as we can. We'll need to work out the tides. But once we've dropped our mines, there won't be much of a pursuit. It will mean coming down the river in the dark.'

Jamie nodded. 'It's practical. But come daylight they'll certainly have aircraft out for us.'

'We've been promised support out in the Bay. Happy?'

Jamie grinned. 'No, sir. But it might work.'

'We'll make it work. I'm glad we had this chat, Jamie. Just remember, not a word to a soul. The crews will be briefed once we're at sea.'

'Yes, sir. And the off?'

'I'm waiting on the delivery of those nets, and a weather report. But it can't be before the weekend. You can take tomorrow off.'

'Thank you, sir.'

'I know the temptation will be there to say goodbye to your loved ones, but it has to be an ordinary, I'll be off on patrol for the next week or so type thing. Secrecy is absolutely essential. If a word of what we are planning were to get across the Channel we wouldn't stand a snowball's chance in hell.'

'Aye-aye, sir.'

So there we go, Jamie thought, going ashore to catch the bus. He supposed they, and he in particular, had been simply having it too good. Now . . . but failure was not something to consider. He had to believe that no matter what happened, he personally would come through. Which meant that *Forty-One* would have to come through as well.

Meanwhile, there was her ladyship. She had been on his mind ever since that disastrous meeting with the American woman, because she had definitely been very annoyed. With him! Quite illogically. He had been given an order and he had carried it out. That he might have enjoyed doing so was one of the occasional perks of being on the receiving end of orders.

But then Kristin was not a logical person. She lived and acted entirely on instinct and on impulse.

And no matter how optimistic he might be about coming back from this raid, he had to be sufficiently realistic to understand that it was only a fifty-fifty chance. He supposed that she might shed a tear if he did not return. But then, if he didn't, neither would Duncan, and she would have to shed more tears over that.

'Back so soon?' Tim Goring inquired. 'We had the impression you were gone for a couple of weeks. Don't tell me the boat's not ready?'

'Oh, the boat's ready, Dad. It's just that the op, the patrol, I mean, has been put back to next week, so I'm not on duty again until tomorrow.'

'That's great. We'll go down to the pub tonight, and have a drink together.'

'I'd like that.'

Which was the absolute truth. But there was something he wanted more. There was a call box in the forecourt, and he used this immediately after lunch, in preference to risking the house phone.

'Yes?'

'Milady!'

There was a brief hesitation. 'May I help you?'

'Please, milady. I must see you.'

'Why?'

'Because I love you. And . . . this may be the last time.'

'What?'

'I can't explain on the phone.'

Another brief hesitation. 'Where are you?'

'At home.'

'Be at the bus stop in half-an-hour.'

'There you go,' Hawkins said proudly. 'That was quick work.'

'It was indeed,' Duncan agreed, fingering the thick green mesh. 'Any questions?'

The two men were alone in the warehouse.

'I don't encourage questions, Lieutenant-Commander. Not that I'd have had any answers. But anyone can see that these are camouflage nets.'

'I'm sure they can. Now Mr Hawkins, one last job.'

Hawkins looked sceptical.

'I'd like these delivered to my pontoon, but in bags. We don't want anyone else drawing logical conclusions, now do we?'

'When?'

'How about this afternoon?'

'You people are always in a hurry.'

'So, I understand, is Herr Hitler.'

Duncan was on the pontoon when the three large canvas bags arrived. 'One for each boat,' he instructed the driver of the delivery van.

'Are we allowed to ask what those are?' Beattie inquired, standing with Lieutenant Linton, who was commanding the third boat – he was relatively inexperienced, but very keen – to watch the sacks being carted on board.

'No. And I don't want them opened until we're at sea.' He grinned at them. 'No second thoughts, I hope?'

'No, sir.' They answered together.

'And your crews?'

'I have had to make two replacements,' Beattie said. 'They both wanted to come, but they're married men with young children.'

'That was the correct decision. Were you able to replace them?'

'Yes, sir. From Longridge's boat.'

'Mr Linton?'

'Four, sir. Two for family reasons. The other two wanted to come, but . . . well . . . I didn't feel they were up to it.'

'Up to what?'

'Well . . . you described this as a highly dangerous mission.'

'It is, and again you made the right decision. And I assume you have also secured replacements. I'm sorry I can't put you in the picture. My orders are that this is to be done once we are at sea. However, two things you should know. Firstly, when we are at sea, the use of radios is strictly forbidden. You may listen, in fact, you should listen, all the time, but you must not call. We will communicate by means of lights and flag signals. As to what we are setting out to do, we will bring our boats together for a brief conference, as I say, once we are clear of land.

'The second point is that this afternoon, a crew will be along to unship your depth charges and replace them with mines. We will carry twelve mines each. In case this bothers you, I may say that I have carried out a mission of this nature before, off Norway, last April, and it is not as dangerous as it seems.'

'Would that be the mission on which Lieutenant Leeming earned his VC, sir?' Linton asked.

'That is correct,' Duncan said, waiting for the follow-up.

'That was a posthumous award, wasn't it?'

'It was. We found ourselves, inadvertently, in the middle of the German navy. That is extremely unlikely to happen on this occasion. As to exactly where the mines will be dropped, I would prefer you not to speculate. Have any of your crews received shore leave?'

'Those whose families are within reach.'

'Returning when?'

'Tomorrow morning.'

Duncan nodded. 'Once they're back, all leave is off.'

'Aye-aye, sir. Does that mean we leave tomorrow night?'

'We leave, Mr Beattie, as soon as I get the weather forecast I'm looking for.'

It was waiting for him when he rejoined *Forty-One*. Cooper handed him a sealed envelope. 'Delivered by hand, sir.'

'Thank you, Mr Cooper.' Duncan retired to his cabin, sat down, and slit the envelope.

'The High Pressure system presently covering the British Isles and the South-West approaches is expected to last until Sunday morning. It will then decline rapidly as a Low moves in from the Atlantic. This Low will move directly across Biscay and into central and southern France, but it is a big Depression and will affect a large area, including the Channel and southern England. It will be fast moving and should clear the area within forty-eight hours, but it will contain winds of Force Eight or more for a brief period on Sunday night into Monday morning. Winds are expected to decrease on Monday afternoon as the weather improves. During these periods of strong squalls heavy rain showers can be expected. Except in the rain, visibility will be good throughout. Seas will be moderate becoming rough or very rough by Sunday evening, moderating during Monday afternoon. Good luck.'

Duncan remained staring at the paper for several minutes while he calculated. Then he went ashore and up to the Command Building. 'The admiral free?'

'I'm sure he will be, to see you,' Alison said. 'You're looking very serious?'

'Sorry. I need to see him, now.'

'Nothing wrong, is there?'

'Not a thing.'

She didn't look convinced, but escorted him to the inner door and knocked. 'Lieutenant-Commander Eversham, sir.'

'Ah, Duncan. Come in. Had a forecast yet?'

'Yes, sir.' Duncan placed the sheet on the desk, while Alison tactfully withdrew and closed the door.

Lonsdale read, and then raised his head. 'Shit! So, it really can't be on until well into next week, at the earliest.'

'I propose to leave tomorrow afternoon, sir.'

'What? But you can't be there and back in two days. You'll run into that weather.'

'As I explained a couple of days ago, sir, I'd say that is our best chance of survival.'

'In a seventy-two motor boat in a Biscay storm?'

'Even a Biscay storm doesn't have the fire power of the Luftwaffe and the German Navy. I figure it this way, sir. We leave tomorrow afternoon and should be south of Ushant by dawn on Saturday. We then lose ourselves on the edge of the Atlantic until dusk. Weather fine, so they say. We turn in at dusk, and aim to make a landfall at Royan at dawn on Sunday. Weather still fine. We get past Royan at first light, and should be sheltered by fog for most of the morning. During that time we would hope to make some sixty miles, even travelling slowly; we'll be carrying a spring tide. At noon, we take cover, concealing ourselves against the bank with camouflage nets. Weather should now be starting to break, but we're in sheltered water. Just before midnight we complete the journey on the last of the second tide, weather now hopefully pouring with rain and blowing like stink. That should keep the average head down. We shoot the place up, lay our mines, and feel our way back down the river on the ebb. The worse the weather the better for us. We should regain Royan by dawn, Monday.

Weather still severe, but from the south-west. We head into it. If the forecast is right, it should start to clear about noon. But until then, and thus during the crucial period when we are close to the coast, we should have total cloud cover as well as continuous rainsqualls. By the time it clears we should be at least fifty miles off-shore, and once the wind has abated, and the sea conditions have improved, we can make the rendezvous with the cruiser.'

'You make it sound very easy, Duncan. I suppose you have been at sea in a full gale in a small boat before.'

'I have, sir. However, once we're out to sea, the cruiser may be very necessary. I'll need the coordinates for the rendezvous.'

'You shall have them this afternoon. I'm still assuming neither Alison nor your mother know anything about this?'

'Not unless you have told them, sir.'

'Hm.' Duncan knew that he was realizing that he was the one who would have to tell them when it became certain that he was not coming back. 'Well, then, all that remains is to wish you good luck.' He held out his hand.

The Raid

'Will someone please tell me what is going on?' Kristin inquired, using her displeased goddess voice.

'I wish I knew.' Alison threw her cap and tunic into a chair, loosened her tie.

'You're Jimmy's secretary,' Kristin accused.

'Yes. And right now I'm being treated like a junior member of the staff. All I know is what I saw from my window, that at four o'clock this afternoon a flotilla of three MTBs, led by *Forty-One*, cast off and left harbour. The depth charges had been removed from their after decks and replaced with twelve mines each, which would appear to indicate that the operation is a mine-laying one, and that the Admiral has ordered me to come home and be with you. For the whole weekend. So it's something big and serious. I need a drink.'

'Absolutely.' Kristin poured two whiskies, ignored the water. 'Something big and serious,' she mused. 'Very big and very serious.'

Alison managed to raise her eyebrows while drinking deeply. 'How do you know about it?'

'I saw Jamie yesterday afternoon.'

'Oh! And he told you about it.'

'No he didn't. He wouldn't. He was very odd. I didn't mean to see him at all, for a while. I mean, virtually getting into bed with that dreadful woman . . .'

Alison finished her drink and held out the glass. 'I thought she was rather nice. Very . . . vibrant. And he didn't get into bed with her. He was told to look after her, by Duncan, and he did.'

'Ha!' Kristin had also finished her drink, and now she poured again.

'So your nose was out of joint. But you saw him anyway. Why?'

'Well . . . I did want to, of course. And he was so . . . so passionate. Even on the phone, he was passionate. And when we saw each other . . . it was almost like the first time. Or as if it was going to be the last.'

'Oh, God!' Alison got up to put her arms round her mother-in-law. 'The last time. Duncan was almost like that to me, when we lunched together before he said goodbye. See you next week, he said. But it wasn't as if he believed it.'

'So that boy Cooper won't be coming to dinner on Sunday. I suppose that's a good thing: it was an impulse.' She picked up the phone.

'Who are you going to call?'

'Jimmy. I have a right to know . . .'

'You have no right at all,' Alison said.

Kristin stared at her.

'Not even you. There is a war on, which they are fighting in the front line, and we are not. If this is a top secret operation, then it is a top secret operation. For you to start badgering the admiral with hysterical phone calls would be merely to distract him from his duties at a most important time.'

She paused in trepidation, as Kristin was still staring at her, and she suspected that she had never been spoken to like that in her life before, certainly not since she had been expelled from her convent. So she expected an explosion. But after a few seconds Kristin's knees seemed to give way, and she sank into a chair. 'What are we to do?'

Alison handed her her glass, and sat beside her. 'Tonight we will get quietly drunk together. And tomorrow . . . tomorrow we'll play Bagatelle. All day. Sunday, too, if you like.'

By dawn the flotilla was well pass the Scillies and out into the open water where the Atlantic crossed the outer limits of the Bay of Biscay. Ushant was a couple of hundred miles away to the east, and Duncan reckoned he wasn't very far from the site of the naval battle known as the Glorious First of June, when in 1794 Lord Howe's English fleet had encountered the French. That the French had deliberately stationed themselves where they were bound to be found by the British scouting frigates, in order to draw Howe from the path of the huge American food convoy without which the starving French population and Revolutionary Government would

almost certainly have collapsed, and in achieving this object-
ive had actually scored a vital strategic victory, had never
been allowed to detract from the considerable tactical success
achieved by the immortal Black Dick Howe. The French had
lost seven line-of-battle ships, which in the days immediately
before Horatio Nelson had revolutionized naval warfare had
been considered calamitous, certainly as the British had not
lost any.

But however exciting, and indeed glorious had been that
event, and however evocative might be the thought that below
him now would be the mouldering wrecks of the French
vessels and the cadavers of their crews, this was a different
time, a different war, a different enemy, and a different set of
circumstances.

He stopped his engine and had Carling use the Morse lamp
to signal the other two boats to come alongside. It was a bright
clear morning, with almost no wind, thus the sea was calm,
but ominously there was a long swell out of the south-west,
high enough for all three boats to lose the horizon in the
troughs, but long enough not to be uncomfortable. Equally
sinister, the far western sky was streaked with high cirrus
cloud, a certain portent of wind to come.

However, for the moment, the three boats were able to lie
alongside each other, one on each side of *Forty-One*, rising
and falling on the swell, bumping against each other as water
gurgled between their hulls, protected from mutual damage
by the rows of fenders strung along their topsides.

'You'll assemble your crews, if you will, gentlemen,' Duncan
said, using his loud-hailer.

The crews gathered on their respective decks, looking somewhat bemused at this unusual parade.

'You men have all volunteered for what you have been told
is a top-secret and highly dangerous operation,' Duncan said,
his voice reverberating through the trumpet. 'I thank you. I
can now tell you what we are going to do. We are going to
raid, and see if we can destroy, the port of Bordeaux.'

Now the silence was almost tangible.

'For those of you who may not know it,' Duncan went on,
'Bordeaux lies approximately a hundred miles up the Gironde
River, the mouth of which will be our destination tomorrow
morning. Now –' he grinned at them, looking from one boat

to the next – 'I have not actually either lost my marbles or determined to commit suicide and take you all with me. We have a lot going for us. The Nazis have only been in possession of the Biscay coast for a few months. In that time, while there has been a great deal of activity in the Channel and its approaches, there has been very little south of Ushant, therefore not only will we have the advantage of total surprise, but we know from our agents that almost no defences have as yet been constructed for or on the Gironde, and there are very few naval craft down there.

'In addition, we have worked out a very detailed plan of campaign, which we believe will get us in and get us out.' He outlined this to them, watched some appreciative nods, especially when he pointed out the camouflage netting to illustrate the amount of foresight that had gone into his plans. 'Now, lastly, the weather. You are all sufficiently experienced seamen to know there's a blow coming. This won't be comfortable, but it may be an essential part of our escape. I repeat, I have no doubt at all that we can carry out this mission. But also there can be no doubt that it is going to stir Jerry up no end, and that he is therefore going to come after us with everything he has. Again, as I have said, our information is that he does not have much in the water down there, but he can certainly bring up aircraft pretty rapidly. That is where we are going to need all the cloud cover and heavy rain we can find. That it may be accompanied by big seas we just have to accept, and in fact, in relatively small boats, they may also be useful for concealment. Finally, once we have worked our way through the weather, which is not supposed to last more than twenty-four hours, we are going to make a rendezvous with some heavier units which will be waiting to help us out. Just in case anything happens to me, this rendezvous is at forty-five degrees zero minutes North Latitude, six degrees fifteen minutes West Longitude, which is three hundred miles due south of our present position, and that is where we are going now. Course is therefore one eight oh, speed two thousand revs, ETA 1700.' Again he swept them all with his gaze. 'Thank you, gentlemen. We're on our way.'

Duncan lined up the course and speed, and handed the helm to Cooper. 'All well below, Jamie?' he asked into the intercom.

'Purring like a babe, sir.'

'Then join me in my cabin, will you.'

'Aye-aye, sir.'

He was waiting when Duncan got down. 'I didn't want to complicate matters more than necessary,' he explained. 'But you were going to look into the tidal situation.'

'Yes, sir. The flood commences at 0618 tomorrow morning. So if we are on schedule, we will enter the river as it turns. It's a spring.'

Duncan nodded. 'Is that likely to be a help or a hindrance?'

'I think it could be a help, sir. It's not the biggest tide; that's on Monday morning. But it'll carry us up, although it may need careful helming. I reckon between 0600 and 1200 we could do something like eighty miles, even travelling dead slow. Then we'll be within a couple of hours of the port. I know the exact spot where we can lie up for a few hours with the best chance of avoiding detection.'

'Good man. Hazards?'

Jamie grinned. 'You mean apart from running aground? Once we're past Royan, on the starboard side going up, which is the side we'll be using, the only obstacle will be the port of Paulliac. That's about halfway. It's a little place, but it may be manned. On the other hand, we should get past it under cover of the fog.'

'And coming back out?'

'Well, sir, as I understand your intention, it is to remain concealed, if possible, until moonrise. That's about 2200. By then we'll have the flood again, the end of it anyway. It's not going to take us more than two hours to get up the last forty-odd miles, shoot up the port, and start back at say 2400. We'll be able to carry the ebb all the way down, and be out in the Bay by dawn.'

'Jamie, you're a raving genius. Lets get up top.'

But for the apprehension of what lay ahead, it was a delightfully relaxing day. The three boats raced south, a hundred yards apart, under brilliant sunlit skies, although it was very cold and the watch on deck required greatcoats. But it steadily warmed up as the sun rose. The clouds continued to build out in the Atlantic, and as the afternoon wore on the breeze freshened, but this too was warming up all the time.

Best of all their piece of ocean remained empty, both on the surface and in the sky. They could have been the only boats in the world, and Duncan began to feel a growing sense of confidence, that they would not only carry out their assignment but survive. Up till now he had not allowed himself to think of an after; only the task in hand could matter, survival would be a bonus. Now he could remember Alison's face, so crisply handsome, so serious as she had studied him across the luncheon table in the Mess, or Mother's always animated, glowing personality, or Lucifer's huge affection for all living creatures. Now he could look forward to seeing all of them again.

At noon the boats were slowed so that all the officers could take sights and be certain of their position. Then they were off again, into the afternoon. But now the weather was definitely changing. The white cirrus had become dark nimbus, and from streaks had coagulated into huge masses, while the wind continued to freshen and the sea to rise. As they were going into it Duncan reduced speed to ease the ride and reduce the risk of hull damage, as a result of which they arrived at the selected position an hour late, at 1800 instead of 1700, and it was already growing dark.

But they still had two hours to spare before beginning their approach, so he ordered the boats hove to under power, motoring very slowly into the wind to maintain their position, so that the crews could have some rest from the constant pounding, and have their meal in relative comfort.

'You happy with the situation, sir?' Cooper asked.

'Aren't you?'

'I thought this weather wasn't due until tomorrow morning'

Duncan nodded. 'It's a bit early, but that may be to the good. It'll be much easier when we start going the other way.'

As it was, when they got under way again at 2000. Now they were steering almost due east, and the wind was astern. But this was by far the most taxing part of the journey, so far. Duncan had been pretty certain that they had stopped within a mile or so of the selected position, and also that they had largely maintained that position during their two-hour rest period. But now they were blind, with no means of checking that they were exactly on course. The night was very dark, and although the moon rose as expected just after 2100, because of the increasing cloud it only appeared intermittently.

He knew that the only land between them and the coast was the Isle de Yeu, a rocky islet a considerable distance out into the Bay, and although he was pretty sure of seeing that in time to avoid it, or being seen by any watchers on shore; seeing it in the right place was essential as a position check. But he did not know what arrangements the considerable Sable d'Olonne fishing fleet might have come to with their new masters, how many of them might be out. In what was not yet truly a war zone – although no doubt it would be so considered after tomorrow – they would very probably still be showing lights. But as the British ships were not, they would not see them coming. More seriously, he knew the Biscay fishermen habitually trawled a large net between two boats, the line being as much as two miles long. To attempt to pass, however inadvertently, between two vessels engaged in that activity could mean fouling the net and coming to a dead halt.

But they saw nothing, and could as hoped establish their positions exactly when they sighted, in the moonlight, the distant hump of Yeu.

'There's a relief,' Cooper said. 'Think they spotted us?'

'Hardly likely,' Duncan replied. 'We're too low in the water. But as you say, it's always nice to know exactly where one is.'

It was also reassuring to know that his Dead Reckoning navigation, the only means available to him in the absence of any visual marks and sextant measurements, was accurate. DR, known to some as Inertia Navigation, could in fact, if one's figures were right and correctly applied, be the most accurate system of all. It consisted of applying the speed of the boat through the water, from a fixed starting point, and then in laying off all other factors, such as tidal movements – for which every skipper was issued with tidal charts of the area in which he was going to operate – and wind speed and direction, for which he relied on his anemometer and experience, and possible drift, for which he compared the direction of his wake with the course he was steering.

In his situation, Duncan's only problem had been that the 'fixed' starting point had itself been a calculation. Now he felt a great sense of relaxation, but at the same time it was now more than ever necessary to concentrate; they were approaching the coast. At 0400 he ordered a reduction in speed to a thousand revolutions. Throughout the night, as they had streaked to the east, they had created more wind than had been behind them, and the seas had appeared no more than slight. Now, as their speed dropped to fifteen knots, the rising wind, already up to Force Five or say twenty knots, began to whistle around their ears, while the sea became distinctly lumpy.

'This is in our favour,' Duncan told the men on the bridge. 'The coast will mark with surf. We're in your hands, Rawlings.'

'Aye-aye, sir.'

The seaman settled himself against the mast while he levelled and focussed the binoculars. The minutes ticked by, each seeming an eternity. Then he said, 'I have surf, sir.'

'We're looking for a break, fairly wide, and there may even be some lights. Perhaps Red Twenty.'

Rawlings turned the glasses slightly to port, and again the minutes ticked by. 'Aye-aye, sir. Lights bearing Red Sixteen.'

Duncan gave a great sigh of relief. 'Mr Carling, make to flotilla, Line Ahead, speed as Leader. Acknowledge.'

'Aye-aye, sir.'

Within five minutes both boats had acknowledged.

Duncan thumbed the Tannoy. 'How's it down there, Jamie?'

'All correct, sir.'

'Very good. Now we need you up here.'

'Aye-aye, sir.'

He was up in a moment. Now the long line of surf was visible to the naked eye. Rawlings gave him the glasses, and he studied the shore.

'Recognize anything?' Duncan asked.

'Royan on the port bow, sir.'

'Splendid. But shouldn't there be a gap in that surf?'

'There is, sir.'

'I'm damned if I can see it.'

'That's because the river runs north-west as it enters the Bay, sir. We're approaching from a shade too far south.'

'Ah. So?'

'I think we need to alter course fifteen degrees to port, sir. That will bring us in line.'

'Course oh seven five, Mr Cooper.'

'Oh seven five it is, sir.'

Duncan checked to make sure the other boats were following.

'I have a light tower,' Rawlings said.

'That will be the Tour de Cordouan,' Jamie said.

'But no light,' Cooper commented.

'There's a war on,' Duncan reminded him. 'How's our approach, Jamie?'

'That tower marks the southern side of the entrance, sir. There's normally a light on the north side, as well, Point de la Coubre.'

'But not tonight. How wide is the entrance?'

'It's pretty wide, sir. But it's dead low water. There'll be sandbanks to either side.'

'But the passage is free of encumbrance?'

'Oh, yes, sir. It's used by big ships all the time, and is kept dredged.'

'Very good.' Duncan looked over his shoulder again to make sure the other boats were exactly in line as ordered. 'Are you prepared to take us through, Jamie?'

'Aye-aye, sir.'

'Goring will take the helm, Mr Cooper.'

Cooper surrendered the helm, and Jamie wrapped his hands round the spokes.

'How are you going to handle it?' Duncan asked.

'Just to be safe, sir, I think we should go through at dead slow. The tide is slack, so that shouldn't be a problem. And if we're just gliding by they might not even notice us from the town. It's also time to sling those lights, sir.'

Duncan frowned. 'It's clear as a bell.'

'Yes, sir. But when the fog comes up, it'll do it very quickly.'

'Mr Carling, make to *Forty-Two,* stern light, and sling our own.'

'Aye-aye, sir.' Carling hurried aft both to signal with his lamp and to drape the red leading light over the stern.

Duncan, Jamie and Cooper peered into the gloom. But the darkness was beginning to fade as the first fingers of light came out of the low-lying country in front of them. Now they could see the dark stretch of the estuary. Jamie, face tense with concentration, steered directly for the centre while the surf broke to either side, it seemed perilously close, but actually was more than a cable's length on both beams.

'Should we cast the lead, sir?' Cooper muttered.

'I don't think that would do us much good, Mr Cooper.' Even if they were hardly making more than ten knots, that was still too fast for them to be able to react to a sudden shoal. He had elected to trust Jamie's judgement and experience, and it would be utter folly to withdraw that trust now.

Following the course of the river, the increasing lights of Royan, as it began to wake up, were now wide on the port bow. From the careless profusion with which they were being used, it seemed obvious, and reassuring, that the information he had been given about the war not yet having reached Gascony was correct.

'Morse lamp signalling, sir,' Carling remarked.

'They've seen us,' Cooper said, with a note of alarm.

'They've seen, or heard, something,' Duncan said. 'Can you read that signal, Mr Carling?'

'Ah . . . I-D-E-N—'

'They're asking us to identify ourselves,' Duncan said.

'But they're using English!' Cooper said, now definitely anxious.

'No they're not, Mr Cooper. I don't know about the tenses, but I do know that identify in German is identifizieren. Reply, Mr Carling: Ah . . . shit, what's mission in German?'

No one replied.

'All right. Say, P-F-L-I-C-H-T and then G-E-H-E-I-M-I-N-I-S.'

'Sir?'

'Just send it. It means, or it should mean, Duty Secret.'

'Aye-aye, sir.' The lamp started clacking.

'They'll want confirmation, from somewhere,' Cooper pointed out.

'Indeed they will, Mr Cooper, but by the time they wake someone up, and he has called the various stations along the coast to find out what is going on, we should be just about there.'

They were now round Point de Greve marking the end of the south bank, and turning away from the town to head upstream, and a few minutes later the lights faded.

'I'd like to open her up a bit, sir,' Jamie said. 'We need to get as far as we can in the next hour.'

'Carry on. Signal flotilla, Mr Carling: follow Leader, keeping line.'

Now it was daylight, and they looked at the vast expanse of the river, here over a mile wide. Except that at low water it did not look like a river at all. The stream they were following was obviously deep and quite wide, but this was virtually hugging the left bank, their right, where there was a fringe of trees and then an expanse of what looked like pasture. On their left, the distant right bank was still shrouded in gloom, and between them there was a mass of sandbanks and little islets, with only a few patches of water to be seen.

'Does that cover at high water?' Duncan asked.

'Yes, sir,' Jamie said. 'Mind you, even at full tide it's not very deep, and the islets are dry.'

'Would it be deep enough for us?'

'Oh the whole, I would say so. But it would be a bit of a risk; there are no markers as to the channels.'

A bit of a risk, Duncan thought, as Jamie opened the throttle to fifteen hundred revs and the boat bounded ahead, followed after a moment by the other two. This close to the south bank their wakes crashed into the earth, causing a succession of mini landslides.

'If this was peace and we were pleasure boating,' Jamie commented, 'we'd have the river authority out after us for knocking down their banks.'

Now the day was bright and now too the tide was rising, seeming to pick them up and certainly increasing their speed. Cooper surveyed the land streaking by beside them. 'Are we now in claret country?' he asked.

'Yes, sir. Although the vines are a bit further away from the river. This is mostly pasturage. I'd like to reduce speed.'

Duncan was suddenly aware that the initial brightness, and indeed warmth, had gone from the sun, and that the sun itself was suddenly no more than a watery glow, rapidly disappearing. 'You do that, Jamie,' he said. 'Signal the flotilla, Mr Carling: Reduce speed, follow the light.'

Jamie eased the throttle back, and *Forty-One* came off the plane. *Forty-Two* took a couple of moments to respond, and closed right up to the stern of the leader before sinking off her plane; Beattie, on the helm, held up his hand to acknowledge his nearly catastrophic lack of concentration. But then he was

gone, only the very prow of the boat being visible, and that
hazily.

The fog seemed almost tangible, lying around them in a
solid mass. 'Can we go on?' Cooper wondered.

'I think so, sir.' Jamie moved even closer to the bank, now
spending more time staring to his right than straight ahead.

Carling suddenly held up his hand. 'What's that sound?
Some kind of siren.'

'My God! We've been spotted,' Cooper gasped.

'That, sir,' Jamie said, 'is a cow mooing. I think we may
be too close in.'

He made a slight alteration of course to port, just in time.
As he did so, there came a slight scraping under the hull, and
then they saw the fence, looming above them, and the cow,
looking over it.

'Shit!' Carling said. 'I beg your pardon, sir.'

'Be my guest, Petty Officer,' Duncan said.

'I'm sorry about that,' Jamie apologized.

'You're doing a great job, Jamie. But I'm going to leave it
to you to explain to my wife and mother, when we get home,
why my hair has suddenly turned white.'

'Signal from aft, sir,' Rawlings said.

Their heads turned. '*Forty-Seven* aground,' spelt out the
lamp.

'Cut your engine,' Duncan snapped. 'Drop you stern anchor.
Signal flotilla.'

The kedge went over the stern, and the boat came to a halt.
Now for the first time they realized the strength of the rising
tide, which bubbled past them at some four knots, and of the
wind, which was bending the trees to and fro, while now too
it started to rain.

'You'd think this would blow the bloody fog off,' Cooper
complained.

Forty-Two had also come to a halt. Duncan went aft. 'Can
you see him?' he called.

'No, sir,' Beattie replied.

'But you saw his signal.'

'Yes, sir. Then he disappeared. We were still under way.'

'Still, he can't be that far back.' The temptation to go back
himself and sort things out was enormous. But it was his duty
to lead and remain in overall command. Yet he had to break

his own orders and take an enormous risk; the alternative was to write off a third of his little fleet. 'Use your radio on the lowest possible power,' he told Beattie. 'Signal Mr Linton to inflate and put down his dinghy with two men, and float it up to you. They must have sufficient line to reach you, and they must be secured to a heavy warp for towing. No further conversation, please.'

'Aye-aye, sir.'

'Signal when you are ready.'

He had kept his own radio on all night. Now they listened to the brief exchange of signals.

'Think it'll be overheard, sir?' Carling asked.

'I think the odds are in our favour. That signal won't have carried more than fifteen miles. How close are we to a possible listening position, Jamie?'

'I would say we're about twenty miles from Paulliac, sir. Then we should be all right.'

'They make some high quality wines around Paulliac,' Cooper mused. 'One in particular, Chateau Batailly, it's like drinking liquid velvet.'

'Then I'll buy you a case when we get home,' Duncan promised.

The waiting was hard on the nerves, but at last Beattie signalled that they were ready. The tide having risen steadily, *Forty-Seven* came off easily enough. Half an hour later they were abeam of the little dock at Paulliac, suggesting that they might have been closer than Jamie had estimated. There was a fairly large vessel alongside. 'That's an odd shape,' Cooper commented. 'Do you think it's some kind of warship?'

Duncan studied it through his glasses. 'It's a dredger, Mr Cooper. And I'd say the crew's ashore, having a drink until the fog lifts.'

The town beyond the dock was barely visible through the mist, and there was no suggestion that anyone on shore had been alerted as to their presence, or had even seen them as they ghosted by, and a few moments later even the docks were lost to sight.

By half past ten the fog had turned to mist, and they could see the other boats behind them.

'How much further do you reckon?' Duncan asked.

'Another half-hour, sir, and then we should be in a wooded area. The trees come right down to the bank. With our nets, we should be able to lie there for the rest of the day.'

There would just be time, Duncan estimated; the fog was definitely thinning. In fact they saw the little wood at a quarter of a mile distance, and virtually as they did so the rain became very heavy. He signalled the other boats to reduce speed and prepare to moor, and then Jamie negotiated them into the bank. Two seamen were waiting to leap ashore with warps to make fast to trees, cursing as they found themselves in a bank of nettles, but completing the job and returning on board to be doctored by Wilson.

'Nice job, Jamie. Get that net in place, Mr Carling,' Duncan said, himself going ashore to walk back to where Beattie and Linton had their men also spreading the camouflage nets.

'Sorry about that snafu back there, sir,' Linton said. 'Just a moment's lack of concentration.'

'Could've been worse,' Duncan reassured him. 'We nearly killed a cow.'

'How long are we here, sir?' Beattie asked.

'Till 2200. I'm afraid it will be necessary to have a look-out, but each man should do only an hour. For the rest, have your men not on duty, and yourselves, get some sleep. When we start moving again, it's for the night. I want every man in a life jacket and a steel helmet, as we must expect to be shot at. Now listen carefully. In another hour from here we will reach the confluence of the rivers Dordogne and Garonne, which come together to form the Gironde. The Garonne is the right-hand stream as we approach it, and that is the one we will take to get up to Bordeaux.

'I have no idea what we are going to find at Bordeaux, but I am told it is almost certain that there will be at least one and possibly several large cargo vessels moored alongside. There will be no time for directions, so as we enter the port we are going to spread out – the navigable river is pretty wide there – and attack separate targets with our torpedoes. Just don't get in each other's way. If there is only one ship, I will take it and you will launch your torpedoes against the docks themselves. Use your cannon to shoot up everything you can see, particularly things like fuel dumps. Then make back down river to the confluence and drop your mines. Just make sure we are all together when you do this; we have to be in line abreast. The tide will still be in flood, so the mines will either be carried further upstream to interdict traffic out of the locks, or better yet against the bridges to blow them apart. Then we get out of there. It'll still be dark, so you'll need to follow me. Any questions?'

He was sure they both had a few, but neither asked.

'Very good.' He shook hands with each of them. 'We won't communicate again, except in an emergency, until the attack is completed.'

He returned on board *Forty-One* to give his crew the same orders. Wilson had prepared a hearty lunch, and after eating he retired to his cabin; he would take the 2100 or last, watch. Once he hit his bunk he was asleep in moments; he had not realized how exhausted he was, or how cold and stiff, and the gentle murmur of the river flowing past the hull, the very quietude of the hull itself after the previous forty-eight hours, with the whole overlaid by the steady drumming of the rain on the deck immediately above his head, was soporific.

Thus the slowly approaching grinding noise only gradually penetrated his consciousness. That and a steady tapping on his door. He opened his eyes. 'Yes? Come in.'

It was Carling, who had been on watch. 'Sorry to wake you, sir. There's a craft approaching.'

Duncan had only removed his boots, cap and tunic before turning in. Now he merely reached for his oilskin top to lead the petty officer up to the mess cabin and peer through the large port.

The grinding sound was steadily approaching, coming up-river. 'I don't think that's a warship,' Duncan said. 'In fact . . .' and a moment later the dredger came into view. It was 1700, and as he had surmised, she had clearly only been waiting out the ebb in Paulliac.

'Will she see us, sir?' Carling asked.

'Only if she has reason to look. I have an idea she's concentrating on getting up to Bordeaux before dark.' Although she could be attracted. He looked back at the other two boats. Beneath their nets it was impossible to discern anyone on watch, but he knew they were there. An over-reaction now could be fatal.

But there wasn't one, and the dredger slowly drew abeam.

Duncan levelled his binoculars and could make out the faces of the two men on the bridge – the remainder of the crew were sheltering below from the rain – but as he had estimated they were both peering ahead to maintain their position in the main stream, and sparing no glances to either side.

'Ships that pass in the rain,' he remarked. 'But thank you for calling me, Mr Carling.' He went back to bed.

The entire crew was up at 2000, for dinner, totally refreshed and feeling ebullient. Duncan gathered that only one or two had even heard the dredger, while the still pouring rain had meant they were safe from any strolling passer-by on the shore.

He accompanied Jamie to the engine room after the meal. 'How's our fuel standing up?'

'Fine, sir. We're still well over half.'

'Very good. Now tell me what effect this rain is going to have.'

The tide was now racing past the three boats, extending the mooring warps as it pulled on the hulls. The water level was certainly high, and in places bubbled against the top of the embankments, but as yet there was no sign of flooding.

'Well, sir, it'll certainly make a difference, but it takes time. It'll increase the flow of the streams feeding the river, and this will increase the flow of the river itself. But it's not likely to happen before dawn tomorrow.'

'In time for the next flood tide. You suggested these were the conditions to create a mascaret.'

'Yes, sir, they are. But that's good for us.'

'Tell me why?'

'We should be at the river mouth by dawn. Before then in fact. The tide will turn about 0700. Now we may shake up Bordeaux tonight, but they'll recover and want to come after us with everything they have. Hopefully, they'll be a few hours behind us. In other words, they'll still be halfway down the river, at best, when the tide turns. If there is a mascaret, they'll run into the full force of it before they reach Royan. The Gironde is no river to come down against a mascaret.'

'We'll hope you're right. We'll need you on the bridge for the run in.'

'Aye-aye, sir.'

*   *   *

At 2200 the nets were stowed, the crews donned their safety gear, the engines were started, the warps brought in, and the three boats moved away from the sheltering trees. With total, low cloud cover and still pouring rain, there was no hope of assistance from the moon; the night was utterly dark. But Jamie was as confident as ever, and they slipped quietly upstream, now riding the last of the flood so that only an hour after resuming their voyage they came upon the bifurcation of the river. The confluence of the two smaller rivers created a wide area of deep and navigable water, and now they could see lights in the distance.

'Action stations, Mr Carling,' Duncan said.

The orders were conveyed verbally, and the crew took up their positions. They rounded a slight bend, and in front of them was the city.

There did not appear to be any blackout restrictions in force, and although at eleven o'clock on a Sunday night most people were in bed asleep there was still an immense glow of light from street lamps which even extended along the esplanade on the right hand side, where the bulk of the city lay. The port was down stream of the residential area, and thus also of the bridges, which were all low and designed to cope with barge traffic out of the canal rather than ocean-going ships.

Disappointingly, there was only one of these alongside a dock on the right bank. But behind it . . . 'Holy Jesus Christ!' Jamie muttered. 'That's a destroyer.'

'Then that's our target,' Duncan said. 'Let me have it.'

Jamie surrendered the helm and Duncan thrust the throttle forward. 'Torpedoes, Mr Carling,' he bellowed. 'Fire when we bear.'

There was no need to call for the range, they were certainly within two miles, and the need for concealment was over; now it was a matter of doing the job and getting out as quickly as they could. But they were not going to get away with a destroyer behind them.

Yet at the moment no one on either the ships or the shore seemed to realize what was happening, although the roar of the engines as the three boats opened their throttles together must have cascaded across the houses. Then someone reacted quickly enough to fire a Very pistol, and the red light carved it way briefly through the rain. This was followed by the wail of a siren.

Duncan brought his boat round in a wide sweep, sending shock waves of wake crashing into the docks behind them as he lined up. Carling was gazing straight ahead, and now he pressed both levers without waiting for the usual command: he had already received it.

Knowing that at this range they could not possibly miss, the moment the two giant fish left the tubes Duncan swung away violently, anxious not to be too close to the coming explosion. 'Gun, Mr Cooper,' he called.

They were now tearing past the south bank, and the cannon opened fire, sending its twenty-millimetre shells searing into the smaller boats moored alongside, while Rawlings' machine-gun crews sprayed them with bullets. As he did so there was a succession of huge explosions. Duncan looked over his shoulder to see plumes of flame and black smoke rising from the destroyer, which was already listing on to her beam ends. But by far the greater explosion had come from the freighter moored just along the docks from her and as he gazed at the huge plume of red-tinged black he realized that she must have been carrying explosives.

This time the shock wave hit the MTB, and she went over on her beams ends, scattering the men on deck. Duncan fought the helm while reducing speed to bring the boat back under control, looking aft as he half expected to see the mines, and the boat also going skywards. But they seemed intact. He lined the boat up again and someone shouted, 'Man overboard!'

'Shit! Where away? Jamie!'

'Aye-aye, sir.' Jamie slid down the ladder and ran forward, where men were just picking themselves up.

'Hallo!!' someone was shouting out of the darkness, and Duncan recognized the voice: Carling!

'Find that man,' he bellowed. 'Use the searchlight.'

'Sir?' Cooper queried. The light would delineate their position to any watcher on shore.

'Use it!'

Having given the order he brought the boat round again, seeking to retrace his course, if that were possible. The light blazed across the water, but almost immediately became diffused in the teeming rain. There came another series of explosions as the third boat loosed its torpedoes, and no longer having a worthwhile ship to aim at, had sent them against the docks themselves. Again smoke and flame shot skywards, and a machine-gun that had opened fire from the land at the sudden light was silenced.

A boat loomed out of the gloom. 'Do you require assistance?' Beattie called.

'We have a man overboard.'

Forty-Two also commenced a slow sweep, also using her searchlight, and now *Forty-Seven* joined them. For the moment the three boats were inviolate, as all around them were explosions and flaring lights, sirens still blaring and frantic activity as both the destroyer and the freighter rolled on their sides, mooring warps popping and men trying to get ashore or leaping into the water. But Duncan knew that their security was going to be no more than momentary. The Germans would recover soon enough, and messages would be going out all over the Biscay coast as to what was happening. Even a few minutes further delay in getting out would endanger the entire flotilla; it would be the height of irresponsibility to risk his entire command for the sake of one man, however valuable and however much a friend. Carling was either already dead or, if he made the shore, he would be taken prisoner, hopefully honourably. Equally, the three boats had to leave together, as they all had to drop their mines in unison.

There was no longer anything to be gained by radio silence, at least at that moment. He thumbed the VHF. 'Leader to flotilla. Call off the search, and form line abreast to drop mines.'

'Dowse that light, Mr Cooper,' he called, and turned *Forty-One* downriver, still at dead slow. 'Bridge, Jamie.'

The light went out, and Cooper and Jamie arrived on the bridge together. 'Do you think he's gone, sir?' Cooper asked.

'I sincerely hope he isn't,' Duncan said. 'But we cannot wait for him now. You'll have to get aft and prepare the mines for dropping, Mr Cooper. Jamie, I need you to lead us out.'

'Aye-aye, sir.'

The other boats were obeying orders, also switching off their lights and lining up. Duncan led them downriver to the confluence, the huge racket growing behind them, waited for them to come abreast, then thumbed the radio again. 'Drop mines.'

The thirty six canisters went into the water almost simultaneously.

'Nice work,' Duncan said. 'Now follow me home.'

'What speed do you reckon?' Duncan asked.

'A thousand revs, sir,' Jamie replied.

'Is that all? We want to be clear by dawn.'

'The tide is turning now, sir, and the river will be running pretty fast after this rain. Control is going to be difficult. In fact . . . they know we're here now, and they know there is only one way we can go, so trying to conceal ourselves is a waste of time. I think we should use our lights.'

Duncan hesitated only a moment; he knew the boy was right, and not for the first time could only marvel at his clear-headed thinking even in moments of grave danger. 'Very good,' he said. 'One thousand revs. Mr Cooper . . .' the sub-lieutenant had returned to the bridge, 'switch on your searchlight and make to the flotilla to do likewise. But they must stay in line.'

PART THREE
The Sea

'Alone, alone, all, all alone,
Alone on a wide, wide sea!'

Samuel Taylor Coleridge

Tactics

With the lights on, navigation, or at least, pilotage, was that much easier although, as the rain continued to pour, visibility was still limited.

'Still, this is good for us,' Cooper suggested.

'Up to a point,' Duncan corrected. 'Don't you know the old nautical saying?'

'Ah . . . no, sir.'

'It's a ditty, which goes, when the wind comes before the rain, soon you may make sail again, but when rain comes before the wind, then your sheets and halliards mind. For the purposes of the rhyme, wind is here pronounced poetically as wynd. Now, you see, the wind hasn't actually arrived yet.'

Although it was certainly fresh, blowing the rain into their faces.

'Will you ask Rawlings to come up here, please, Mr Cooper?' Duncan said.

'Aye-aye, sir.'

Cooper left the bridge and returned a few minutes later, accompanied by the leading seaman. 'Sir!'

'I'm very sorry about Mr Carling, Rawlings.' He knew that the pair had become good friends over the past few months.

'Thank you, sir. So are we all.'

'You understand there was nothing else I could do.'

'We understand that, sir.'

'Well, I am appointing you brevet petty officer. The rank will be confirmed when we get home.'

'Aye-aye, sir. And thank you.'

'Now, I need Goring on the helm. Will you take a couple of men and check out the bilges, make sure we suffered no damage from those blasts.'

'Aye-aye, sir.' Rawlings left the bridge.

'Do you reckon he'll be all right?' Cooper asked.

'Yes. Right now, he's pretty shaken up. They all are, as are we. But we have a busy day ahead of us. By the time that's over, I reckon we'll all just be happy to be alive.'

Cooper gulped.

As the tide turned, the river began to grow rough. The wind was from the west, the tide was flowing west, with increasing speed, and even in the relatively shallow water the combination was throwing up wavelets and flurries of spray. What it was going to be like out in the Bay did not bear consideration.

But they had to get there first. Duncan stood beside Jamie. 'Let me know when you need a spell.'

'I'm all right for the time being, sir.'

Duncan nodded. They were already back at the little wood, and half an hour later the lights of Paulliac came into view. This was their first real obstacle, and while he was pretty sure there was no combative craft in the port, it would certainly have a garrison, however small. 'I think we have to rush this, Jamie,' he said. 'They'll know all about us. I'll tell you when.'

'Aye-aye, sir.'

Duncan used the VHF. 'Leader to Flotilla. I estimate that we are about to come under fire. We shall go up to two thousand revs. Douse your lights, but reduce speed again as soon as our light comes on. Acknowledge.'

'Message received and understood, sir,' Beattie and Linton replied.

Duncan watched more lights come into view, and now a searchlight cut across the water in front of them. 'Whatever guns they have will be trained along that beam. Mr Cooper, open fire on that searchlight as soon as we bear.'

'Aye-aye, sir.' Cooper slid down the ladder and went forward, summoning his gun crew to accompany him.

Duncan switched off his own light. 'Take us through, Jamie.'

'Aye-aye, sir.' Jamie drew a deep breath and thrust the throttle forward. As he did so, there came a huge explosion, from behind them. 'Hallelujah,' Duncan said. 'Someone's struck a mine.'

Forty-One had gathered speed and was making thirty knots. They raced towards the beam of light, and the twenty-millimetre

opened fire, sending a series of small shells towards its estimated position. But the beam remained on as they reached it,
then went out, even as a stream of machine-gun bullets whirred
about them. As the boat never trembled, none seemed to have
hit, but Duncan knew he had to make sure. 'Reduce speed,
Jamie.' He switched on his light to warn the others, then heard
the chatter of the gun again, competing with the deeper bangs
of the other two quick-firers. Looking back, he saw that another
searchlight had appeared. 'Shit!' he muttered. It hadn't occurred
to him that they'd have a spare. 'Petty Officer Rawlings!' he
shouted.

'Sir!' Rawlings appeared at the foot of the ladder.

'Check for casualties and damage.'

'Aye-aye, sir.'

All three boats were now past the obstacle, and had slowed
to continue their passage. Rawlings returned from his inspection. 'No hits, sir, and no casualties.'

'Excellent, Mr Rawlings. We should have a clear run now.'

'Until Royan, sir,' Jamie suggested.

But at that moment the VHF came to life. '*Forty-Seven*
reporting, sir. I am sinking.'

'What?' Duncan snatched the mike. 'How fast?'

'We can stay afloat another half-hour, sir. We were hit several
times below the waterline, and the pumps cannot cope.'

Well, Duncan supposed, they had just been too lucky, so
far. 'Very good, Mr Linton. Reduce speed, Dead Slow, Jamie;
maintain just sufficient way to keep control. Same for you,
Mr Beattie. Mr Linton, bring your boat alongside *Forty-Two*
in the first instance, and transfer six crew members, then drop
down to us and we will take the remainder. Stand by, Mr
Beattie.'

'Aye-aye, sir.'

Jamie was now having to wrestle the helm to and fro to
maintain his course as the ever increasing river flow threatened to pick the MTB up and sweep it away.

'Stand by, Mr Rawlings,' Duncan said, as he looked astern
and saw *Forty-Seven*, already low in the water, pull alongside
Forty-Two and transfer six of her men. 'Stand by your gun,
Mr Cooper,' he called.

'Aye-aye, sir.'

Forty-Seven slipped forward. The crew of *Forty-One* already had the fenders out, and now they took the warps from the stricken vessel. The men clambered aboard. Linton was still on the bridge.

'Put your helm hard to starboard, Mr Linton,' Duncan called. 'And then secure it.'

There was a brief hesitation. Duncan could guess that the young officer was almost traumatized at the prospect of losing his command. 'It has to be done, Mr Linton,' he called, and then looked forward. 'Stand by, Mr Cooper. You're aiming for the fuel tanks.'

'Aye-aye, sir,' Cooper acknowledged. The gun had already been trained on the sinking vessel.

Linton now pulled himself together, and secured the helm hard to starboard; the boat, engine still running, now strained against the mooring warps. Linton scrambled over the rail, and warps were cast off.

'Hold your fire, Mr Cooper.' Duncan said. 'Searchlight, Mr Rawlings.'

Forty-Seven swerved away into the rain, but remained picked out by the light. Duncan waited until it was as distant as possible before fading from view, and then shouted, 'Fire!'

The twenty-millimetre opened up, pumping shells into the sinking hull, with immediate results; there was a huge whoosh of flame and smoke and shock waves swept across the bridge of *Forty-One*. *Forty-Seven* became a blazing wreck, slowly settling into the water. 'Let's get out of here, Jamie,' Duncan said, and thumbed the VHF. 'Follow, Mr Beattie.'

Linton arrived on the bridge, wiping tears from his eyes. 'I am so very sorry, sir.'

'You have nothing to be sorry about, Mr Linton. That could have happened to any one of us. Look on the bright side: that Jerry gun could have hit those tanks instead of below them. Then you would have gone up with it.'

They hurried into the darkness, increasingly conscious of the wind, that was now howling about them as they approached the coast. 'I need your eyes, Mr Rawlings,' Duncan said, as they saw the lights of Royan; it was now past 0400.

Rawlings braced himself as he levelled the glasses. 'There is no visible movement, sir.'

'I was thinking of the coast.'

'Ah . . . yes, sir. Rollers on the beach.'

'Thank you. Can we do without the light now, Jamie?'

'Yes, sir.' Jamie's voice was hoarse with exhaustion.

'Very good. Just get us through and then you can stand down. Kill the light, Mr Cooper.' He picked up the VHF. 'We will be at sea in a few minutes, Mr Beattie. Conditions look severe. Remember at all times to head the seas, maintaining as much speed as safe. You are not, I repeat not, to assist us should we get into trouble. You have the co-ordinates for the rendezvous. By the time you get there the weather should have improved, and you should be able to set a course for home. I will see you either at the rendezvous, or in Portsmouth. Good fortune.'

'Aye-aye, sir,' Beattie replied.

Duncan rejoined Jamie, Cooper and Linton at the helm. The river had now eased its pace as the tide slackened before the flood, which would be in a couple of hours time, by when they needed to be well out to sea. He levelled his binoculars at the lights of Royan, steadily approaching as the river took them nearly up to the harbour before bending away again to the estuary. They would of course know that the British MTBs were coming, and they would have received an update from Paulliac. But that was several hours ago, and they would have been expected sooner than this; Paulliac would not have known about the delay caused by the scuttling of *Forty-Seven*. For the same reason, even if they were spotted, the Germans would be looking for three boats.

But in the utter pre-dawn darkness, there was no reason for them to be spotted, he told himself. They were travelling at about ten knots, and thus there was very little visible wake at any distance, and the growl of the engines was lost in the roar of the surf on the beach.

'Altering course now, sir,' Jamie said.

Duncan looked astern. The red light was glowing, and all Beattie had to do was follow it. Another five minutes . . . there was a huge splash some hundred yards away to starboard, followed almost immediately by the roar of the explosion.

'Shit!' Linton gasped.

'That's a four point seven,' Cooper said. 'How the hell did they spot us?'

'I think someone saw our tail light where there shouldn't have been a light at all,' Duncan said. 'I think we need to open up a bit, Jamie.'

'Aye-aye, sir.' The throttle was pushed forward, and the boat gathered speed, just in time, for the next shell plunged into the river very close to where they had been.

Duncan looked astern, and could make out *Forty-Two* still following; as she was showing no lights at all the watchers on the shore had not yet seen her. A few minutes later they were at the entrance, plunging into the seas that broke to either side of them on the beach, sending showers of spray high into the sky.

'Very good, Jamie,' Duncan said. 'You've done a great job. Now go below and get some sleep.'

'If he can,' Linton muttered, as the bows soared to the waves and then crashed down into the following troughs. Duncan reduced speed to a thousand revs to limit the risk of damaging the hull, and was glad he had done so as dawn broke. He knew that the average yachtsman tended to overestimate the size of the seas he encountered, and accepted entirely the professional judgement that whatever one's first impression, one should halve it to get the true wave height. On the other hand, the MTB's bridge was twelve feet out of the water, and the waves were certainly higher than that, with a foaming, breaking crest another couple of feet on top, while the fact that they were going into a wind of perhaps forty knots meant that their real situation was very close to hurricane conditions.

The saving factor was that as they plunged further into the Bay and left the shore behind them, the waves grew longer; *Forty-One* seemed to develop a mind of her own, and as each wave reared up and looked about to crash down on top of her, always snaked out the other end into a trough before confronting the next monster, so much so that Duncan very rapidly abandoned the idea of using the throttle to escape the worst and just let her get on with it, concentrating on helming to stop her falling off and getting rolled up.

It was exhausting work, but it was also exhilarating, and grew more so as the morning wore on, and the low, heavy clouds began to break up. By the time he gave the helm to Cooper, to rest his aching arms and back, there was even the occasional glimpse of the sun, and the wind had definitely started to drop. But when he looked behind himself, he discovered they were alone.

'Damnation,' he commented. 'When did they go?'

'They were there at first light,' Linton said. 'And then we lost them. After your instructions, we didn't think you'd want to be distracted. I mean, in those seas, they could've been only a wave away.'

'They could still be pretty close,' Cooper put in.

'Of course,' Duncan agreed. 'You acted correctly.' He had now been on his feet for fourteen hours, 'I'm going to turn in for a couple of hours, but I want to be called if anything crops up. Anything at all. I reckon we're at least sixty miles off shore, but those long range Condors will have no problem with that.' He pointed at the now rapidly clearing sky. 'Those patches of blue are what we have to worry about, so keep a sharp lookout. Course is two six five for the time being, and as the seas go down you may increase speed to fifteen hundred revs. I'll be up at noon, then we should be able to fix our position.'

'Aye-aye, sir,' they answered together.

He went below, checked the engine room himself. Everything seemed in order, and as they had operated only for short bursts at even two thousand revolutions, the tanks were still half full. He rolled into his bunk and was asleep instantaneously.

Duncan awoke to a brilliant day, with only fleecy white clouds, the wind fresh instead of strong, the seas still showing the occasional whitecap but not in the least uncomfortable.

'Where's the war, sir?' Linton asked as he handed over the helm. He was very closed to hysterics, Duncan estimated, following the excitement of the night, the loss of his command, ands now the almost balmy boating conditions.

'I have an idea it may still be there, Mr Linton. Now, you go below and have a nap. Use my bunk.'

It was just on noon. Duncan gave the helm to Rawlings while he took a sight. 'We seem to have been blown a bit to the south of our track, Mr Rawlings. Course will be two seven five.'

'Aye-aye, sir.'

'Now tell me, how are things forward?'

'Tight as a drum, sir.'

'I was thinking of morale.'

'High, sir. Obviously they're sorry to have lost Mr Carling, but they know we've done a great job.'

'Thank you, Mr Rawlings.' He replaced his sextant in its box, clipped it shut. 'I'll take her now. Seen anything hostile?'

'Not a sausage, sir.'

'And have you had a watch below?'

'Yes, sir. Three hours. I'm fresh as a daisy.'

'Good man. I'd like you to use your eyes for a while.'

'Aye-aye, sir.' Rawlings levelled the binoculars, sweeping the sky. 'Absolutely nothing. I reckon they've given us up.' He brought the glasses down to the visible horizon. 'Well, what do you know, sir. There's an MTB over there. Maybe three miles away.'

'Well, glory hallelujah. As we don't seem to have any other company . . .' He thumbed the VHF. 'Report, *Forty-Two*. Are you intact?'

'Aye-aye, sir,' Beattie replied. 'And yourselves?'

'Yes. I think you can close up.'

'Aye-aye, sir.'

'Begging your pardon, sir,' Rawlings said. 'But we do have company.'

'Eh?'

'I have smoke, red ten. Shall I sound action stations, sir?'

'Wait for identification.'

The smoke was now clearly visible, and beneath it . . . 'That's a heavy cruiser, sir, and four destroyers.'

'Right where they should be,' Duncan said. 'Let the crew sleep, Mr Rawlings. Our mission is completed.'

Alison parked the Sunbeam, but remained seated for several minutes before getting out. She knew that she was in a state of suspended shock, which some time, some time very soon she suspected, was going to overwhelm her.

She had prepared for the possibility of this moment from well before her marriage. From, indeed, the moment Duncan had left her on that headland at Scapa Flow, to take his ship to sea, and combat. But it had always seemed a remote scenario, too remote and too ghastly seriously to consider.

She approximated it with one day going to the doctor with a pain in the stomach and being told that you had inoperable cancer. Why should it ever happen? And unless and until it did, why even consider the possibility?

But now . . . she had never had to share grief before, but that was because she had never had any grief to share. And she had no idea how Kristin was going to take it; how real, and how deep, was that veneer of careless insouciance, of dominating courage, that was her mother-in-law's visible persona. And, of course, as Kristin had pointed out when last they had discussed the subject, she would have two lives to mourn.

She drew several deep breaths, then got out of the car and went to the front door, opened it, and only then remembered that she was not braced for the inevitable welcome. But to her relief, although she could hear Lucifer barking in the garden, as he would have been alerted by the car engine, the dog was not present. Instead . . .

'You're back very quickly,' Kristin said from the head of the small staircase. 'Tell me about it.'

Alison looked up, again drawing deep breaths. She had seen her that morning, at breakfast, before she had gone into Portsmouth, her weekend leave being over. They had, as Kristin had determined, spent a curiously intimate weekend, talking about every subject under the sun, save for the one subject they both wanted to talk about. Kristin loved to reminisce in any event, and she had told Alison about her various lovers – enough to fill at least two normal lifetimes – beginning with that tumultuous session in the cabin of the then Lord Eversham's yacht in the Mediterranean, when she had been fifteen years old. 'I was quite something then,' she had said. As if she wasn't quite something now?

Then there had been nothing to do but experience the trauma of waiting, and somehow, when she had set off for work that morning, she had suddenly felt absurdly optimistic. The flotilla had left on Friday afternoon, carrying a full cargo of mines. Wherever they had been going, it had to be German controlled coastal waters, and there were no German controlled coastal waters that were further than a day's range from England, for an MTB. Equally, as presumably they would maintain close to full speed, their fuel capacity would not extend longer than two days. So, as Sunday evening had come and gone, without a word . . . she had half expected to see them sitting alongside their pontoon.

As she had entered the office she had been summoned to the admiral. 'Good morning, Alison,' he had said. 'Please sit down.'

'I'll just have to get my book, sir,' she had responded.

'No book, Alison. Just sit.'

It was then the first lumps of lead had started to gather in her stomach.

'I think you need to read this,' he had said, holding out a sheet of paper. 'It is the transcript of a news bulletin put out by Berlin radio this morning. We received it an hour ago.'

I don't want to read it, she had thought. But she had already been doing so.

'Last night, three British motor torpedo boats, having surreptitiously made their way up the Gironde River, attempted to carry out a raid on the port of Bordeaux. This raid was a complete failure. German forces were waiting for them, and two of the boats were sunk. The surviving boat, badly damaged, managed to get back down the river, but then disappeared in a violent storm that was raging at the time, and is presumed sunk. There was only one survivor from this unfortunate sortie, a petty officer named Carling, who was blown overboard when his ship exploded. He is now in hospital.'

Alison had raised her head. 'Petty Officer Carling was . . .'

'Yes. He served with Duncan.'

Slowly she had laid the paper on the desk.

'This report is, of course, unconfirmed,' Lonsdale had said. 'We would hope to obtain some more details from the French Resistance, which is quite active in that area.'

'But you believe it.'

'I believe it may well contain an element of truth,' Lonsdale had said, carefully. 'Duncan's flotilla was certainly sent to attack Bordeaux. Unfortunately, the fact that Petty Officer Carling has been taken prisoner off an exploding MTB . . . there is no way the Germans could have invented that, as they could not possibly have known Carling's name until he was captured.'

'And we know he served with Duncan. So . . . QED.'

He had gazed at her for several seconds. 'Are you going to be all right?'

Alison had drawn one of her deep breaths. 'I will be all right, sir. In a few minutes.'

'Well, I would like you to go back home, and stay there for a while.'

'Sir, I have a job to do. Don't I?'

'Indeed you do. And I am asking you to do it.'

Her head had come up. 'Oh, shit!'

'Kristin has to be told, before the news is released, which it will be within the next few hours. She is such an unpredictable character that there is no knowing how she will react. She obeys no rules, whether moral or religious. It's just possible that with Duncan gone, she might say to herself, oh, what's the use? And take one of her unilateral decisions. I would not like that to happen.'

Alison had stood up. 'Neither would I, sir.'

'I know this is a shitty job I am giving you, but I feel you are the best equipped to handle it. She is very fond of you. What I would like you to do is give me a ring this afternoon and tell me if you think it would be a good idea for me to come over.'

'I will do that, sir.'

'And take this.' He had handed her the paper. 'Use it, if you think it would be better for her to read it than for you to tell her.'

The paper was folded into her handbag, and now she was faced with an ebullient Kristin.

'Or did you forget something?' she asked.

'My leave has been extended. Can we go upstairs?'

Kristin raised her eyebrows, then led the way. She did not speak until they had gained the sitting room, then she said, 'Tell me.'

'Would you like to sit down?'

'I have never fainted in my life,' Kristin pointed out.

Alison hesitated, then opened her bag. 'Admiral Lonsdale gave me this when I reached the office. Apparently it had just come in.' She held out the paper.

Kristin took it, looked at it, looked at Alison, and unfolded the sheet. Alison stared at her as she read, but there was no change of expression, save for a slight flaring of the nostrils. 'This is from the Germans.'

'Yes, it is.'

'Then it is very likely to be propaganda.'

'The admiral is hoping to obtain some confirmation, or a clarification, from the Resistance. But—'

'You believe it.'

'Petty Officer Carling served on Duncan's boat.'

Kristin gazed at her for several seconds. Then she went to the sideboard and poured herself a goblet of brandy. 'You?'

Alison shook her head.

Kristin drank, deeply, put down the empty balloon. 'Walking that dog absolutely exhausts me. Are you home for lunch?'

'I'm home for as long as . . . well . . .'

'You feel I need you. Or you need me. Would you let Lucia know?'

'Of course.'

'I am going to lie down for a little while.' She went to the bedroom door.

'Kristin . . .'

Kristin looked over her shoulder. 'I am not going to kill myself, Alison.'

She went inside, and closed the door. Alison remained seated for a few moments, then got up, stood at the door, and listened . . . to a succession of heart-rending sobs.

How strange, she thought, that Kristin should have broken down, while she, by far the weaker character, had not yet shed a tear. She could not help wondering if Kristin was mourning Jamie Goring more than her own son. But that was a terrible thought.

She went downstairs to tell Lucia and Harry, who were clearly stunned, then put on brogues and a heavy coat, a furry hat and thick gloves, and took Lucifer for a walk. He was delighted at this unexpected second pleasure of the day, and his bounding energy as he darted to and fro, looking for rabbits and repeatedly returning to nuzzle her hand, was heart-warming, so much so that when she said, without thinking, 'It's you and me, now Luce, just us chickens,' she did burst into tears.

But that was acceptable, out in the open sir, with no one around, save Lucifer, who, when she dropped to her knees, hurried back to lick her face, while she hugged and kissed his mammoth head and shoulders.

She walked for longer than she had intended, partly because she had no idea what she might find when she got back to the house. She even considered returning to the road and visiting Goring's Garage, but decided against it. They would have been officially informed, and to them she was a stranger. They would want to be alone with their grief.

It was half past one before she opened the door and allowed Lucifer, who had lost none of his energy, to go bounding down the hall to the kitchen. She followed. 'Lucia! I'm terribly sorry I'm so late. I didn't keep track of the time.'

'It is not a problem, Donna Alison. It is hot whenever you wish it. Donna Kristin is not down yet, anyway.'

'What?!'

'Donna?'

'Ah . . . she must still be sleeping. I'll call her.'

She ran for the small staircase, almost fell up the steps, stumbled across the sitting room, knocked on the door. 'Kristin?'

There was no reply.

Oh, my God! She thought. Oh, my God!

'Kristin!' she shouted.

Still no reply. She tried the handle. The door was unlocked. She opened it, stepped inside, gazed at the bed. This was empty, although the sheets were tousled. She had never been in here before, and she found herself staring at the nude above the bed, a very young, very beautiful Kristin, erotically posed, exuding sex from every pore. Oh, Kristin!

Then she heard a splash. She ran to the bathroom door, hesitated. 'Kristin?'

'Come in, Alison.'

Alison drew a deep breath and opened the door. Kristin sat in her tub, hair piled on top of her head, the rest of her tastefully disguised beneath a froth of bubbles, but hardly less compelling for that.

'You look distraught,' Kristin remarked.

'I . . . I was walking Lucifer.'

'Which is enough to make anyone distraught.' To Alison's consternation, Kristin stood up, and stepped out of the bath, thereby reducing the portrait to insignificance. And all this she was currently dispensing to that little boy! No, no . . . *had* been dispensing.

'Well,' she said. 'I'll leave you to it. I'm sorry. I didn't mean to interrupt your bath.'

'But you came up to tell me something,' Kristin pointed out, picking up her towel.

'I . . . ah . . . oh . . . um . . . oh, yes. Lunch is ready.'

'Well, it should be. I'll be down in a few minutes. Would you ask Harry to open a bottle of the Bollinger?'

'A bottle . . . yes, of course.' She hurried from the bathroom as there was a knock on the bedroom door.

'Milady!' Harry had given up attempting to specify.

Alison looked over her shoulder. Kristin had wrapped herself in the towel and was unpinning her hair; she showed no sign of adding anything further or of closing the door. 'Lucifer is barking,' she pointed out. 'We must have a visitor. You'd better see who it is.'

Alison cautiously opened the door, a crack. 'Yes, Harry?'

'Rear-Admiral Lonsdale is here, milady.'

'What?' She looked past him at Lonsdale, just reaching the top of the stairs, looking slightly dishevelled.

'Whew!' he said. 'Every time I come here I am nearly torn to pieces.'

'You were going to wait for my telephone call,' Alison accused.

'Well, I couldn't. You see—'

'Jimmy!' Kristin emerged from the bedroom, still wearing only her towel. Both men took an involuntary step backwards. 'Have you come to join the wake? Harry, Admiral Lonsdale will be staying to lunch. Will you tell Lucia, and open the bottle now.'

'The . . . ah . . .?'

'Bollinger,' Alison said, urgently.

'Right away, milady.' He went to the stairs.

Lonsdale had got his breath back. 'Kristin . . . I had to come.'

'Of course.' Kristin advanced towards him, bare feet leaving damp impressions on the carpet. 'You are doing your duty.'

'No, no. I mean, yes. Well . . .' he drew a long breath. 'An hour ago we received a radio message from *Cornwall*, that is the cruiser I sent down there to see the flotilla got home safely.'

Both women stared at him.

'She reports that she has made the rendezvous with two MTBs. It seems that one was lost.'

'Duncan's.'

'No, no. *Forty-Seven.* But her crew was taken off. In fact, there was only one casualty in the whole operation, poor Carling. And we know that he is at least alive, even if he is a prisoner.'

Alison's knees gave way, and she sank on to the settee.

'All the rest survived?' Kristin believed in being certain of her facts.

'Yes. Not a single other casualty. And more than that. The raid seems to have been a tremendous success. A German destroyer was sunk, and a munitions ship exploded. The docks were badly damaged and a carpet of mines laid at the confluence of the Garonne and the Dordogne. In fact, the crews claim to have heard some explosions behind them as they descended the river, so it is possible that other vessels were sunk as they tried to follow them.'

'Where are they now?' Kristin asked.

'On their way home. They should be here tomorrow. What are you doing?'

Kristin had dropped the towel. Now she put both arms round his astounded neck and kissed him. 'I am happy. I had not supposed I would ever be happy again.' She released him and went to the door. 'Harry!' she shouted. 'Open four bottles. We shall want one each, and you and Lucia must have some too. Oh, and give a bowl to Lucifer.' She came back into the room. 'I shall get dressed,' she announced. 'And after lunch, Jimmy, I shall show you something. If you'll let me come into Portsmouth tomorrow morning to be there when they dock.'

Whistles blasted and sirens blared as the two MTBs entered the harbour and slid alongside their pontoon. It seemed that everyone was there. Fitzsimmons was first on board to shake Duncan's hand, and then do the same to Linton and Beattie and Cooper. 'I think there may be gongs for all of you,' he said.

'And our crews, sir,' Duncan said.

'Indeed.'

Bruton was behind him. 'Quite a show, Lord Eversham. Congratulations.' He also extended his hand, and Duncan shook it.

Hawkins was waiting, casting a sceptical eye over the two hulls. 'I suppose these have to be patched up by tomorrow, my lord.'

Duncan looked at Fitzsimmons.

'You can take your time, Mr Hawkins,' the captain said. 'Neither these boats nor their crews will be going anywhere for the next couple of weeks. Now, Lieutenant-Commander Eversham, Rear-Admiral Lonsdale is waiting to see you, with your officers.'

Lonsdale shook hands with each of them, while Duncan had eyes only for Alison, standing to attention at the side of the room. Then he was allowed to see her in private, save for Kristin. 'When we heard the German bulletin,' she said, holding him close, 'I really thought the end of the world had come.'

Duncan kissed her and looked at his mother. 'What is it you always say, Mother?'

'Only the good die young,' she agreed, and took him in her arms in turn. 'But they sounded so definite . . .'

'They always do. But they had to. They've had a severe bloody nose. And they have to start wondering where we're going to turn up next.'

'You,' Alison said, 'are not turning up anywhere outside of the English Channel. The admiral has given me his word. In the meanwhile, he wants a full report as to the action, for submission to the Admiralty, before you start your leave.'

'But you are getting leave?' Kristin asked.

'Well, you see, the boats have a few holes that need patching.'

'So he, and all his crews,' Alison said meaningfully, before Kristin could ask a leading and perhaps incriminatory question, 'will be off duty for the next week or so.'

'Splendid,' Kristin said. 'Lucifer will be so pleased. Well, I had better leave you two to it. I know you have a lot to do, and I'm trespassing anyway. I will see you later.'

She closed the door behind herself.

'How did she take the news that I was dead?' Duncan asked.

'In public, with the stiffest of upper lips. In private, she had a good blub. So did I. I don't think either of us have a lot going for life if you're not there.'

'I am here,' he reminded her. And took her in his arms again. 'For always.'

'Mr Williams is here, Mr Chadwick,' announced Mrs Bainbridge, and lowered her voice to an arch-whisper. 'I think it's about *her*.'

'And about time,' Chadwick said, and stood up. 'Come in, Harold. I hope you have something for me.'

Harold Williams was a small man who wore a perpetually harassed expression. 'You won't like it.'

Chadwick gestured him to a chair. 'So sit down, and ruin my day. Mrs Strong has defected to the enemy.'

Williams sat down, cautiously. 'No, no. We have had a report from Stockholm.'

'Well, that's something, seeing as how the only thing they have given us so far is that she arrived safely. And we already knew that from the RAF.'

'Apparently, she warned them off. Being too interfering, I mean. She seems to be a somewhat positive young woman.'

'Yes,' Chadwick agreed. 'She is.'

'She pointed out that for them to appear overanxious might just put the old boy's back up. Seems he isn't really keen on working for us. Or he wasn't.'

'Thank God for that last sentence.'

'So she said it had to be a softly-softly catchee monkey approach. And of course, presumably, as they had not seen each other for some time, there was a good deal of reminiscing and indeed, getting-to-know-each-other all over again, before she could get down to the nitty-gritty.'

'Yes,' Chadwick said, a trifle wearily. He had forgotten his colleague's tendency to turn every sentence into a paragraph. 'But she has succeeded at last?'

'Professor Hallstrom appears to have been persuaded that if he is going to work for anyone, it should be us.'

'Hm. Not quite the enthusiasm for which we had hoped. But I assume that means he is coming out. Now, arrangements.'

'Ah.'

Chadwick looked down his nose at him.

'We may have a problem there,' Williams said.

'Do you know, those are the exact words used by Mrs Strong when she was sitting there.'

'Then you know what the problem is.'

'The old man doesn't like flying. She was going to talk him out of that nonsense.'

'She hasn't succeeded.'

Chadwick blew air through his lips; the sound was very close to a raspberry. 'For one of the world's leading scientists, this character seems to think in a very woolly fashion. He's agreed to work for us. But he doesn't want to come to us. So what is his solution to the problem?'

Williams looked more anxious than ever. 'He sees no reason why he cannot be transported across Finland into Russia, and come out through there. After all, he says, there is no war going on up there any more.'

'Now we know that he's barmy. Does he really suppose we can get him into, and then out of, Russia, without the Soviets knowing about it?'

'Yes, but they're neutral. Aren't they? What reason would they have for interfering, providing all his papers, and hers, are in order? We'd see to that.'

'Harold,' Chadwick said, his tone suggesting he was addressing a small child. 'Russia is not neutral. Russia has never been neutral. Russia never will be neutral. She may not actually be at war with anyone at this moment, but the rulers of Russia, whether they were tsars or are now commissars, have always been and are now interested in only one thing: the power and welfare of Russia. They also have some of the world's leading scientists working for them, men who are completely aware of who Professor Hallstrom is, and what he is working on. Do you suppose that if the Soviets ever discovered he was on their territory they would let him go again? At the very least they'd sell him to the highest bidder, which in view of the fact that they are presently playing footsie with the Nazis, would probably be Germany. I'm sorry, but you will have to get back to the Embassy and tell them that Mrs Strong will just have to work harder. We've been waiting a couple of months already. We can wait another couple of weeks to get hold of him.'

'Ah!'

'Now what? Don't tell me the old lunatic is suffering from

terminal cancer? Our last report was that he is as fit as a fiddle. Except perhaps in the head.'

'He is, as fit as a fiddle. But he could be suffering from a case of terminal exposure. An additional report from Stockholm says that they are quite certain that he is being shadowed, and his house watched. They have not yet identified the nationality of this surveillance team, but they are certain that it is not the Swedes, and we know that it is not us . . .'

'Shit!'

Williams raised his eyebrows. His colleague was not given to expletives. 'In fact, in all the circumstances,' he said, beginning to examine his finger nails, '*were* the old boy to be suffering from terminal cancer, and pop off rather sooner than expected . . . well, it would solve a lot of problems. Wouldn't it?'

He raised his head, and flushed as he met Chadwick's gaze. 'Of course, we would then never have access to his knowledge and expertise . . . but neither would Jerry.'

'And Mrs Strong?'

'Well, of course, she would probably have to go too. But we could easily arrange an accident.'

'If,' Chadwick said, 'you were not my friend, my colleague, and a member of my club, I'd throw you out of that window.'

'Steady on, old man. We're fighting a war of survival, a war for the future of mankind, a—'

'Spare me the bloody rhetoric, and shut up for a moment, will you? I'm trying to think.'

Williams relapsed into silence, remembering that Chadwick had once been known as the Boy Wonder of MI6.

Chadwick pointed. 'I assume Hallstrom would not be averse to coming out by sea?'

'I have no idea. I can find out. But that's surely a non-starter. What are you thinking of? Sending *Hood* through the Kattegat? I don't think even Winston would accept the idea of risking our biggest warship for a scientist. Even an atomic scientist.'

Chadwick stared at him; was it possible that he, Harold Williams, was making a joke? 'There is more than one way to cook an egg,' he riposted. 'How does the idea of using the North Cape take you?'

'The North Cape? In April? Anyway, Sweden doesn't have a sea coast up there.'

'Agreed. However . . .' he got up, went to the bookcase and

selected an atlas, which he opened on the desk, finding the right page and then indicating it. 'If you will study that, Harold, you will see that at the very north of Sweden, the border, at, for instance, this place Kilpis, is just twelve miles from the head of the Lyngen Fjord. Twelve miles.'

Williams peered at the map, then at the legend printed on the side. 'Kilpis is situated exactly on the seventieth parallel. That is within the Arctic Circle. And, I repeat, it's April. You're talking about snow and ice, and God knows what else. How old is this fellow Hallstrom, anyway?'

'I believe he's sixty-five.'

'Oh, my God! I thought you said you didn't want to take chances with his life?'

It's not *his* life I'm interested in, Chadwick thought, remembering the vision of Rebecca Strong in bed in that nightie, but he decided to keep that to himself. 'According to his daughter, he is perfectly fit, and you have just confirmed that. Anyway, it'll be May by the time we get this thing set up.'

'Same difference. Bloody Lapland! Given what we know of his character,' Williams said, 'he'll never go for it.'

'You get on to the Embassy, and tell them to have a private chat with Mrs Strong. She should be informed just how close the Nazis are to moving in. Tell them to lay it on with a trowel. But to tell her that if she can get her dad to Lyngen Fiord, we can bring them out.'

'A pipe dream,' Williams groaned. 'I mean, take this place Kilpis. Don't you suppose there's a Jerry post just across the border?'

'There probably is. But if you will look at the map again, you will see that to the east of Kilpis, there is nothing but open country until you get to the Finnish border. I cannot believe that border is very heavily patrolled: Sweden is determinedly neutral, and Finland is pro-Nazi.'

'You're still asking the old boy to tramp twelve miles across the snow. Anyway, what the devil are you going to send up there to pick him up? It may be only a dozen miles to the fiord, and you may be right that the area is so remote there will not be a lot of Germans about, but it is one hell of a long way down the coast of Norway and across to Scotland. And that is certainly well patrolled, and sewn with mines, too. I don't think even a destroyer could get through.

A sub might, but we know what Hallstrom thinks about subs.'

'I was thinking of something much smaller and much faster than either a destroyer or a sub,' Chadwick said. 'After all, Mrs Strong already has been rescued by an MTB, once. I should think she'd be happy for it to happen again.'

Crisis

'Mr Chadwick is here, sir,' Alison said.

'Who?'

'He telephoned, sir, and asked for an appointment. Said it was urgent.'

'Always urgent,' Lonsdale commented. 'MI6, isn't he? Any reason why he wants to see me? Won't Captain Fitzsimmons do?'

'Apparently not. It seems that Mr Chadwick is here with the blessing of the First Sea Lord.'

'What? Oh, good Lord! You'd better show him in.'

'Yes, sir.' Alison withdrew to the outer office, and returned a moment later. 'Mr Chadwick, sir.'

The two men regarded each other, then Chadwick held out his hand. 'Admiral Lonsdale? Robert Chadwick, MI6.'

'Good heavens!' Lonsdale shook hands. 'Don't tell me we have a spy in my department?'

'That would be the business of MI5, sir. Do you think we could close the door? What we have to discuss is top secret.'

'Hm. Thank you, Lady Eversham. Please close the door, and I am not to be interrupted until I ring.'

'Yes, sir.' Alison withdrew.

Chadwick stared after her. 'Did you say, Lady Eversham?'

'I did. It's her name, you see.'

'What a remarkable thing.'

'No doubt you are about to explain that,' Lonsdale suggested. 'But do sit down. MI6. Of course, you are counter-espionage and that sort of thing.' He always found it useful to appear slightly dim to officials from other government departments.

Chadwick seated himself before the desk. 'That sort of thing. We deal with matters which are normally outside the remit of government departments, or of which the government does not wish to know until they are resolved.'

'I assume you are going to explain that as well,' Lonsdale remarked. 'Or at least, what I have to do with it. Are you saying that Second Officer Eversham is involved in something that is being investigated by MI6?'

'No, no. Nothing like that. But you addressed her as Lady Eversham. May I assume that there is a Lord Eversham?'

'You may.'

'And would I also be correct in assuming that he is a lieutenant who commands one of your MTB fleet?'

'You would be right in assuming that Lieutenant-Commander Lord Eversham commands one of my MTBs.'

'Ah! I see. But he would be the same Lord Eversham who rescued an American lady named Rebecca Strong from drowning after the ship on which she was travelling was torpedoed, immediately after Christmas. Or perhaps you don't know about that?'

'Mr Chadwick,' Lonsdale said, 'I know everything that happens to any ship or any man in my command.'

'Ah! Well, then . . .'

'So tell me, would you be responsible for the arrest of Mrs Strong when she was about to have dinner with some friends?'

'You know about that?'

'I was one of the friends.'

'Good lord! And these friends were the Evershams. I see. Tell me, Admiral, did Mrs Strong tell you, or them, why she was in England?'

'No, she did not. Now you can tell me where she is and what has happened to her.'

'Mrs Strong is in Stockholm, with her father. She only, ah, stopped over here.'

'Because she was torpedoed? I understand she was on a Portuguese vessel out of Lisbon. If she originated in the United States, that seems a very odd way to get to Sweden.'

'She was here at our request.'

'Now that you will *have* to explain.'

'Does the name Hallstrom mean anything to you?'

'No.'

'Professor Hallstrom is an internationally known scientist.' Chadwick's tone indicated astonishment that anyone, and certainly an admiral, did not know this.

'And what has Mrs Strong got to do with him?'

'She's his daughter.'

'Good lord! And you, MI6, have been engaged in making
it possible for her to visit her father? I suppose it is reassuring
to know that you have nothing better to do.'

Chadwick looked down his nose. 'I am not going to bore
you with the details, Admiral, which are in any event classified, but Professor Hallstrom is engaged in research which it
is felt, at the very highest level, may be of the utmost importance in winning the war. And which, in the wrong hands,
could go a long way to making sure that we lose it. Thus we
want him here, in England. He has always been reluctant to
leave Sweden, so having exhausted what we may call normal
channels of persuasion, we finally determined to try the powers
of his only child, of whom he is very fond.'

'And nearly got her drowned.'

'But she did not drown, Admiral, thanks to Lord Eversham's
MTB.'

Lonsdale started to frown.

'So we got Mrs Strong to Sweden, and after some time she
has persuaded her father to come out. The caveat is that he
won't fly.'

Still frowning, Lonsdale stroked his chin.

'So then we thought of a submarine, but he suffers from
claustrophobia. So that brought us down to a surface craft.
But a vessel of any size would be too liable to be spotted and
attacked by the Germans. What we need is something very
small, but very fast, able to nip in and nip out.'

'How simple you make it sound,' Lonsdale commented. 'So
you want the use of my MTBs. How many?'

'Oh, just one. There will only be Professor Hallstrom and
Mrs Strong to bring out. And one is more likely to escape
detection than a flotilla.'

'Yes.' Now Lonsdale's expression indicated that at last he
was getting a glimmer of sense. 'Where is this pick-up to be
made? I'm not sending one of my boats into the Kattegat.
She'd never get back out.'

'We understand that. We were thinking of one of the fjords.'

'The Atlantic fjords are all Norwegian, and therefore in
German hands.'

'We understand that also. But what about in the vicinity
of the North Cape. Could one of your boats get up there?

We were thinking of Lyngen Fjord. It's head is only twelve miles from the Swedish border.'

Lonsdale gazed at him for several seconds, then got up and went to the huge map of the Western Seaboard of Europe pinned to the side wall of the office, using a wand to point. 'Lyngen Fjord.'

Chadwick joined him. 'We make it just on twelve hundred statute miles from Scapa Flow. Say—'

'One thousand and fifty-six nautical miles.' The Admiral had dropped his guise of innocent bewilderment.

'Can your boat do that, and back, on one fuel load?'

'It may be possible.' Lonsdale returned behind his desk and sat down. 'When?'

'They're ready to come out now.'

'It's only the sixteenth of May.'

'Another reason for hurrying. In another few weeks there won't be any darkness at all.'

'Agreed. But right now there's still a chance of ice. In case you weren't aware of it, Mr Chadwick, an MTB is made of plywood.'

'Great Scott!'

'Quite.'

'You mean it's not on until all the ice has melted?'

'All the ice never does melt up there, Mr Chadwick.'

'Are you saying it can't be done?'

'It can be done, with the right skipper. He'll have to be a volunteer, of course. And his crew.'

'Ah.'

'Now what?'

'Well . . .' Chadwick actually looked embarrassed, which would have surprised Mrs Bainbridge. 'This brings us back to square one: Mrs Strong being fished out of the English Channel by Lieutenant . . . I beg your pardon, Lieutenant-Commander Lord Eversham.'

Lonsdale's stare was beginning to remind him of the fabled basilisk.

'It seems that Mrs Strong was most impressed,' Chadwick went on, 'by the behaviour of Lord Eversham and his crew. I understand that there had just been an action.'

Lonsdale continued to glare at him.

'Anyway, the point is, when we first proposed sending an

MTB to pick her and her father up, neither was happy with the idea. But then she apparently thought a bit, and said, 'It might work. Would Lord Eversham be in command?' Our man in Stockholm didn't know how to reply to that. I mean, he'd never heard of a Lord Eversham. So he assured her that whichever boat came to her rescue, it would be competently crewed. She didn't seem happy with this, did some more thinking, and then said, 'OK, we'll come out by MTB. If it's Lord Eversham's boat.'

'So now you want to have her running the Royal Navy.'

'Well, you say you've met the young lady.'

'I have,' Lonsdale said, remembering.

'Then you'll understand that she is, ah, of a somewhat positive disposition.'

'You could say that. However, positive or not, what she wants is simply not on.'

'He's not injured is he?'

'No, he is not. But a couple of months ago he had to carry out an extremely hazardous mission.'

'At which he was successful, I trust.'

'He was successful. But I think it would be unacceptable to ask him to undertake another, no less hazardous, mission, so soon. In fact, I have assured him that it will not happen. Therefore . . .'

'Ahem.'

'Yes?'

'I was hoping that it would not come to this, Admiral Lonsdale. But as it has . . .' Chadwick took an envelope from his breast pocket. 'The First Sea Lord was kind enough to give me this, for use if I considered it necessary. I'd like you to read it. It's quite brief.'

Lonsdale took the envelope, which was not sealed, and opened it, extracted the single sheet of paper, which was on Admiralty notepaper. 'Dear Mr Chadwick, in view of the discussion held this morning, and the extreme gravity of the situation you outlined, and which has been confirmed by the Prime Minister, I am writing to agree that you have carte blanche to requisition whichever of His Majesty's Ships you consider necessary to carry out the transference of Professor Hallstrom to this country, and also that you are empowered to select the crews of such vessel if you consider this to be

essential to the successful completion of this project. D
Haskins, Secretary to the First Sea Lord.'

Lonsdale folded the sheet of paper, replaced it in the envelope, and handed it back. Chadwick restored it to his pocket.
'Believe me, Admiral Lonsdale, I am truly sorry to have had
to resort to this.'

'And you consider that the war is liable to be lost if there
is any delay, such as might be occasioned by making a further
effort to persuade Mrs Strong and her father that any of my
MTB skippers would be capable of carrying out this project?'

'That may indeed be the case.'

'You'll forgive me for wondering if this is not a little
extreme.'

'What I have not told you, sir, is that we are not the only
people interested in Professor Hallstrom's experiments. Our
Stockholm Embassy is convinced that there are German agents
actively watching the Hallstroms, and that it is only a matter
of time, perhaps a very short space of time, before an attempt
is made to remove them to Germany.'

'Can't they take steps to prevent this?'

'Not without risking a serious diplomatic incident. Neither
Professor Hallstrom nor his daughter are British citizens, therefore we have no right either to protect them in a foreign
country or to ask the Swedish police to do so, even supposing
they were prepared to undertake such a responsibility, which
might involve a clash with Nazi agents, in view of the determination of the Swedish government to remain neutral.'

'And Hallstrom is that pliable, that he'll work for whoever
happens to get hold of him?'

'Admiral Lonsdale, you are a sailor, and almost by defin-
ition, sailors fight clean, decent, even noble wars and battles.
Our luck is to fight very dirty wars indeed. But even we do
not fight as dirty as some of our enemies. If the Gestapo were
to get Mrs Strong into one of their torture chambers and illustrate to Professor Hallstrom just what they propose to do to
her if he does not cooperate, he will cooperate.'

Not for the first time Lonsdale stared at him for several
seconds. But he was not actually seeing Chadwick's face; he
was seeing Rebecca's face, twisted in agony as she suffered
. . . he did not actually know what.

'When?' he asked.

'When can you be ready?'

'The day after tomorrow. We will leave at dawn and go up to Scapa to top up with fuel. We will leave at dawn the next day, and be at Lyngen Fjord at dawn two day's later. That is Wednesday the twenty-first. Can you set it up for that?'

'Four days. That should be time enough. I'll get on to Stockholm right away. But . . . did you say, we?'

'Did I? Slip of the tongue, old man. I mean, our boat will leave the day after tomorrow.'

'With Lieutenant-Commander Eversham in command?'

'Yes.'

'Well, thank you, Admiral.' Chadwick stood up. 'You have been most cooperative.'

He shook hands, and went to the door. Lonsdale waited until he had had time to clear the outer office, then pressed his intercom. 'Will you come in please, Lady Eversham.'

Alison appeared, and with her notebook and pencil.

'No dictation.'

'Very good, sir. Actually, there is something I would like to discuss with you.'

'Can it wait? There's rather a lot on at the moment.'

Alison hesitated. Then she said, 'Yes, sir. Of course.'

'Duncan was not on patrol today, was he?'

'No, sir.'

'Therefore I assume he's at home.'

'Yes, sir.'

'Then I would like you to invite me to dinner.'

Alison stared at him with her mouth open. 'Oh, my God! You . . .'

'I know. I'm going to have to break my promise. I have received direct orders from the First Sea Lord.'

'And they want Duncan . . .'

'For a special mission, yes.'

'And you can't tell me what it is.'

'I will, tonight. So if you could telephone Kristin . . .'

'I will do that, sir.'

'Jimmy!' Kristin said, opening her arms. 'How lovely to see you. Do let go of the admiral's hand, Lucifer; you don't know when last he washed it.'

Lucifer obeyed his mistress, and Lonsdale counted his

fingers. 'I should come here in boxing gloves. Or steel gauntlets.'

Kristin embraced him. 'He loves you.'

'I certainly wouldn't like him to hate me. I hope you don't mind my imposing. Again.'

'You could never impose, Jimmy.' She held his hand to lead him into the drawing room, where Duncan and Alison waited, Alison having arrived only a few minutes before the admiral, and having also been greeted by Lucifer, was still looking somewhat tousled. 'Although the again bit bothers me. The last time . . .'

'I know.'

She glanced at him, then said. 'Give the admiral a drink, Duncan. You can add the arsenic later.'

Duncan poured.

'I think we should all sit down,' Lonsdale suggested.

'But keep it handy,' Kristin recommended, and sat beside him. 'What torture are you considering inflicting upon us now?'

Lonsdale sipped his drink. 'As I explained to Alison, this was not my idea. In fact, I disliked the whole thing . . . until I learned all the facts.'

'Which you are about to tell us,' Kristin pointed out.

'Yes, Kristin,' the admiral agreed. 'And I would be obliged if you would not interrupt. Otherwise I shall take Duncan into the study for a private chat.'

Kristin blew a raspberry, and held out her glass for a refill. 'I shall be as mum as Caesar's wife.'

'Her crime was infidelity.'

'Which can hardly apply to me, as I have no one to be faithful to.' She gazed at him with enormous eyes. 'At this moment. But I shall not say another word.'

'Thank God for that. Now listen very carefully.' The admiral looked around their faces. 'And remember that everything I tell you is classified.' He outlined his conversation with Chadwick. 'So you see . . .' he gazed at Duncan. 'You seem to have made quite a conquest.'

Duncan looked at Alison, who was looking at Kristin. But Kristin was giving a quick shake of the head. Alison turned back to the men. 'What about mines?' she asked. 'That whole area is thick with them. At least up to the North Cape.'

'They're virtually all magnetic, which are not a hazard to wooden hulls.'

'Virtually.'

'Those that are not magnetic are anchored to the sea bed, and ride not less than six feet beneath the surface. They present no hazard to a three-foot draft wooden boat.'

Duncan was still looking at his wife. 'You mean you have no objection?'

'If it'll help to win the war . . .' she wrinkled her nose. 'Anyway, on a tiny boat . . . I assume you won't have to put her to bed.'

'I sincerely hope not.' He grinned. 'If it crops up, I can always hand her over to Jamie.'

Kristin snorted, very loudly.

'The point is,' Lonsdale said, deciding to ignore her, 'can it be done, fuel-wise?'

'You say we're going to top up at Scapa. Then it'll be close to two thousand four hundred miles there and back. At cruising speed, say twenty knots, we have a range of two thousand five hundred miles.'

'Oh, my God!' Alison commented.

'I made it just over two thousand,' Lonsdale argued.

'There and back in virtually a straight line, sir. That won't be possible, either going or coming. We will have to lose ourselves a couple of hundred miles offshore to be sure of escaping detection.'

'Then you're saying it isn't on,' Lonsdale said. 'Shit! I beg your pardon, ladies.'

'I should think so too,' Kristin declared, coming to life.

'It can be done,' Duncan said. 'I admit it leaves us no room for manoeuvre, but if we could follow the same plan as we did in Biscay in February, and rendezvous with a ship, say a hundred miles north of the Shetlands . . .'

Lonsdale snapped his fingers. 'Of course!'

'I have never heard such rubbish in my life,' Kristin declared. 'You . . .' she addressed the admiral, 'are proposing to send my son virtually to the North Pole, to rescue an American tart who has got herself into this mess . . .'

'Kristin!' the admiral said, with unusual severity, at least when addressing his favourite woman. 'That was quite uncalled for. Mrs Strong got herself into this mess, as you call it, through trying to help us win the war. And the rescue is not of her, per se, although I would not like to think of her in the hands of the Nazis, but of her father, who is of such vital importance.'

'I still think that you should just put the rocks to her,' Kristin said. 'If necessary, kidnap her and her beastly father, put them on a plane, and fly them back here whether they like it or not.'

'Kristin,' he said, now clearly exercising great patience, 'we want Professor Hallstrom to work for us, not hate us.'

'Ha! I still think that you're sending Duncan, and his crew,' she added, 'into great and unnecessary danger.'

'I am not sending Duncan anywhere,' the admiral declared, with slightly defensive dignity. 'I am going with him.'

'What?' All three spoke together.

'You can't do that, sir,' Alison protested. 'What about your command?'

'I have been informed by the doctors that I have been over-working and am suffering from stress. They have recommended, in fact they are insisting, that I take at least a week's rest. I intend to do that, starting tomorrow, and the best possible rest I can think of is an ocean cruise.' He looked at Duncan. 'I am coming as an observer, Duncan, and in no other capacity. I shall not interfere in any way in your command.'

'Of course you are welcome, sir,' Duncan agreed, without total conviction.

'And you call that having a rest from stress?' Kristin inquired.

'A change is as good as a rest.'

'You are stark, raving mad. But in the circumstances . . . I think you should stay here tonight.' She looked at her son and daughter-in-law, the admiral being temporarily speechless. 'Admiral Lonsdale has made it perfectly clear that everything that has been said here tonight, or may be done here tonight, is classified. Shall we have dinner? I feel like an early night.'

Her look at Alison was again meaningful.

Rebecca regarded the rather nervous young man seated on the settee. 'That seems rather extreme, Mr Trent,' she remarked. 'Do we have to go all the way up there? And then walk, for twelve miles? Won't there be snow on the ground?'

'We are trying to arrange transport for you, Mrs Strong,' Trent explained. 'Through the Norwegian underground. As for being extreme, well, yes, I suppose it is. But it is apparently the only way the Royal Navy can get to you, and get away again.'

'And it will be an MTB, captained by Lord Eversham.'

'As you required. That is our understanding, yes.'

'Well, then, we must do as they require. When is this happening?'

'It is a little over seven hundred miles from Stockholm to Kilpis. The roads in places are not very good, so we have to allow twenty-four hours for the journey. We will leave at dawn tomorrow morning, drive for twelve hours, spend the night at Lykesele, and be at Kilpis by dusk the following night. The MTB is due in Lyngen Fjord at dawn the next morning. That is Wednesday the twenty-first of May. You will have to travel overnight to be there by dawn . . .'

'Twelve miles, on foot, in the dark, through the snow.'

'You will have a guide, and as I have said, if possible, transport. If not, you will have to walk it, but . . . they estimate that you and your father will be in England, or at least, Scotland, by Friday.'

'Well,' she said. 'It's something to look forward to.'

'I hope you know what we're doing,' Johann Hallstrom remarked, as the car bounced its way over the rather uneven surface. He was a small man who seemed to be rendered top-heavy by his shock of thick white hair, but there could be no question as to where Rebecca had got her very fine features. Now he looked out of the window of the car with disfavour. Yesterday had been merely boring, having to be driven all day. But the hotel had not been very comfortable, and today, as they moved further north there was more snow to be seen in the fields to either side, although the road was clear.

'It's the best I could come up with, in all the circumstances.'

'Supposing this cloak and dagger stuff is necessary at all.'

'Would you really like to be kidnapped by the Nazis, and forced to work for them?'

'Do you really believe all of that rubbish? This is 1941, not the Dark Ages.'

'Daddy, we are on the verge of another dark age. These people mean to dominate all Europe, and they are not going to let anything stop them, if they can help it.'

'I still cannot believe they would torpedo or strafe a Swedish merchantman.'

'Bound for England, and with your name on the passenger list? They had no compunction in torpedoing that Portuguese ship, and they didn't even know I was on board.'

'And that is the root of all the trouble, isn't it? You're just scared of being torpedoed again.'

'I won't deny that.'

'But you're prepared to go on a thousand-mile trip in a small wooden motor boat.'

Rebecca sighed. She loved her father dearly, and she conceded that he was a genius, but he did like to worry a subject. Which, she supposed, went with the mentality to be a genius. But it could be tiresome. 'Seeing as how you won't fly . . .'

'I must have been a fool to let you talk me into this.'

She squeezed his hand. 'You just have to accept that you're famous. People want you to work for them. It had to be your choice, whether you want to work for the good guys or the bad guys. I think you made the right choice.'

'I should never have published that paper,' he grumbled.

Trent, seated in the front beside the driver, looked over his shoulder. 'We shall be in Kilpis in half an hour. From there you will be in the hands of the Norwegian Resistance.'

'But we'll still be in Sweden?' Rebecca was suddenly anxious.

'Oh, yes. They will take you across the border and deliver you to the fjord.'

'But you won't be with us.' Over the last couple of days she had come to regard the young man as a very reliable aide, who had seen to their every requirement.

'Well, no. If I cross the border I become an enemy alien.'

'And we do not?'

'You are an American citizen, Mrs Strong. And your father is Swedish. There is nothing to prevent either you, or him, going anywhere you please in the entire world.'

'It's nice to hear you say that,' Rebecca conceded, wishing she could believe it. But then she told herself, why shouldn't I believe it? It's true. Isn't it?

* * *

But she felt almost weepy, as she said goodbye to Trent and his driver, who were starting their return journey immediately. They, or their superiors, obviously felt that every minute spent in such close proximity to German-occupied territory was a risk.

Now they were in the hands of a rather rugged-looking young man, who was accompanied by a woman, also young and craggy of feature. 'I am Bjorn, Ja?' he announced. 'And this is Greta. We are to take you, Ja?'

'Where do we go?'

'First we eat. It is early, Ja? We wait for dark, Ja?'

That made sense. Although it was eight o'clock it was still quite light. Trent had told her that at these latitudes, in May, it was only truly dark for about three hours in the middle of the night; in another couple of weeks it would not get dark at all.

Bjorn and Greta took them to the village inn, where the food was surprisingly good, and certainly warming. There were only a few people in the establishment, but then, Rebecca had gained the impression that there were only a few people in the entire place; the steeply sloping red-roofed wooden houses clustered around a small square and the village church, and eyes peered at them from behind lace curtains.

But in the small restaurant everyone was entirely courteous, and apparently not at all inquisitive as to what two strangers might be doing in their midst.

'So what's the drill?' she asked over the meal.

'I do not understand. Drill?'

She realized that his English, if actually very good, had not reached the idiomatic stage. 'I meant, what exactly do you wish us to do?'

'Ah. You come in my car.'

'You have a car?'

'Of course. I am a doctor.'

'What? Wow! I mean . . .' you don't look like a doctor. But she decided against saying it. 'That's great. And you have patients on both sides of the border?'

'That is it.' He seemed impressed by her intelligence. 'The doctor here is not here, Ja. So they sent for me. Your father is not well, Ja? So we take him across the border to my little hospital for treatment, Ja?'

'The Germans do not object to this?'

'No, no. I treat them also when they are sick. The Germans, they do not like being stationed up here. It is the midges, and the mosquitoes, Ja?'

'Ah,' she said. She had noticed a sudden concentration of bugs when getting out of the car, but they had not seemed relevant against the general background of this adventure. But now she saw two men, who had been seated at an adjacent table, get up and wrap their scarves tightly round their faces before pulling their caps down over their ears, to leave only their eyes exposed as they went out.

'The mosquitoes only live for about three months,' Bjorn explained. 'But perhaps because of that, they are voracious. Imagine, having to live your entire life, from birth to death by old age, in three months.'

'Kind of makes you brood on the number of seconds we humans waste every day, don't it,' Rebecca agreed, hoping they were not going to get into a philosophical or intellectual discussion when she had so much on her mind.

But actually, talking to Bjorn, or rather, listening to him, as he told her about the enormous contrasts involved in living so far north, the months when there was no daylight, and the brief period, which they were just entering, when there was no dark, was intensely interesting and reduced the stress of waiting for their adventure to begin. She felt quite sorry for her father, exposed to the conversational gambits of Greta, whose English was not half so fluent as Bjorn's, It came as a surprise when the doctor suddenly said, 'It is time, Ja?'

'What?' Rebecca looked around herself, realized the restaurant was empty, save for the waitress who had served them, and who was quietly snoring in a corner. 'Oh, good Lord! I hadn't realized the time.'

Suddenly she was afraid. Once she stepped out of this doorway she was launching herself, and her father, into the unknown. But Bjorn and Greta were totally reassuring, and, she reminded herself, only twelve miles away were, or would be, very soon, Duncan and that delightful boy Jamie.

They went out into the night, brushed aside the hordes of insects who welcomed them, and got into the small car, Rebecca and Hallstrom in the back, Greta and Bjorn in the front. 'Now, you must remember, sir,' Bjorn said, 'that you are not well. You have stomach pains which need to be investigated, urgently. If anyone speaks to you, it might be helpful for you to groan a little. Ja?'

Hallstrom blew a raspberry, and Rebecca squeezed his hand. Bjorn started the engine, and they drove out of the little town and along a fairly good road before arriving at a barrier. There was no one on the Swedish side, but on the other a German soldier stamped his feet outside of a small building. Bjorn drove up to the barrier and blew his horn. The soldier came forward, and spoke in German, to which Bjorn replied in the same language. The soldier leaned on the counterweight and the barrier rose. Bjorn drove through, and the soldier held up his hand.

The car stopped, and the German came forward and peered into the car, using a flashlight. Hallstrom played his part, arcing his body forward with both hands held to his stomach, and grunted; Rebecca put her arm round him protectively. The soldier made a comment and switched off the light. Bjorn replied, and drove on. 'There, you see,' he said. 'There is no problem. Now it is only a short drive.'

'To the head of the fjord?'

'No, no. We go some distance further. There is a little port, you see, Skibotn. We go past that. You should not have to walk at all.'

Rebecca gave a great sigh of relief. And they saw a bright light in the distance.

Bjorn made a comment in Norwegian which Rebecca had to assume was an expletive. She felt like uttering one herself. The light had now divided into two, and was clearly a pair of headlamps, and were situated on a vehicle parked exactly in the centre of the road. In front of it stood a German officer, holding up his hand.

Bjorn braked. 'What must we do?' Rebecca asked.

'I do not know. This should not have happened.'

Oh, my God! Rebecca thought.

The officer advanced, and he was now supported on either side by a soldier armed with a tommy gun. Rebecca could only stare at them; her brain seemed to have gone entirely blank. She felt her father's fingers closing on hers, but not even that was reassuring.

The officer shone a flashlight into the front of the car. 'Dr Roeder,' he remarked, very pleasantly, but ominously, he was speaking English. 'And Greta. How nice to see you.'

'Good evening, Herr Hauptmann. Why are we being stopped?' Bjorn asked; his voice was trembling.

'Because I understand that you are being a naughty boy,' the captain said, and shone his light into the back of the car, where Hallstrom was again doing his dying swan bit in Rebecca's arms. 'Professor Hallstrom, I presume. May I ask where you are going, Professor?'

'My father is on his way to hospital,' Rebecca said.

'Ah! You must be the glamorous Mrs Strong.' The light played over her. 'One seldom believes every piece of information one receives. But in this case it is being proved absolutely correct. You are glamorous. Will you get out of the car, please. And your father.'

'I think you should know,' Rebecca said, grateful that her voice was not trembling, although she was scared stiff, 'that I am an American citizen. Would you like to look at my passport?'

'I know you are an American citizen, Mrs Strong. Unhappily for you, America at this moment is a very long way away. Now, will you get out of the car, or would you like my men to drag you out?'

Rebecca drew a deep breath, but her father opened the door and got out, hugging his briefcase, so she followed.

'Thank you,' the captain said. 'Now you, doctor. And Greta.'

The engine had still been running. Now Bjorn pressed his foot on the accelerator. The car bounded forward, the soldiers having hastily to jump aside.

'Shoot it!' the captain snapped, himself drawing his Luger pistol. Bjorn raced at the parked car and swerved round it. The road wasn't wide enough, with the car occupying the centre, and there was a crash as their sides collided, then Bjorn was past and careering into the darkness, followed by several shots from both the soldiers' rifles and the captain's pistol. One of the soldiers shouted something, and the captain answered disparagingly. Having never experienced anything like that before, Rebecca and her father remained standing absolutely still. 'Foolish fellow,' the captain remarked in English. 'He had not actually been charged with anything. Now he is dead.'

'Dead?!' Rebecca cried.

'Well, Wolfgang is certain he struck the car, more than once. He saw it swerve out of control.' He gave orders in German, and the two soldiers set off, tommy guns at the ready. 'Now you will come with me.'

'Are you arresting us?'

'Yes.'

'For what reason? What are we supposed to have done?'

'I'm afraid I only obey orders, Mrs Strong. I received orders that it was possible that Professor Hallstrom and his daughter, known to have left Stockholm two days ago in the company of an official from the British Embassy, might be meaning to enter Norway. All border posts were so informed, and when I learned earlier this evening that two people answering your descriptions were in Kilpis with Dr Roeder, well, my task became very simple.'

'Those bastards in the restaurant,' Rebecca said.

'You are perceptive. Now, my instructions were that you are to be held pending the arrival of a Gestapo officer from Oslo. He should be here in a day or so. I will try to make you comfortable for that time, but there are one or two questions I need to ask you myself. So . . .' he indicted the waiting car.

'Daddy,' Rebecca said. 'Can they do this?'

'They are doing it.' The Professor was a man who dealt in facts. 'I knew this whole crazy idea was going to turn out badly.'

'So what are we to do?'

'Cooperate. There is nothing else we can do.'

'Oh . . .' Rebecca felt like stamping her foot, but instead gazed at the captain, who had been talking to his driver.

'The car is kaput,' he said disgustedly. 'When that maniac slammed into it, he burst some pipes in the engine. We will have to walk. But it is only a few kilometres.'

As her father had said, there was nothing for it. The captain was clearly only obeying orders, and apparently had every intention of continuing to do so. While to attempt to run away in the darkness was a non-starter, for several reasons: he had the pistol, and she had no desire to be shot; there was no way her father was going to be able to run very far or very fast;

and she had no idea in which direction they should run to find the fjord where Duncan was going to arrive in a few hours time. She wondered how long he would wait, how long he would dare wait, and if it mattered, if she was never going to make it anyway?

The German post was situated in the little town of Skibotn, which was actually, as Bjorn had said, a tiny port on the fjord itself. But it was two miles away, and she felt exhausted by the time they got there, while Hallstrom was panting and unsteady on his feet. The town itself was in darkness at two o'clock in the morning, but the three soldiers, who, together with a sergeant, manned the post, all looked benevolent. 'I am afraid that the only accommodation we have are our cells,' the captain said. 'But they are quite comfortable, and there are two of them, so you may have one each. Unfortunately, that scoundrel Roeder drove off with your luggage, so you will have to do without it until my people return with the car. They should not be long. In any event, it is past midnight, and I know you have had a long journey. You will wish to sleep. I will take the briefcase, Professor.'

Hallstrom hesitated, but continuing his policy of cooperating, handed over the small valise. They were given a cup of cocoa each, and gazed at each other as they drank. There was nothing to say that might not incriminate them. But there was nothing to say in any event. Rebecca felt that they were a pair of butterflies, helplessly fluttering their wings in a gale, with never a hope of success. She had not really believed Trent's insistence that the Germans were watching and waiting. But in fact, he was as helpless a butterfly as either of them, in his belief that by leaving Stockholm clandestinely in the early morning they could be got to safety before the Germans realized they had left. Now . . . but it was better not to think about now, or what came next, save that she must play her trump card of being an American citizen to its maximum. But whether she would be able to use it to help her father she did not know. The worst thought of all was that Duncan and Jamie and their men might be sailing into a trap.

Rebecca had never been in a cell before, and presumably, as cells went, this was quite acceptable, if decidedly primitive. There was a cot, which contained a folded blanket but no pillow, and a table, and two straight chairs . . . and a slop bucket with a lid. This was presently clean, and smelt of disinfectant, but if she was going to be here for two days . . .!

Most disconcerting was the fact that the wall facing the corridor was just bars, as in some Western movie. This did not mean she was constantly overlooked, because the cells were down a corridor from the main building and all she faced was a blank wall on the other side of the corridor. But it did mean that she would be totally exposed to anyone who took it into his head to wander down the corridor to have a look at her, no matter what she might be doing at the time. On the other hand, as she had no clothes to change into, and no desire to take anything off, it was not an immediate problem.

There was a naked bulb dangling from the ceiling, but this was switched off, and the only light came from a matching bulb hanging in the corridor, and this was not opposite her bars in any event. It was perfectly warm. She took off her coat and folded it to make a pillow, then lay on the cot and pulled the blanket over her. She was exhausted, but she suspected that she was not going to sleep; her brain was rushing round in ever decreasing circles. She closed her eyes, and opened them again as there came a considerable noise from the outer office. As she did not speak German she had no idea what was being said, but the voices were raised and vehement. Then she heard footsteps in the corridor, and her door was unlocked.

She sat up, and the captain came in, carrying her suitcase. 'Are you awake, Mrs Strong? Ah. Here are your belongings. I'm afraid this senseless escapade has cost a life.'

'Dr Roeder?'

'Oh, his also, I suspect. But Greta, his nurse . . . that is unfortunate.'

'You mean your thugs shot her?'

'You should be careful how you phrase things.' He placed the suitcase beside the cot, and sat on one of the straight chairs. 'Greta was shot, yes. Roeder's car was as badly damaged as mine. One of the wheels had been knocked off centre, and in fact it seems to have come off after a brief while, so that the vehicle rolled over into a ditch. It would appear that both Roeder and Greta were dazed by this, and they were just recovering when my men caught up with them.

They called upon them to surrender, and the foolish people would not. Greta, who had twisted her ankle, actually drew a revolver. So my men shot her. Roeder ran away into the darkness. They fired after him, and hit him. They know this, because when they followed they found blood on the ground. But then they came to a stream and lost him. Not very efficient, but there you are. However, the doctor will either die from loss of blood or be found when it is daylight.'

'Do you expect me to believe all of that mush?'

He shrugged. 'I do not care whether you believe it or not, Mrs Strong. It is what happened. Now you need to consider your own position.'

'My position,' Rebecca said, speaking slowly and carefully, 'is that my father and I, neither of whom have anything to do with this ridiculous war you are waging, have been illegally arrested. You may feel that we should have had some kind of visa to enter this country, but we were not advised of this in Stockholm. And in any event, if we have entered this country illegally, your correct course is to deport us. Now. Not hold us like condemned criminals.'

He regarded her for several seconds. 'You present a very good case. Are you a lawyer? Or you husband, perhaps?'

'My husband is a billionaire industrialist, who has a great deal of clout. When he learns about this the explosion is going to be heard in Berlin, and will involve anyone who has behaved illegally.'

The captain did not look overly concerned. 'Sadly, Mrs Strong, the case you present is badly flawed. If you entered this country, illegally but for an entirely innocent purpose, although I cannot imagine what that may be, unless you intend to study reindeer in their natural habitat, why did your escort oppose us when we sought to discover what was going on?'

'Well . . . does anyone want to be arrested by you people?'

'Very droll. But as they are no longer in a position to answer my questions, I am afraid you will have to.'

'What questions? I told you . . .'

'Yes, yes. You and your father are innocently roaming around Lapland. You really should not assume that everyone in the world, except you, of course, is a fool. You came here, because it is the closest the Swedish border comes to the sea, except where it is actually on the sea, as in the Kattegat or the Baltic, and those waters are too dangerous for British vessels to penetrate. So you are waiting to be taken off, by . . . I imagine it is to be a submarine. Now, as I am sure you know, in this area there are several fjords, such as the one outside, inlets which lead to the ocean, any one of which can be navigated. I do not have the men to guard them all. So I need you to tell me, now, where this submarine is supposed to enter to pick you up, and at what time.'

'I have no idea.'

'Oh, please, Mrs Strong. You came here to make a rendezvous.'

'Even if I knew, I'd see you in hell before I'd tell you.'

The captain stared at her for some moments. Then he got up and sat beside her on the cot. He put his hand on the nape of her neck, and moved the fingers up into her hair. His touch was very gentle, almost loving. 'I do think, Mrs Strong, that you need to consider your position very carefully. Or you will indeed find yourself in Hell.'

Rescue

'I have land, sir,' said Petty Officer Rawlings.

'Thank you, Petty Officer,' Duncan acknowledged, and peered into the mist. He could see nothing himself, but he had every confidence in Rawlings eagle-like vision.

They had spent the previous two days well out at sea. As he had warned Lonsdale, this had added a couple of hundred miles to their journey, but as they had been travelling at a steady fifteen hundred revs they had kept their fuel consumption as low as possible, given the time scale on which they were operating. And again as he had told the admiral, remaining a good distance offshore had lowered the chances of their being observed; there was little activity up here. They had also been sheltered by the persistent mist, sometimes degenerating into fog, that had made the relatively tiny boat no more than a speck, and although they had heard aircraft from time to time, they had seen none and had no evidence that they had themselves been seen. The only real hazard had been the occasional ice floes, but these had been small and isolated and easily avoided. Now it was three o'clock in the morning, and already light. And according to Rawlings, they were there. He wondered if their luck would hold all the way back?

Rear-Admiral Lonsdale appeared, wearing a greatcoat like everyone else, and slapping his gloved hands together. 'Any idea where we are?'

'Yes, sir. We have just made our landfall.'

'Have we?' He in turn peered into the mist. 'Where, exactly?'

'We'll have to get closer.' Now he could himself make out the dark humps of the islands. 'It should be either North Kvaloy, Vanna or Fugloya. They all mask the entrance to Lyngen Fjord.'

'Well, if you're right, I congratulate you.'

Duncan couldn't blame the old boy for being sceptical; they had made almost the entire journey by Dead Reckoning, being able to check their position only twice, once when the mist had lifted sufficiently at noon to give a glimpse of the sun, and the other during the night just ended, when again a brief clearance had allowed a glimpse of the stars. Both of those fixes had been reassuring, but in any event with the weather so settled – there had hardly been a breath of wind throughout the voyage – and the sea thus remaining calm, there was no reason for them ever to lose their calculated track.

Lonsdale had actually been surprisingly good company, somewhat of a tyro for all of his vast experience because he had never voyaged on a small motor boat before. He had been as good as his word, never interfered or permitted any reference to his rank. But neither had he offered the slightest reason for being there at all. Duncan had some ideas, but he knew they had to be kept strictly to himself.

Cooper appeared, looking slightly dishevelled: the Admiral was using his bunk, and he had been doing the best he could in the mess cabin. 'Good morning, Mr Cooper,' Duncan said. 'I'll have the Pilot Book up, if you please.'

'Aye-aye, sir.' He ducked back down the hatch.

Duncan listened to the sound of the pump, which meant that Jamie was also up. He thumbed the Tannoy. 'All well down there, Jamie?'

'Aye-aye, sir. Purring like a babe.'

'Fuel?'

'Just on half, sir.'

'Hm. Very good.'

'What do you reckon?' Lonsdale asked.

'It's about what we calculated, sir. It should certainly get us back to the cruiser you have waiting for us.'

'If we can find her in this muck.'

The humps of the islands in front of them, now within a few miles, were becoming clearer by the moment. Cooper arrived with the Pilot Book, and opened it at the appropriate page. 'Small headland, cove to the left, then an abandoned house,' he read.

'I have that, sir,' Rawlings said.

'Mr Cooper?'

'I make that Vanna, sir.'

'Very good. We leave that to starboard.' He reduced speed to a thousand revs.

'What about water?' the admiral asked.

'Fifteen fathoms, sir,' Cooper said.

The MTB slipped between the two islands, and the high cliffs of the mainland appeared before them. It was broad daylight now, and both Rawlings and Cooper swept the land to either side.

'How far up?' Lonsdale asked.

'Not too far,' Duncan said. 'There's a little town on the left hand side, and it may be garrisoned. Mr Rawlings, steel helmets and life jackets for all, and then we need action stations. But quietly. No bell.'

'Aye-aye, sir.' Rawlings slipped down the ladder while Duncan reduced speed still further, so that they were barely gliding through the dark water, now encased by the cliffs.

'There's someone signalling,' Cooper said.

'Oh shit. I suppose things were going just too well.'

Cooper levelled his glasses. 'He's a civilian, and he's definitely signalling. And . . . he's got blood all over him.'

'What?' Duncan put the engine into neutral, and the boat came to a stop.

'It might be a good idea just to shoot him,' Lonsdale suggested.

Duncan looked up at the cliffs towering above them. 'A shot in this vault would sound like a sixteen-inch gun. Besides, I think it may be worthwhile hearing what he has to say. If he's been shot, it can only be by the Germans.'

Rawlings reappeared with the helmets and lifejackets, while the crew came up to man the machine-guns and the quick-firer. Now Duncan himself took the glasses to study the rather grotesque figure standing on a spur of rock only just above the water level. 'Take the bow with a boathook, Mr Rawlings,' he called. 'The gun, Mr Cooper. Cover the land behind that fellow.'

Cooper left the bridge and hurried forward.

Duncan spun the helm and put the boat slow ahead. It inched towards the rocks. Rawlings lay on his stomach in the bow, prodding over the side with the eight-foot-long boathook. 'No bottom.'

'It is steep-to, up to the rocks,' Roeder called.

A moment later there was a gentle nudge, and the doctor scrambled over the bow, assisted by Rawlings. He immediately sank to the deck. Cooper knelt beside him, looked back at the bridge. 'He is wounded. I think badly.'

Duncan had put the boat astern, and she had eased out into the stream, then he put the engine into neutral and let her drift: there was no current, and anchoring in what was still some eighty feet of water would be both noisy and time-consuming. 'Mr Rawlings,' he commanded, 'take that man below. Mr Cooper, keep your gun trained on the land. You too, Morrison,' he told the Leading Seaman who was in charge of the machine guns.

He and Lonsdale went into the Mess cabin, where Roeder had been placed on the table, and Wilson was holding a mug of brandy to his lips. But blood continued to seep through his clothes, and his complexion was pale.

'We'll get you bandaged up,' Duncan said. 'Jamie!'

Jamie had come up from the engine room. 'Aye-aye, sir,' he acknowledged, and returned below to fetch the first-aid kit.

'There is no time,' Roeder said. 'I am a doctor. There is no time. Listen.'

He panted out his story, while Jamie cut away his clothes. He had been hit twice, in the back, and it was a miracle of courage and determination that he was still alive, and became even more so when the horrified officers learned that he had been hit three hours earlier.

But they had come to do a job. 'Is the professor all right?' Duncan asked.

'And Mrs Strong?' Lonsdale was pale with anxiety.

'They were taken into custody,' Roeder said through gritted teeth, having been rolled on his face so that Jamie could attempt to clean the wounds, and apply antiseptic.

'Taken where?' Duncan asked.

'Skibotn. It is on the fjord, a few miles away. The left-hand side.'

'You are sure they're still there?'

'Yes.' Roeder burst into a fit of coughing, spitting blood.

Duncan looked across the stricken body at Wilson, who was shaking his head.

'Goddamn!' Lonsdale said.

Duncan looked at his watch. 'Four o'clock. If they were arrested at midnight, they're probably all asleep. Dr Roeder, I'm sorry, but can you tell us how many German soldiers are in Skibotn?'

Roeder's head had sagged on to the table. Now he raised it again. 'Six and officer.' His head sagged again.

'He needs a transfusion, sir,' Wilson said. 'He's losing too much blood. I just can't stop it.'

Duncan put his mouth to Roeder's ear. 'Doctor, there must be a hospital close by.'

Roeder sighed. 'There is a clinic, in Skibotn.'

'Very good. We'll have you there in fifteen minutes.'

'The garrison . . .' Lonsdale said.

'We have to take them out, sir. At the moment, we have every advantage.' He looked around the faces; nearly the entire crew had crowded into the Mess cabin; most were still wearing their helmets and life jackets. 'Mr Cooper, you and your people man the gun. Morrison, you and two men take the heavy machine guns. But no firing until, and unless you have a clear line of shot on an enemy; we can't take any chances with the lives of the Hallstroms. Mr Rawlings, I want you and the remaining men armed with rifles and bayonets. Understood?'

'What about me, sir?' Jamie asked.

'Well . . .'

'I came ashore with you in Guernsey, sir. If I hadn't been there we mightn't have got her ladyship out.'

'By God, you're right. No, no, not you, Wilson,' he said as the cook opened his mouth. 'We need you here in case any of us come back with a hole. Now, gentlemen, we are going to take over the village, dealing with the enemy first. Our priority is to rescue Professor Hallstrom and his daughter. Once the enemy has been neutralized and the Hallstroms are on board, we will take Dr Roeder to his clinic for treatment. Lieutenant Cooper, should anything happen to me, you're in command.'

'Aye-aye, sir. But . . .'

'Don't worry about it. I've never been hit yet. Well, gentlemen . . .'

'Ahem,' Admiral Lonsdale commented.

'Ah! With the utmost respect, sir, I do feel that as you have never handled an MTB . . .'

'Of course Mr Cooper should take command were something to happen to you. But I am not staying here like a stuffed dummy. I can handle a rifle and bayonet as well as anybody.'

'But if anything were to happen to you, sir . . .'

'Lieutenant-Commander Eversham, I am assuming command of the shore party. Your crew will bear witness that this is my decision, and I take full responsibility for my action.'

Duncan hesitated for a moment, then he said, 'Aye-aye, sir. Mr Rawlings, provide Admiral Lonsdale with a weapon. The assault starts now.'

Duncan took the helm, Lonsdale and Jamie on the bridge beside him. Cooper had his men on the foredeck, and Morrison's crew were also in position. Rawlings and his two armed seamen waited beside the Mess cabin.

At slow ahead *Forty-One* inched through the still water, the little port coming into view as they rounded a bend in the fjord. It was 0530, and the town still slept, but as the MTB came alongside the little dock a man in a green uniform emerged from the doorway of one of the few large buildings, situated opposite the landing stage. He carried a Swastika flag in his hand which he was clearly about to set on the adjacent pole, but while he nearly dropped it as he saw the boat nosing alongside, his presence instantly delineated the German post.

Duncan put the engine into neutral. 'Secure, Morrison!' he shouted, picked up his rifle and left the bridge, Lonsdale and Jamie behind him.

Rawlings and his two were already on shore, and opened fire as the soldier turned back towards the door and began to shout. As he was using German, the only word they recognized was 'Achtung!', and that was brief, as two bullets slammed into his body. Then Rawlings was past him and entering the open doorway.

Duncan and Jamie had by now caught him up, and they entered the outer office together. Two more men were emerging from the back, still half asleep, and they immediately went down as well. 'Take out the rest,' Duncan snapped, having spotted the corridor to the cells.

He ran down this, came to the first, where Professor Hallstrom was sitting up, looking bewildered. 'Stand clear,' Duncan shouted, and fired into the lock.

As this shattered, spewing metal fragments left and right, they heard Rebecca shout, 'Duncan!' and then give a gasp.

'Get her!' Duncan snapped, pulling the Professor's door open.

Jamie ran along the corridor and checked: the door to this cell was open. He stood in it, stared at Rebecca, naked, half on and half off her cot, a German officer behind her, one arm round her waist, the other holding a Luger to her head. 'Is this what you've come for?' he asked. 'Throw down you weapon or she dies.'

Rebecca was panting in terror, and Jamie hesitated, unable to decide what to do; he had never been in a situation like this before.

There was heavy breathing at his shoulder, and a shot rang out. The captain's head seemed to disintegrate, blood and bone flying in every direction; Rebecca screamed, as it cascaded across her hair and shoulders. Jamie turned his head, and Lonsdale, still panting from the exertion of keeping up with the younger men, stepped past him. 'My God, sir,' he said. 'Suppose you'd missed?'

'I never miss,' Lonsdale said. 'I once won a trophy at Bisley.'

The captain was slumped against the wall behind the cot, his arms still round Rebecca's waist. The admiral hurried forward to extricate her and wrap her in the blanket, lifting her into his arms. She gazed at him with enormous eyes. 'I know you,' she muttered.

'James Lonsdale. We met at Lady Eversham's.'

'You're an admiral.'

'Ah . . . yes.'

She was looking past him at Jamie. 'Always coming to my rescue, Jamie.'

'Well, ma'am . . .' Jamie was embarrassed. 'It was the admiral . . .'

'Let's get you out of here,' Lonsdale decided, still holding her against him.

'My clothes . . .'

'Do you know where they are?'

'Well . . . no. That man took them away.'

'See what you can find, Goring. Come along, young lady.'

He carried her to the door, and encountered Duncan and her father. 'Rebecca?' the Professor asked. 'Are you all right?'

'I'm getting better. Lord Eversham! Duncan! My knight in shining armour!'

Duncan looked as embarrassed as Jamie had done. 'We heard a shot . . .'

'It was the admiral. He shot the bastard who . . . well . . . who was holding me.'

'And I am taking her back to the boat,' Lonsdale declared, in a tone that indicated he had no intention of yielding his trophy to anyone.

'Well done, sir. I think we should all get out of here.'

'My briefcase,' Hallstrom said. 'I must have my biefcase. It has my papers.'

'Is this it, sir?' Rawlings held it up. 'It was in the office.'

'Thank God for that!' Hallstrom clutched it to his chest.

From outside there was quite a clamour as people ran on to the street to find out what was happening.

'Jamie!' Duncan shouted.

'I'm here, sir.' Jamie returned, empty-handed. 'I'm afraid I couldn't find anything, ma'am.'

'We'll fix you up on board the boat,' Lonsdale assured her, and carried her into the main office, where she promptly buried her face in his shoulder, for the place was a shambles, with six dead German soldiers scattered about the floor.

Outside it seemed that nearly the entire village had assembled, together with their dogs. At the sight of the naval uniforms they burst into applause. One man, who seemed to be important, stepped forward. 'Is there anything we can do for you, Captain?' He spoke English and addressed Duncan, Lonsdale's rank being obscured by various pieces of blanket and Rebecca.

'Yes,' Duncan agreed. 'We have a wounded man on board. Your doctor. He has lost a lot of blood and needs a transfusion. Can you take him to his clinic?'

'Of course we will do that, sir.'

'And will there be any repercussions?'

'Are there any Germans still alive?'

'No.'

'Well, then, as we are in telephone connection with Bergen we will have to inform them what has happened, of how we were invaded by the Royal Navy, about whom we could do nothing. When would you like us to make this report?'

'Would twelve hours be too long?'

'Not at all. Twelve hours it shall be. Shall we say you came by submarine?'

'That would be most helpful.'

The mayor shook hands. 'May God go with you, sir.'

'That was a brilliant operation, Duncan,' Lonsdale commented, as they returned down the fjord at some speed, their wake crashing into the rock walls to either side.

'We haven't got home yet, sir.'

'But you are confident we shall.'

'If the weather stays misty, and Jerry does indeed look for a sub, I think we have every chance. How is Mrs Strong?'

'She is a strong character, if you'll pardon the pun. She is pretending that she is more concerned about her lack of clothes than about what happened to her. I am sure that it must have been pretty traumatic.'

'Did she tell you what it was, exactly?'

'No, she did not, and I felt it would have been inappropriate to ask.'

'Oh, quite.'

'Although the mere fact that she was stripped . . . it makes the blood boil.'

'Absolutely, sir. Still, we must do all we can to put her mind at rest.' He thumbed the Tannoy. 'All well, Jamie?'

'So far, sir. But . . . we're under half.'

'Very good. Now, I would like you to visit our passengers. See that the professor is all right, and get him anything he wishes. Then I would like you to offer Mrs Strong the use of one of your shirts. I assume you have a clean one?'

'Ah . . . yes, sir.'

'Very good. When you have done that, report to me on their condition.'

'Aye-aye, sir.'

They had reached the mouth of the fjord, and were threading their way through the islands. Visibility remained poor, but had risen to five hundred yards, which was sufficient for their purpose. Cooper arrived on the bridge, and Duncan gave him the helm. 'Course two seven oh as soon as we're clear.'

'Two seven oh it is. Speed?'

'Keep it at fifteen hundred revs. We have to watch our consumption.'

He joined the admiral at the back of the bridge. 'You're steering due west,' Lonsdale commented. 'How long do you feel you must maintain that course? It's not going to help our consumption.'

'I think we need to go out the same way we came in, sir, that is, maintaining a position at least two hundred miles off shore before Jerry starts looking for us, sir. If that cruiser you promised us is on station, we should be all right.'

'And you're confident of finding her in this?'

'Yes, sir.'

'Hm. Now look here. This woman Mrs Strong . . . she has nothing on.'

'I understand that, sir.'

'But you've sent that boy Goring down to her.'

'He's done it before.'

'What?'

'He was the one who attended to her when we recovered her from the Channel, in January.'

'Good heavens!'

'And she seemed very appreciative of his attentions.'

'Remarkable. But still, to offer her one of his shirts . . .'

'He's done that before, too. For Mother.'

'What did you say?'

'You remember, sir, that Mother and Alison were both inadvertently on board when my flotilla received orders to make immediately for Dunkirk to assist in the evacuation. In the circumstances, I decided to take them with me, intending to put them ashore in Dover at the end of our first run.'

'Yes, yes, I remember all that. And they stayed with you for three days.'

'Circumstances got a little out of control.'

'I still don't see how this boy Goring got involved. With your mother.'

'Well, sir, both Alison and Mother were absolute bricks, helping wounded men on board, and looking after them too. And Mother's dress got soaked in blood. Well, she couldn't go on like that for an indefinite period, so Jamie lent her one of his shirts.'

'Hm. Let us hope he never gets around to writing his memoirs. I think this fog is lifting.'

'Jamie Goring,' Rebecca said, nestling in Cooper's bunk. 'My other knight in shining amour.'

'I wouldn't say that, Mrs Strong. I've brought you a shirt. It's one of mine, I'm afraid. I hope you don't mind.'

'I think that is enchanting. Let's try it on.' She sat up, discarding the blanket.

'I'll leave you to it,' Jamie said.

'You stay right there.' She swung her legs out of the bunk and stood up, having to hold on as the MTB, although only cruising on a calm sea, still surged from trough to crest. 'How do I look?'

Jamie swallowed as he gazed at the hardened nipples. 'You look just splendid to me, ma'am.' He held out the shirt.

She ignored it. 'Will you give me a hug?'

'Ma'am?'

'I want to be hugged, by you, very tightly. Just the way I am.'

He licked his lips, closed the door, and took her in his arms.

'That feels so good,' she whispered, and kissed him on the mouth. 'I had to have that,' she said. 'After what . . . I had to have that.' She released him and put on the shirt. 'Am I respectable enough to come on deck?'

'Ah,' he said. Her breasts were very clearly delineated beneath the material. 'It's pretty chilly up top. I'll get you a coat. And a pair of socks. You won't mind?'

'Not if they're your socks.'

'Mrs Strong!' Duncan and the admiral spoke together. Duncan was again on the helm, and the time was 0900. As the admiral had suggested, the mist had definitely thinned, and there was even a trace of a watery sun, behind them, as they were still steering due west. 'How splendid to see you looking so well. Is your father all right?'

'He's sleeping. I think he's found the last three days pretty exhausting.' She pulled Jamie's duffel coat closer about her; from the thighs down her legs were exposed, as far as the ankles; her feet were encased in woollen socks. 'This is thick. You guys have any idea where we are?'

'I think so,' Lonsdale said. 'We'll have you home in a couple of days.'

'A couple of days,' she mused. 'Say, can this boat cross the Atlantic?'

'Not in her present condition,' Duncan said. 'I think the admiral was referring to England.'

It was one of the most peaceful days that Duncan could remember. They ploughed steadily westward for fourteen hours, the sea remained calm, and visibility remained thick; if it improved during the morning, it closed in again that afternoon. They had no idea what was happening behind them, or indeed, anywhere. As with the voyage into Biscay in February, only more so as here was only the one boat, they could have been the only people in the world, their isolation increased by the intimacy enforced by their over-crowded space.

Rebecca soon found it too chilly to remain on deck, and so took herself to the Mess cabin, where it turned out that the Watch Below preferred to spend their time instead of, as was more usual, the warm comfort of their bunks.

Professor Hallstrom came up for lunch, having largely recovered his spirits, and the admiral had no choice but to join in, thus continuing to gather, Duncan reckoned, a valuable insight into the inevitable intimacy of living in such close contact with one's fellows necessitated by a small boat. He had no doubt that the old boy would have loved to find himself alone with Rebecca, but the only way he was going to do that was by taking her to Cooper's cabin and closing the door, and there was no way he was going to be that obvious about his feelings.

Jamie kept a low profile, preferring to spend most of his time in his engine room, although he came up for meals. While Rebecca herself, aware that she was an object of admiration to everyone on board, was the life and soul of the party, making much of the admiral for firing the shot that had saved her life, and becoming solicitous as dusk approached.

'But where are you guys going to sleep?' she asked.

'We'll doss down in here,' Lonsdale said gallantly.

'But that's not right, you being an admiral and all. I can sleep in here and you can use my bunk.'

'Definitely not, my dear girl.'

The crew had actually offered to give up three of their berths to the officers, but of course that had also been declined. Duncan left them to it; he had other things on his mind. At 1900 he joined Jamie in the engine room. 'Estimate.'

Jamie peered at the sight gauges. 'At this speed we have fifty hours, sir. Say a thousand miles. But that means running the tanks dry. If we have to move up a gear . . .'

'We shouldn't need that. In one hour we'll be at the way point. There'll be no means of verifying that, of course, but with the weather this good I can't see any reason why we should be off course. Then it's south by south-west for eight hundred miles to the rendezvous. That should be within our range.'

'That's how far north of the Shetlands, sir?'

'The position is one degree three minutes of West Longitude, sixty-two degrees thirty-five minutes North Latitude. That's something more than a hundred miles north of the Shetlands. Can you scrape that up?'

'As long as the weather holds, sir.'

Duncan slapped him on the shoulder. 'We've been in tighter spots than this, Jamie. And we're still here.'

At 2000 he altered course. 'One nine two until further notice,' he told Rawlings. 'I'm going down for a kip, but keep a sharp look-out, and call me if anything crops up. Mr Cooper will take the Middle Watch.'

'Aye-aye, sir.'

Wilson had served an early dinner, and the ship was already quiet save for the steady hum of the engine. He used the crews' heads rather than disturb the Hallstroms; he reckoned that although they were both showing a great deal of resilience, they were both also suffering from delayed shock. As for what had been done to Rebecca . . . that did not bear thinking about, although he could not stop himself wondering if she would ever speak of it. There was certainly no reason for her to confide in any of them . . . save perhaps Jamie. There was an odd relationship, he thought as he dozed off.

Used as he was to the comings and goings on a small yacht at sea he was not disturbed by the watch changing at 2400, but with a seaman's built-in mental clock was awake at 0350, and up to receive a mug of cocoa from Wilson before going up to the bridge to relieve Cooper. In the eight hours since they had turned off they had covered a hundred and sixty miles away from the high latitudes, and the night was utterly dark, but to his surprise and relief he could see some stars.

'I think it may lift tomorrow,' Cooper remarked, handing over the helm.

'That would be perfect timing,' Duncan agreed. 'See you in the morning.'

Cooper went below, and Duncan was joined by Leading Seaman Morrison equipped with binoculars, with which he studied the sky. 'They all seem to be in the right place, sir,' he commented.

'That's good news. Like a spell?'

'Aye-aye, sir.'

'Course one nine two, and steady on fifteen hundred revs.'

'One nine two it is, sir.'

Duncan took the glasses and himself studied such stars as were visible. As the seaman had said, they indicated that they were on the right track. Another thirty-two hours to go, which was good timing; they should approach the cruiser in daylight tomorrow.

The hours dragged by; and seemed to grow steadily colder. The sky lightened by 0400, and Jamie arrived with cocoa. But now the mist closed in again and they were back in a grey, featureless world. At 0730 Rebecca appeared, wrapped in her duffel coat. 'Wow! Do you have any idea where we are?'

'Believe it or not, but we do,' Duncan said.

'How?'

'It would take too long to explain. I'm about to go off watch. Ask Mr Rawlings how we do it.'

The petty officer was at that moment emerging.

'Still one nine two, fifteen hundred.'

'Aye-aye, sir.'

Rebecca chose to accompany him down to the mess cabin, where Wilson served them breakfast, together with Morrison and the seaman who had shared the watch with them. 'Doesn't that guy ever sleep?' she asked in a whisper.

'Like any seaman, he's trained to get his naps in two or three hour spells. Which is what I intend to do now.'

'Oh. Right. I guess I'll go back to bed. Would you just tell me what day it is? I've completely lost track.'

'It is Thursday, 22 May.'

'That's great. See you later.'

Duncan was asleep in seconds, to awake again it seemed only a few seconds later, as the engine revolutions suddenly dwindled. He sat up. 'What the . . .?'

Lonsdale was seated at the table drinking coffee. He put down his cup with a clatter. 'Something's gone wrong.'

Cooper, asleep on the other settee berth, also woke up.

Able Seaman Norton came down the hatch. 'Compliments from Mr Rawlings, sir. Will you please come up.'

Duncan looked at his watch: it was just past 1000. The two officers pulled on their boots and greatcoats and with the admiral went up together, followed by Jamie, clearly worrying about his precious engine.

'There, sir.'

The mist had again lifted to a certain extent, and there, certainly less than a mile away, were . . . 'Holy Jesus Christ!' Duncan said.

Lonsdale snatched the glasses. 'That's a battleship. With a heavy cruiser. Well, that should solve all of our fuel problems. Although what a battleship is doing up here . . .'

Cooper had also been using his glasses. 'Excuse me, sir,' he said. 'But that is not one of ours.'

'Eh?'

'It is pretty big,' Duncan conceded. 'I suppose it could be *Hood*.'

'With respect, sir,' the lieutenant said. 'That is not *HMS Hood*. *Hood* has two funnels. That ship has only one. And I would say she's bigger. Anyway, would *Hood* be up here, with no destroyers and only a cruiser for company?'

Duncan looked at Lonsdale. 'The boy is right,' the admiral said. 'But if it's not one of ours . . .' he levelled the glasses again. 'It's a monster.'

'Mr Rawlings,' Duncan said. 'See if you can make out the flag.'

Rawlings levelled the glasses at the very indistinct flutter of colour on the stern of the vessel. 'Swastika, sir.'

'But then . . . Great Scott!' Lonsdale stared at Duncan. 'It can only be *Bismarck*. We knew she was completed and working up in the Baltic. But if she's out here . . .'

'She's heading for the Atlantic. Convoys destruction. And

maybe a rendezvous with *Scharnhorst* and *Gneisenau* out of
Brest. Do you think our people know she's coming out?'

'In view of this mist, I very much doubt it.'

'Are we going to attack her, sir?' Cooper was eager.

'I don't think our two torpedoes will have much of an
impact on a ship like *Bismarck*,' the admiral said. 'Just let's
be happy that they haven't spotted us.'

The two big ships were fading into the mist.

'We have to warn the Home Fleet, sir,' Duncan said.

The two men gazed at each other.

'You realize that Jerry will be monitoring all frequencies,'
the admiral said. 'And that he will possess the latest direction-
finding equipment. At this range our signal will just about
puncture his eardrums.'

'I still think it has to be done, sir. If she gets out into the
open sea before we start doing something about her . . .'

'You're right, of course. Do you have the latest code book?'

'No, sir. For our purposes, we always use clear.'

'And where we are, you'll have to use maximum strength,
if you are going to get the range.' Lonsdale took off his cap
and looked inside it, as if seeking inspiration. Then he said,
'Very good, Lieutenant-Commander. Send your message in
clear, and then let's get out of here at full speed.'

Duncan looked at Jamie, who was wearing a stricken expression. 'Must be done.' He checked the chart. 'Mr Cooper, make
to Commander-in-Chief, Scapa Flow, in clear: Have sighted
Bismarck and unidentified heavy cruiser estimated position
one degree thirteen minutes West Longitude, sixty-five degrees
thirteen minutes North Latitude, steering West North West.
Timed 1045. *MTB Forty-One* on detached duty.'

'Aye-aye, sir.' Cooper got to work with the Morse key.

Rebecca had joined them. 'What's happening? Why are we
stopped?'

'We have hostiles about,' Duncan explained.

'Begging your pardon, sir,' Rawlings said. 'That cruiser is
coming back.'

All their heads turned. The enemy squadron had just been
fading into the mist, but now the heavy cruiser was taking
shape again, her bow pointing towards them.

'Holy shit!' Lonsdale said. 'I beg your pardon, Mrs Strong.'

'Be my guest,' Rebecca smiled.

'So they did see us,' Duncan said. 'And now they've heard our transmission. Action stations, Mr Rawlings. All hands stand by for full speed.'

Rawlings rang the bell, and Duncan thrust the throttle forward. As he did so, there was a flash and a smoke cloud, and they heard the whine of the shell, which hit the water about four hundred yards astern.

'What's he got?' Lonsdale asked.

Cooper had finished sending his message. 'If she's either *Hipper* or *Prinz Eugen*, eight eight-inch, two by two in two forward turrets. Range about fifteen miles.'

'Oh, my God!' The enemy ship was no more than three miles off.

'Speed?' Duncan asked.

'Thirty-two knots.'

'We need to hurry.' He had the throttle hard forward, and the boat was bouncing over the shallow waves at forty knots. But the cruiser was firing again, and this shot landed in front of them.

'Wowee!' Rebecca commented.

'He's thinking,' Duncan said. 'And he's got the range. Jamie, get below and make sure everything is all right. I'm going to have to zigzag.'

'Aye-aye, sir.' Jamie slid down the ladder.

'I think you should go down as well, Mrs Strong,' Lonsdale suggested.

'Aw, Admiral, don't be that way. This is something to tell my grandchildren, if they ever turn up. Anyway, if we get hit, won't I stand more chance up here than down there?'

'Well . . .' Lonsdale looked at Duncan, who caught his eye in-between putting the helm hard to port.

'It's a point, sir. But put a life jacket on, and hold on.'

'Aye-aye, sir,' Rebecca said.

She was enjoying herself, and he reckoned that, after her ordeal, it might be good for her, psychologically; there would be no point in telling her that if they got hit there would be no survivors, whether on deck or below.

Forty-One was now screaming East, and still a shell burst perilously close. 'Check the bilges, Mr Rawlings,' Duncan commanded, bringing the boat round in a tight turn to make south again, But he was eight knots faster than the German and he reckoned that the big ship, if she was on a mission as support for *Bismarck*, could not afford to be drawn too far out of position.

His calculations were correct. Fifteen minutes later the warship had faded from sight and the guns were silent.

'Wheee!' Rebecca commented, taking off her steel helmet and letting her hair blow in the breeze. 'Are we all right, now?'

'We still have to get home,' Duncan reminded her.

His first problem was that avoiding the cruiser at full speed had thrown his DR calculations. But it had only been for a short time, and he estimated that he was within twenty miles of where he should be, while if the mist were to clear sufficiently for him to gain a glimpse of the sun he should be able to re-establish a fixed position.

The second problem was far more serious. 'Message from Commander-in-Chief, on board *King George V*, sir,' Cooper said, his expression revealing concern.

Duncan took the sheet of paper, read the transcript aloud. 'Well done *Forty-One*. All units concentrating to find and destroy enemy. Suggest you make Lerwick for re-fuelling. Good luck.'

Lonsdale held out his hand and read the message for himself. 'Just like that,' he commented.

'Well, sir,' Duncan said, 'I suppose getting hold of *Bismarck* is more important than recovering us.'

'Not from where I'm standing. Can you do it?'

Duncan gave Rawlings the helm and went below to study the chart, Lonsdale at his elbow. 'We are roughly here.' He made a mark.

'Roughly?'

'I wasn't keeping track with that cruiser breathing down our necks. Now, Lerwick is on the eastern coast of the main island. I make that . . . just over four hundred nautical miles. At our present speed, say twenty hours.'

'And we have fuel for . . .?'

Duncan pressed the intercom. 'Jamie! What's our fuel position?'

'We burned a bit while wriggling, sir. But at our present speed, oh, we have seventeen hours left. That should take us to the rendezvous with a couple of hours to spare.'

Duncan looked at Lonsdale. Then he said, 'Come up, will you, Jamie.'

'What the fuck are we going to do?' Lonsdale inquired.

Jamie appeared. 'Sir?'

'There is not going to be a rendezvous,' Duncan said. 'Every ship is needed to chase the Germans. We need four hundred miles as opposed to two hundred.'

Jamie looked from one to the other of his superiors.

'Well?' Lonsdale inquired.

'If we reduce speed to a thousands revs, sir, we might squeeze another few hours out of her, but that won't get us there.'

'What exactly does that mean?'

'Well, sir, right now we have roughly seventeen hours endurance. At fifteen hundred revs, that is, twenty knots, that gives us three hundred and forty miles If we operate at a thousand revs, say fifteen knots, we would also increase our endurance to perhaps twenty-five hours, say three hundred and seventy-five miles.'

'That still leaves us twenty-five miles short. Can't we reduce any further?'

'No point, sir. Five hundred revs would give us perhaps thirty-five hours, but at ten knots, if that, we'd still be fifty short.'

'Shit!'

Duncan was studying the chart. 'One thousand revs it has to be.'

'But . . .?' Lonsdale asked.

'It is four hundred miles to Lerwick. But that is virtually the bottom end of the group. Herma Ness, the northernmost point on Uist, is sixty miles north. If we can make that . . .'

Lonsdale peered at the map. 'There's nothing there.'

'There are bound to be some crofters. And even if there isn't, if we can make a landfall and anchor in an identifiable position, surely to God Lerwick can get some fuel up to us.'

'Twenty-five hours,' Lonsdale mused. 'This time tomorrow.'

'Well, sir, you said you had a week's leave. You might just make it.'

'And if the weather breaks?'

'As they say, man proposes and God disposes. We just have to hope He's on our side, this time.'

*   *   *

'This is heavenly,' Rebecca remarked. She was seated in a folding canvas chair in the stern of the boat, Admiral Lonsdale beside her. 'Do you know, these last few days have been quite the most exciting of my life. I mean, I have never been, well . . .' she changed her mind about what she would have said.

'Do you think it would help if you spoke of it?' Lonsdale asked.

She glanced at him, and looked away again. 'Not right now. Maybe . . . maybe in a few days time. But I've never been shot at before, either. And now, this, we could be on a pleasure cruise.' She gazed into the afternoon mist. 'If the sun were to come out, it would be just perfect.' She tapped the metal contained at her elbow. 'What are these?' She gestured at the other one.

'Depth charges. We drop them on submarines.'

'Wow! Is that a fact?'

'That is, if we see a submarine, which we are hoping not to do on this voyage. Our business is to get you and your father to England.'

'And I'm grateful, believe me. But we're going to be a day or two late, right? Won't your wife be worried?'

'I don't have a wife, right now.'

Rebecca turned her head to look at him. 'No wife? And you an admiral, and all?'

'One doesn't have to be married to be an admiral,' he pointed out. 'I suppose I just haven't met the right woman yet.'

'That's tough. You know what you should do, Jimmy? You should marry Kristin.'

'Kristin?'

'Don't you like that idea? I mean, she's beautiful, she's rich, and you know what? I have an idea she may have something going for you.'

'Do you think so? Kristin, well . . . she's a bit of a handful.'

'You think about it,' Rebecca said. 'You could do a whole hell of a lot worse.'

These were the longest twenty-five hours of Duncan's life, but he suspected that went for everyone on board. It was utterly unreal for a boat like *Forty-One* to be ghosting across the ocean at fifteen knots, ghosting being an appropriate word because of the unnatural quiet; at this speed the engine was no more than a hum. They listened to the radio, but for the moment there was nothing of importance. No doubt the entire Royal Navy was concentrating, but *Bismarck* and *Prinz Eugen* seemed to have utterly disappeared.

Duncan kept the crew to normal watches, and on Friday he was on the Morning Watch, 0400 to 0800. The mist remained thick, and the weather remained calm. The day brightened perceptibly at 0500 to suggest that the sun might have risen, but there was no sight of it, and no possibility of making a fix; they had now been blind for two days. He remembered reading that Christopher Columbus had been in this position at the end of his 1492 transatlantic voyage, with no fix for two days because of mist. He hadn't even been absolutely certain that there *was* any land in front of him. But Columbus had been under sail, and therefore possessed of an unlimited range. What would I give, he thought, to be on the helm of *Kristin*, then I wouldn't give a damn, either.

Jamie came up, gazed into the mist.

'I'll have the bad news first,' Duncan said.

'There's not more than five hours left, sir. I'm afraid there isn't any good news.'

Lonsdale appeared. 'Well, Duncan, where's this land you've been promising us?'

'Still fifty miles away, sir. If my DR is accurate.'

Rebecca appeared, wrapped in Jamie's duffel coat, and gazed at the non-existent horizon. 'So . . . where are we? There doesn't seem a lot of land about.'

'It's there,' Duncan said, getting all the confidence he could into his voice. 'We should see it in the next couple of hours.'

He handed over his watch to Cooper but remained on the bridge. In fact, by mid-morning every man on board, including the professor, was on deck, peering into the murk.

'I think it's lifting, sir,' Rawlings ventured.

'So find something.'

The petty officer levelled the glasses for the hundredth time.

Jamie appeared. 'We have run out of fuel, sir.'

As he spoke, the engine suddenly stopped. The silence was uncanny; even the slapping of the sea against the hull seemed to be muted. For several minutes no one spoke, and Cooper continued to clutch the useless wheel. Then Rebecca asked, quietly, 'Do you guys have a plan B? I mean, we have a radio, right?'

'Right,' Duncan said. 'Mr Cooper, put out a Pan message. What do you reckon visibility is, Mr Rawlings?'

'Maybe half a mile, sir.'

'So we'll assume my DR has been accurate. Give our position as approximately five miles north of Herma Ness, Uist. Send it in clear on 2182. We are out of fuel and need a tow.'

'Aye-aye, sir.' Cooper got to work.

'Who's this guy Pan?' Rebecca asked. 'Shouldn't you be sending SOS or Mayday or something?'

'No, we should not,' the admiral said. 'SOS or Mayday should only be used if the situation indicates imminent loss of life. If we send that, every ship that picks it up is, by the laws of the sea, bound to come to our assistance. Pan means we need help, urgently, but are not actually in a dangerous situation.'

'I get you. Kind of amber instead of red. But doesn't that mean that no one *has* to come, if he's got something better to do?'

Lonsdale looked baffled, so Duncan said, 'That is absolutely correct, Mrs Strong. So we keep our fingers crossed.'

'I have a reply,' Cooper said. 'Very loud. For him, too. Says we nearly blew his headphones off.'

'I have a ship, sir,' Rawlings said. 'Green ten. A trawler.'

'Put up a flare, Morrison,' Duncan said, 'just to make sure he sees us. Then prepare a tow line.'

'He wants to know,' Cooper said, 'if we realize that we gave out the wrong position. Herma Ness is forty miles away, due east.'

'Ignore that,' Duncan recommended. 'Tell him to take our line.'

'He also says a tow as far as Lerwick will be expensive. He's a Scot, you see.'

'Tell him,' Lonsdale said, 'that we are a Royal Navy vessel, and that he has been requisitioned. He will receive a standard fee . . . if he tows us into Lerwick. If he refuses, we will regard it as a hostile act and sink him.'

'Now you see,' Duncan said, 'how important it is always to have an admiral on board.'

*   *   *

It was Monday afternoon when *MTB Forty-One* slipped into her berth in Portsmouth Harbour. Duncan had called ahead, but as the operation had been top secret only a handful of people were waiting for them. Fitzsimmons shook the admiral's hand. 'Thank God you're back, sir.'

'*Bismarck*? We heard about the *Hood* disaster.'

'They've caught her, sir. Seems she's been crippled by torpedo strikes, and she's being brought to battle by *KGV* and *Rodney*. They should have her in a day or so.'

'There's a relief.'

'Yes, sir. This fellow . . .' he jerked his head. 'Claims to be a Secret Service wallah. Has all kinds of authorization from the Admiralty . . .'

'I know him.' Lonsdale shook hands. 'Good afternoon, Mr Chadwick.'

'Admiral Lonsdale! We really hadn't intended you to undertake this mission yourself.'

'But you did say it could be vital to our security.'

'Well, yes, sir. Ah, did you . . .'

'Here they are.'

Duncan was assisting Professor Hallstrom ashore, while Cooper looked after Rebecca.

'Professor!' Chadwick shook hands. 'Robert Chadwick. Welcome to England.'

'That remains to be seen,' Hallstrom said enigmatically, and turned to the two officers. 'Thank you for all you've done, Admiral, Captain Eversham. I only hope it was all worthwhile.'

Rebecca had embraced Jamie, to his obvious embarrassment. Now she joined the officers. 'It was great fun. I can't thank you all enough.'

'You're not dashing off?' Lonsdale asked.

'Well . . .' She looked at Chadwick.

'I'm afraid this is all still top secret, Admiral. We don't want anyone to know that Professor Hallstrom is here. Our object now is to get Mrs Strong back before anyone realizes that she ever left.'

'Well . . . like I said, thanks for everything.' She faced the crew, who were assembled on deck. 'All of you. I'll never forget you.' She turned back to the admiral. 'Well, sir. It's been fun.'

He held her hand. 'Ships that pass in the night.'

'Ships always return to port, Jimmy. I'll see you again.'

She followed Chadwick and her father to where Alison and Kristin waited. 'Don't tell me he had to put you to bed again,' Kristin remarked.

'How else do you think I got here?'

'And what on earth are you wearing?'

'The gear belongs to that boy Jamie. Isn't he sweet? I'll see you around. Maybe.'

Alison hurried off to embrace Duncan. 'I've been so worried.'

'I told you that they always miss me.'

'Absolutely. You are far more accurate. My resignation is on the admiral's desk.'

'What? You? Giving up the Navy?'

'Reluctantly. The Navy doesn't approve of pregnant officers.'

Duncan looked past her at his mother, who waggled her eyebrows, 'We were going to tell you last week, when we had the results of her test. But we didn't think we should when the admiral outlined this jaunt, as we knew you'd need to concentrate.' She went past him to Lonsdale. 'Jimmy! I'm so glad you made it.'

'Kristin!' He kissed her. 'Will you invite me to dinner tonight? There is so much I want to talk about.'

'Tonight?' Kristin looked over his shoulder at the crew, still assembled on the deck, picked out Jamie, who was gazing at her. 'Well . . . are those poor fellows on patrol tomorrow?'

'Good lord, no. After what they've been through, I think they deserve a few days off.'

'I'm so glad. I tell you what, Jimmy, could we make it tomorrow night? I have an appointment, first thing tomorrow morning, and I think I should be early to bed.'